STREET SMART

WORK FOR IT BOOK #1

ALY STILES

WWW.SMARTYPANTSROMANCE.COM

COPYRIGHT

This book is a work of fiction. Names, characters, places, rants, facts, contrivances, and incidents are either the product of the author's questionable imagination or are used factitiously. Any resemblance to actual persons, living or dead or undead, events, locales is entirely coincidental if not somewhat disturbing/concerning.

Print Edition:
978-1-949202-57-1

PART I
DEFINE

1—REED REEDWEATHER, III

MARCOS

Mr.

Reedweather

Will

Be

With

You

Shortly

Seven words I never thought I'd hear. And yet, here I am, wrecking all kinds of statistics in my dash to break the mold and achieve every MBA grad's wet dream. Yep, on paper I belong in prison. In practice, I'm a soon-to-be Yorkshire University alum who just landed an internship at Reedweather Media, a marketing subsidiary of the legendary Sandeke business empire. *Paid* internship, I might add. Suck that, Mr. Gary of the Bellevue Group Home for Boys.

My leg seems less confident as it vibrates against the waiting room chair. And by chair, I don't mean the uncomfortable doctor's office variety that look like they were upholstered with scraps from your gram's tub of weird basement crap. These are legit leather beasts, like the kind mob bosses use when they're ordering hits and stuff.

I lift two fingers and point them at the wall. Pretty sure it's what powerful people do to get things done. Lefty Two Eyes… dead. Bourbon on the rocks… ordered.

Shit. Gets. Done.

My roommate Nate and I were just discussing this last night. He came up through the foster system too, but with three more years of experience, he's also more educated in the *intangibles.* You know, the real skills you need that they don't teach in business school.

Golf.

Scotch-tasting.

Cigar-smoking.

Oh, and that handshake where you squeeze with just the right amount of too-hard pressure while narrowing your eyes in ominous *I'm-too-important-to-fuck-with*-ness.

"Everything okay?" the executive assistant calls over from his desk.

Crap. I'm still two-finger-saluting the wall and probably squinting super ominously.

"Fine." I force my eyes un-squinted and drop my hand back to the soft leather armrest. Yep, these chairs also have armrests. The dumpster rescue chair in my living room doesn't even have armrests.

The assistant's phone buzzes, and he answers without averting his wary stare from my direction. Clearly no one taught him about *The Handshake* or he wouldn't be so concerned.

"Mr. Reedweather is ready for you," he says, nodding toward a pair of imposing walnut doors. I resist the urge to lift two fingers as I pass, pretty sure he doesn't know about that either.

With a deep breath, I push through to The Promised Land. And freeze. Seriously, this office—nay, *suite*—is the standard backdrop for every business magazine feature photo from 1992 to 1995. Mahogany bookcases, mahogany desk, even a mahogany sideboard with one of those obscene hutch things towering on top. Why have a hutch? Because you have so much money that buying a giant useless cabinet isn't enough—it needs a roof. Damn, how many trees had to die to furnish this place? There's even a matching table that could host at least twenty people. What would a twenty-person meeting that couldn't take place in a conference room even be about?

"You're looking at genuine West Indian mahogany, son."

A deep voice interrupts my revelry, and I tear my gaze away to land on the emperor himself: Reed Reedweather, III. The man, the myth, the reason I was up until 2 AM practicing that stupid handshake.

Game time.

"It's very impressive, sir."

I'm a pro at using "sir." Plenty of years of addressing authority figures who love that word. It melts on the tongue like butter, way smoother than my attempt at *The Handshake*, it turns out.

Shit.

But Mr. Reedweather's grip? Pure art. I shudder in the wake of the ominous eye-squint, discreetly flexing my hand to ease the cramp as I take the seat he offers— another leather chair *with* armrests, of course.

After returning to his throne behind the desk, my new boss steeples his fingers in perfectly executed *Thoughtful Appraisal*. Damn, he's good. No wonder he's a gazillionaire.

I'm not sure what to do with my own hands, though, and settle on clasping them loosely in my lap once the blood flow returns to my fingers.

Several seconds pass, and I'm sure this is another calculated business thing I should know. *Thoughtful Pausing*—not to be confused with *Thoughtful Appraisal,* which is more advanced. And so we stare. Him looking thoughtful, and me... Well, I'm aiming for thoughtful as well, but my face feels like it might be leaning toward confused.

Also in the silence, I can't help but notice that Mr. Reedweather is the perfect accessory to all his mahogany accents. Tailored suit, smooth jaw—he even rocks the medium-length salt-and-pepper hair slicked back at an angle that lets you know he stands in front of the mirror each morning and gives himself a wink of approval. *Look at you, rock star. Go slay some P&L reports.* Finger gun and out.

"You have an impressive résumé, Mark."

"Oh, um, Marcos."

"Mark-O, yes."

5

"Marcos, actually. Like... with an *s*."

Wait, how does he have a facial expression that makes me feel bad he can't pronounce my name? This dude is a freaking business ninja.

"Oh right. They mentioned you were Mexican."

"Well—"

"I think that's just great, Mark-O. See, we're all about diversity here at Reedweather."

I can tell him I'm Brazilian another time.

"Actually, many of our employees are native Spanish-speakers."

And that Portuguese and Spanish are different languages.

"You may have noticed my assistant is male."

True.

"*Rapid Inclusivity*, Mark-O. *There's* a term you need to learn if you're going to survive in the twenty-first century."

Rapid Inclusivity? Pretty sure that's not a thing.

"But here at Reedweather, it's not enough. No, my *amigo*. Our mantra is what I like to call *Rabid Inclusivity.*"

Yeah, definitely not a thing.

I nod gravely, focusing on the weird desk sculpture that looks like an avocado to keep a straight face. Note to future CEO self: Source a bronze avocado.

"You know what? I already like you, Mark-O."

"Thank you, sir."

He nods as if to assure himself of that fact and drops another pause that has me shifting to the edge of my seat. It's uncanny, really. I study his manicured eyebrows to see if those dynamic weapons are playing any role in this witchcraft.

"You know, I don't do this often, but I already feel like you and I have a special bond."

"Oh, um—"

"You a scotch man, Mark-O?"

Shit. "Uh…"

"Well, never mind. I can tell you will be if you're not already. I can read these things. *Acquired Intuition* they call it."

They don't. Almost positive.

"Like I said, I don't do this often." He says this with a slick swipe at a desk drawer that tells me he definitely does.

In another graceful movement, he deposits a decanter and two tumblers on his giant desk calendar. Yes, he still has one of those enormous paper calendars covering half his workspace. From my vantage point, I mostly see doodles and notes on Fridays that look suspiciously like tee times.

"Picked this up two years ago on a trip to your part of the world," he says proudly, handing me a glass.

"Pennsylvania?"

With a hearty laugh, he swirls his cup in salute. "You're funny. I knew I liked you."

I force a smile and swirl my own, still not sure about the protocol for drinking within the first twenty minutes of employment at a new job. I play along and mirror his movements, pretending to smell something divine before tipping the glass ever so slightly toward my tongue. Truthfully, it smells like booze, and when a drop sneaks its way past my lips, tastes like it too.

"Ahhh," he breathes out. "Heaven, am I right?" He swirls the glass again, and I follow suit, figuring that's what you do *after* drinking scotch as well as before. Maybe you're supposed to swirl it with every swallow? Or is it a timing thing? Every twenty-three seconds? I grip the glass, waiting to see what he does next.

"Well, now that we're relaxed, let's talk business. I've seen your portfolio, Mark-O. Impressive stuff, impressive stuff." He nods and takes another sip from his glass, this time without a swirl. I file that away.

"You are quite the artist. What do they call these cartoon books again?" He waves at his screen as if I can see it.

7

"Graphic novels?"

"Yes! That's it. Graphic novels. I remember when we called them the funny pages. You ever read *Dagwood*, Mark-O?"

I nod because I'm not sure but have zero confidence he can verify my story either way.

"Good stuff, good stuff. So listen."

He places his glass on "Wednesday April 3" and leans forward to bore his stare into mine. I swallow hard, forgetting I'd brought the glass back to my lips a second before, and have to choke down a huge gulp of scotch.

"We'll be starting you off as an entry-level assistant. I'm sure you understand the politics involved. Or as we like to call it here at Reedweather: *Dogmatic Positioning*. You study *Dogmatic Positioning* at Yorkshire, Mark-O?"

I have no idea how to answer that. "Well—"

He waves me quiet and resumes his laser stare. "Never mind. Doesn't matter. You're here to learn, am I right? We'll only be hiring one intern to a permanent position at the end of this quarter, but you do well, impress us with your hard work, and the sky's the limit for go-getters like you. You feel me, Mark-O?"

I nod, still fighting back tears against the alcoholic burn in my throat—and now a fresh tickle from whatever *Dogmatic Positioning* is supposed to be.

"I can't hear you," he says, adding a creepy big-toothed grin that I think is intended to be playful.

"I—*feel* you," I rasp out.

I put the glass on the edge of the desk before it does more damage. Naughty scotch. Another note to future CEO self: Avoid desk drinking.

"Great. Well, then, I think it's time we hook you up with your new boss. You ready for the big leagues, Mark-O?"

I nod yet again, not sure what other response I could give to that or most of these questions. One day I'll be the man who only gets yeses.

He seems to like it and makes quite the show of leaning over to push a button on his phone. (Which also answers my question about why he still has a phone that requires you to lean over and push a button.)

"David, can you do me a favor and see if my daughter is ready to meet her new intern?"

2—EVANGELINE REEDWEATHER

MARCOS

"Ms. Reedweather?"

My fist stalls on the door to the office when its owner looks up from her desk. Well, damn. This is a pleasant surprise. Or a dangerous one.

They say we all have a doppelgänger—some human on the planet who is our clone in every way for no explicable reason. If we also have a polar opposite doppelgänger—someone who doesn't have a single identifiable trait in common with another person—that would be Evangeline Reedweather and her father. Intelligent, brown eyes bore into me, sizing up my entire existence in one swift appraisal. Her matching dark brown hair is twisted back in some severe style that screams, *I'm young and beautiful, but none shall enjoy this fact. Especially you, asshole.* My asshole brain is clearly not heeding said warning. Because —*damn.*

"Marcos Oliveira?"

I swallow and nod, suddenly aware that only the top half of my body is in her office. Her gaze slides from my face to my partial torso bending around the door frame. It's an athletic pose, at least. Does she notice the strain of my pecs and abs required to pull off this daring position? The slightest of smiles flickers over her lips, making me think she notices just fine.

"Feel free to come in." She even adds a wave, like maybe I'm not well versed in human interactive protocol. *You see, Marcos, in many cultures, door-knocking leads to door-entering...*

I shake off my stupid. "Right. Yeah. Duh." Then cringe when I hear my private thought-words out loud. She smiles to herself again. Probably a sad-polite gesture because she just realized she lost the intern lottery. *Which one of you wants the dude who doesn't know how to walk through doors and speak words?*

"Sorry, Ms. Reedweather. You're just—" Shit. *Abort!* My fingers, still holding the door frame, clench around the wood in protest at my stupidity. *How were you going to finish that sentence, genius?*

"I'm just, what?"

"Uh..."

Hot as fuck. No.

A challenging, intelligent woman—a.k.a. my kryptonite. Also no.

"You okay, Marcos?"

"Yeah, fine. Just." I clear my throat. "Allergies."

Oh my god. Somewhere my professors are groaning into their locally sourced, sustainable kale-based lattes. Your star student, ladies and gentlemen. Straight-As be damned. I could desperately use a locally sourced, sustainable kale-based latte to groan into right about now. Or more of Mr. Reedweather's weird desk scotch.

Another slight smile skims over her lips. "Why don't you sit, and we can chat?"

She rounds her desk and takes a seat at a small, normal-sized private office table, which, like everything else about her, sits in direct contrast to her father's tastes. In fact, her entire office is the sophisticated and modest opposite of Reedweather's flamboyant ode to mahogany. It probably ruined his year that she passed on the hutch when she designed her space. Motioning toward the chair across from her, she studies me with an unreadable expression.

I follow instructions like a functioning human this time and place my zippered portfolio on the table. She eyes it curiously, and I pray she doesn't have x-ray vision because there's nothing in it. A blank legal pad and a pen—that's what I brought for my epic corporate crusade. Hashtag *warrior*.

"Look, I'm going to be up-front with you," she says, all humor draining from her face as she settles her stare back on me. "I'm not a fan of this internship program. My father enjoys the brutality of the competition and the slick political games you young, hungry suits love to play, but I personally find it tedious and counterproductive. I know you think you're God's gift because you come from some fancy school and bought that fancy tie, but I assure you, I've watched twelve other clones of you work at those desks over the last three years and all it does is make my life harder. I'm not impressed by who your parents are, how many yachts they own, or which senator signed your letter of recommendation. Your money and connections have zero impact on your ability to do this job, got it?"

Is now a bad time to mention that I got myself through school by stripping? Her gaze narrows coldly. Probably.

I nod instead, trying to suppress a smile of my own this time. That was quite possibly the hottest speech I ever heard.

"Got it," I say.

She lifts a brow, clearly surprised by my casual response. I'm hoping it's because I'm intriguing and unexpected, and then I remember it's probably because those were actual human words spoken in a normal human voice at a socially accepted interval.

He can *comprehend his environment after all! Bravo.*

"You *got it*?" she repeats, mimicking my tone. There's a flash of stifled humor again. It's like it physically pains her to smile and she must avoid it at all costs.

I nod. "Yep. None of that should be a problem. I don't know any senators, and I'm, like, ninety-nine percent positive Rita and Steve didn't have a yacht."

"Rita and Steve?"

"Last set of foster parents before the group home. I'm a *hundred* percent sure Bellevue didn't have a yacht. Just that stupid canoe with a hole that took up half the garage. No one wanted garage-cleaning duty, trust me."

Her lips press into a thin line that makes me feel a little better about not being the only one who can't get words out sometimes.

"Oh, and I borrowed this from my roommate." I tug the blue silk tie and stare down at it for a beat. "Is it too much?"

The amusement finally leaks out, skimming over her face as she studies my tie. "No, it was a good choice. Brings out the blue in your eyes."

Is she joking? My pulse picks up when her smile spreads to her own dark irises, softening the professional façade into a glimpse of the young woman behind it. She scans me again—this time with a perusal that evokes inappropriate thoughts about the employee handbook's stance on manager–intern chemistry.

She clears her throat, shifting just enough to make me think the room is suddenly a little warm for her also.

"Okay, well, they've explained to you how this program works?" she asks, returning to a professional, no-nonsense, hair-twist Vice President of Promotions.

"Two interns, one job opening, right?" Shit. Zero chance that's not an office porn movie. Hopefully, she's too distracted to notice my weird description.

Her expression remains flat, giving me hope. "Yes, exactly. For the next few weeks, consider everything a test. Every person you meet, every situation you encounter, assume you are being watched and evaluated. Multiple opinions factor into this decision, not just mine. You will be in direct competition with Chad—" She pauses, clearly fishing for something. "With Chad," she finishes, also clearly not finding it.

"*Chad* sounds formidable," I say evenly.

Another smile slips from her lips, and I unofficially add, *make Evangeline Reedweather smile* to the intern job description they gave me. In related news, I can see if Hallmark is hiring should this job not work out. Yeah, that was sappy.

"He's... intense," she says.

"*Hungry,* even?"

She smirks. "You better be downright ravenous to have a shot at this, Marcos Oliveira."

"*Chad*-Something isn't going to know what hit him, Ms. Reedweather."

"Oh, call me Eva. We'll be too busy for all the formalities."

Eva. I like that. A lot. "And you can call me Marcos. Or Mark-O like your father does. Apparently, that's the Mexican pronunciation."

She almost chokes. "Please tell me you have some Mexican heritage."

I shake my head. "I don't think so. My birth parents were Brazilian, I'm told."

"So you speak…?"

"English. I was raised in Pennsylvania's foster system. I didn't want to disappoint your father, though. He knows so many Spanish words."

"At least thirty."

"Plus, he was super excited about his scotch. Although I'm not clear on where that's supposed to be from."

Her eyes dance, again fighting humor as she straightens in her chair. "Yes, well, it's the curse of being a *Rabid Inclusionist* like he is." Somehow she keeps a straight face as she says this.

I can't, and snort a laugh. "Well, I'm just a lowly intern here to master the art of *Dogmatic Positioning*."

She bites her lip as she nods. "An essential skill, to be sure," she breathes out, so close to losing it her fingers clench into a fist. I'm in awe of her restraint.

"Oh, hey. Quick question. How do I get one of those giant calendars for my desk? Is there a requisition form or something?"

Her laugh bursts out in a sweet melody of triumph.

Finally. One point for Marcos Oliveira.

3—CHAD-SOMETHING

MARCOS

Any humor swirling around Eva's office gets siphoned out by the introduction of my competition. *Chad*, it turns out, does have fancy parents, a fancy trust fund, and a fancy senator on retainer for signing letters of recommendation. None of which is inherently a badge of douchery, of course. What *does* earn him the crown is his whispered assumption that he will, at some point, "tap that tight ass," in reference to our boss while she paused our introduction to take a call. Good news for violence lovers everywhere: Mr. Reedweather's younger, blonder, same-version doppelgänger will be occupying the desk adjacent to mine right outside Eva's door. I scour the area for hidden cameras, certain that placing two competing interns at conjoined desks is a sick blood sport in several obscure autocratic nations.

This season on Bloody Interns, *we have former stripper Marcos Oliveira battling establishment prototype—Chad.*

What hope do I have against a dude named "Chad" anyway? The moniker is business-card ready in its purest form. Pretty sure it's the one on the sample you have to delete to type in your own. I bet that's why he doesn't have a last name. Chad probably also plays golf, can do the Ominous Handshake in his sleep, and has used the two-finger salute since infancy. *Yo, Mom. Boob? Let's get this done.*

I shudder at the thought of Chad's mom's boobs.

"Marcos?"

I blink back to the present, trying not to stare at other, more enticing boobs as Eva hovers between our desks. It's an unfortunate (and very fortunate) eye-level challenge, and I force my gaze up to her razor-sharp stare. I also notice, with some ire, that Chad doesn't try as hard. I'm guessing he's of the *women secretly like to be objectified* school of flirtation. Consequently, I add *never invite Chad as a wingman* to my list of life survival hacks.

"You're okay with that?" Eva asks, eyeing me curiously. Can she tell I'd been lost in Chad-Orbit and have no idea what just happened?

"Absolutely, sounds great," I say, forcing exuberance into my tone to cover any lingering doubt. Doesn't seem to work as she squints for an additional second before clearing her throat.

"Okay, well, if you're sure, then I guess it's settled. Chad will be in charge of creative, and Marcos, you'll cover the analytics."

Wait, what? Shit.

"Oh, um…" I swore a pride of lions couldn't make me lose my cool in front of *Chad*, but suddenly my blood pressure is all kinds of not-cool.

"It's all good, Ms. Reedweather," my nemesis interjects to thwart any mounting offensive. "I have a ton of experience with creative development. And being an Ivy League man, I'm sure my associate here will nail the analytics. We got you covered, ma'am."

Eva studies my dumbstruck face again, looking disappointed. "Okay, I suppose if you both are fine with that, I'll send you each the link to the campaign folder. I'd like to see your slide deck next Friday."

"Perfect. We'll get right on that," Chad says with a wink—*a wink*! I don't even know which of us was supposed to be the recipient of that smarmy F-U, but I keep a straight face as Eva disappears through the neighboring door to her office.

Chad settles back in his rolling chair and tosses me an even smarmier look.

Well.

Shit.

* * *

CHAD IS A PEN-CLICKER. And a desk-tapper. And a portfolio un-zipper, which, for the record, he probably does to show off the wealth of materials stuffed inside. During one of the exposures, I swear I saw a government seal. Does he actually carry his senator recommendation letter with him? Never know when you'll need to prove that a powerful old dude signed off on your existence.

I scowl at my laptop screen, still jotting uninspired notes on my legal pad, when Chad guffaws with the gusto of a railroad baron.

"Cashews!" he cries by way of explanation before typing furiously on his keyboard. I stare at the top of his slicked-back hair for another few seconds before returning to my screen.

What is this project, anyway? Ten minutes into my research on SAT Systems, and I have a sick feeling that I'm not being asked to conduct the typical competitive analysis. It can't be a coincidence that this company is directly tied to a guy named Martin Sandeke. It only takes a few mouse clicks to learn this young entrepreneur isn't just a recent nominee for the prestigious McPherson Fellowship, he's also the estranged son of our Lord Telecom, Denver Sandeke. The son started a non-profit satellite company that could be construed as direct competition to his father's empire?

"Marcona almonds!"

I glance back at my exhilarated coworker. Are we on the same project? I study the campaign summary again and see nothing about nuts of any kind. Satellites, yes. Nuts, no.

"Oh my god. Pine nuts! Hey, Oliveira."

I lift my gaze over my screen.

"Are pine nuts actual nuts?" Chad asks, totally serious.

"Pretty sure," I say blandly.

He smiles and returns to his manic typing.

I read through the directive Eva sent again and sift through the folder of corresponding attachments. Articles, photos, even—wait, is that a blueprint?

I open the file, my heart seizing in my chest. This is a hardware drawing of a satellite. By the document name and date, it's a prototype still in development. I open another file to find what looks like a map of a satellite infrastructure. What the hell is all this?

"What about acorns? Not a nut, right?" Chad calls over.

"Huh?" I clear my head enough to shake it. "I mean, it's a seed with a shell, so yes? Hey, do these files look weird to you?"

"What files?"

"The folder Eva shared with us."

"About the nuts?"

"What the hell nuts are you talking about?" I snap back. Sorry, but there are only so many nut references a guy can handle.

Chad's gaze narrows in a way that tells me he does not appreciate my lack of nut-enthusiasm. He swivels his laptop to face me. I squint at his screen and find the open folder labeled: Nuts for Speed Internet Campaign. Surprised, I glance back at my own display. My folder is titled: X7SATG10. A.k.a. no nuts. Not even an acorn.

Hmm.

"Oh. Gotcha," I force out to Chad, who looks mighty confident now that he knows his competition can't even read.

I wait for him to immerse himself once more in all things nuts, and then slip a flash drive from my pocket to copy the folder. Without knowing how closely these company laptops are monitored, I don't want to risk transferring the folder to one of my cloud drives.

"How's it going over here?" a too familiar voice booms out.

I startle a bit at the intrusion and instinctively shift my screen further from view. Mr. Reedweather approaches with a countenance I can only describe as "gleeful." If he had a mustache, he'd be twirling it sinisterly. His expression deflates the closer he gets, though, until finally he hovers in grim silence. Is he upset about the lack of blood on our particle board cubicles?

"It's going exceedingly well, sir," says Chad, Mr. Exceedingly.

FYI—number of times I've used the word exceedingly: one. To describe Chad-Something just now.

"Excellent," Mr. Reedweather says, brightening. He's also now stroking a pretend beard in my mind. Maybe a tiny dog. Could go either way.

His real hands tuck beneath his elbows when he crosses his arms. "You know who you two remind me of?"

"Cowboys?" Chad suggests.

Huh?

"No. *Me* when I was your age. I hope you know that I wish there was a place for both of you at this company."

Aw, I bet he says that to all the interns. I plaster a grateful smile on my face while Chad murmurs something about being "exceedingly" happy to be here. My secret folder has finished copying, and my hands twitch in my lap to remove the flash drive and close the window. Any action now would mean certain death, however, and those pretend reality TV cameras are watching. Reed Reedweather, too, who seems to have forgotten we actually do work at his company.

"Do you remember that story of the Middle Eastern boy who encounters a sacred vessel that houses a wizard?"

"Aladdin?" Chad's mesmerized expression makes me think he just heard a completely different sentence.

"Yes! That's it. Aladdin." Reedweather rocks back on his heels, his face scrunching into *Considered Wistfulness*. I'm almost positive he's making up this memory on the spot. Fucking genius.

"I used to be that boy, Mark-O." He says this directly to me because I'm the poor kid, I guess? Or the Middle Eastern kid. Or the pursuer of sacred vessels. I don't actually know, but it pisses Chad off, so I'm cool with it. "All it takes is a dream, son. Just. One. Dream." His gaze shifts to a giant framed photograph of a rainbow on the wall that confirms exactly that. *Dare to dream.* Also, pretty sure Aladdin was an unapologetic thief, so *technically*, it takes a dream and a dash of criminal aptitude. Judging by the folder I found, I'm beginning to think it's perhaps more dash and less dream.

"Mr. Reedweather, can I get your opinion on the creative direction for the Nuts campaign?"

I love the flicker of confusion on Reedweather's face before he covers it with a grave, very important nod. "Of course, son. Let's have a look." He circles around

Chad's desk to see his screen, and I use the distraction to eject the flash drive and slip it back into my pocket.

"So you see, the cashew nut, Marcona almond, and macadamia nut are struggling with the internet streaming of the movie they're watching. In walks the pine nut and..."

That's when I learn "biting your tongue" can be a very literal response to a situation.

REAL MARK

MARCOS

We have set breaktimes (I think), but when you work in conjoined-twin proximity to the head of the nut enthusiasts fan club, your need for coffee and bathroom breaks jumps exponentially. It's a convenient cycle, really, since more coffee means more bathroom breaks, which means more time wandering the office instead of listening to orgasmic nut-related outbursts.

I've just stirred in a splash of creamer for the sixth time today when a distinguished man in his mid-thirties breezes into the breakroom. The blue mug in his hand reads "Badass Accountant," and I decide this is my new favorite person at Reedweather Media behind Eva.

"What's up?" he says, shoving his mug into the machine.

"Hey. I'm Marcos. It's my first day."

He stills and surveys me directly. Is that sympathy in his expression? "Marcos, huh? So, I'm *Mark*. Nice to meet you." He holds out his hand, and I shake it with a smirk.

"A real Mark. I like it," I say.

"A real Mark?"

"Mr. Reedweather calls me Mark-O."

"Ah. Yeah." Mark rolls his eyes and pulls his mug from the machine. He opts for a single creamer as well, and I wonder if best friend relationships have ever been built on less. "Well, I'm 'the gay Mark,' so…"

"Wait. What? He actually calls you that?"

"Yeah." He shrugs. "I mean, he's never said those words but… you'll see."

"I already think I do. I'm beginning to get the sense that *Rabid Inclusivity* doesn't mean what Reedweather thinks it means."

He snickers and takes a sip of his badass accountant coffee.

"So, accounting?" I ask, waving toward his mug.

"Yeah, but like, *extreme, hardcore* accounting." He even flexes, and I can't help but notice Mark's got quite the bicep. Wonder if we could be gym buddies. "You? Let me guess, new intern?"

"You got it. What gave it away?"

"Eh, the tie. Also the look of abject horror. You picked a real bull for your first rodeo, my friend."

I laugh and shrug. "I'm a Yorkshire boy. We like our challenges insurmountable and slathered in pâté."

"Now I'm intrigued. What kind of a pâté?"

"Oh. There are different kinds?"

He arches a brow, and I shrug.

"You're not a very good Yorkshire boy, are you," he says, but his smile implies he doesn't hate that fact.

"Not really. I'm pretty sure my scholarship was some kind of social experiment put on by the Psychology department."

Mark snorts a laugh, then sobers when his focus lands on something behind me.

"Here we go," he mutters. "Watch this."

I almost choke on my coffee when I follow his gaze to the entrance of the breakroom.

"I see my two Marks have found each other!"

Reedweather claps our shoulders like what he said is actually a thing.

"You have a good weekend?" Reedweather asks my new friend. Does this guy ever work? All he seems to do is wander around the office preventing others from doing so.

Note to future CEO self: Do shit.

"It was great, thanks," Mark says dryly. He takes another sip of coffee to fill the awkward silence that follows.

"Did you go on any exciting adventures with your *partner?*"

Once again, there are words I recognize that don't sound like words I know. Mark's eyebrows scrunch in confusion as well.

"Well, Carter is pretty busy with the restaurant, but I went to a hockey game with my brother." He adds a shrug.

I mean, that sounds *adventurous* to me, so I offer a reassuring nod. Mark's gaze locks with mine, and I have to stifle a laugh.

"Hockey! Fantastic. Such a great sport," Reedweather says with a vigorous nod. "Carter is Mark's partner," he then explains to me, in case I'm stupid, I guess.

Mark rolls his eyes. I clench my fists to keep from laughing. "Partner? Like for tennis?" I ask innocently.

Mark's eyes flash with amusement—and a warning—but come on.

Reedweather clears his throat, suddenly very interested in the coffee machine. One could even say, *exceedingly* interested.

"Do you play tennis, Mark?" Reedweather asks in my new favorite recovery of all time. His back is to us as he studies the strange machine he's probably never used in his life. He has a male assistant for that.

Mark's gaze snaps to mine, a grin breaking over his lips. "No, just racquetball," he says, and I love that I can't tell if he's serious or not.

"Ah, another sport that can involve partners," Reedweather says with some relief.

"And lots of intense, sweaty, intimate movement," Mark adds. I actually have to bite down on my thumbnail this time. Mark widens his eyes at me, daring me to participate.

23

"Personally, I've never tried *racquetball*, although I've been curious about it at various points in my life," I say, once I can steady my voice. "Maybe you and Carter can show me sometime?"

Reedweather pounds the cappuccino button, obviously convinced that the cup-fill speed is controlled by the button-pressing speed.

"You look pretty fit," Mark says to me. "Even if *racquetball* isn't your sport, I'm sure it'd be fun to show you the ropes."

Reedweather coughs out a curse. "This damn machine is broken," he mutters.

"What about you, Mr. Reedweather?" I ask.

"Huh?" He twists around with a flash of acknowledgment.

"Racquetball. Do you play? It's probably pretty popular at your country club, right? I bet a lot of guys play. Maybe even more than you think?"

He clears his throat. "Oh, uh, sure. Yeah. You need to book the court, though. You can't just go barreling in whenever and with whomever you want." His shoulders relax as he settles into the zone of hearing his own voice. "There's a hierarchy, you see. Bet you didn't know that. A few on top; the rest on the bottom. It's all about positioning and how long you've been around. For example, I'm third generation Pinewood material, so I'm always on top. Always."

Mark and I exchange a look as Reedweather continues his monologue. Our silent pact: *We shall, under no circumstances, interrupt this speech. May it never end.*

"…Because it's only from the top that you get the full view of how far you've come…"

Exactly. *Dogmatic Positioning*. That's what I always say.

* * *

BACK AT MY DESK, the atmosphere isn't nearly as fun as my encounter with Mark and Mr. Reedweather's veiled homoerotic fantasies. Chad is still nut-fervent, and I still don't have a clue what to do about the strange files I've stumbled upon. Eva's frequent glances aren't helping. They're supposed to be discreet. I can tell by the way she averts her gaze when I catch her staring through her open office door. Flirtatious? Maybe, but there's something else—something that has my own gaze lifting in curiosity throughout the afternoon. My heart rate picks up with each collision of our stares. Has she realized she sent me the wrong file? Is she waiting for me to address it or hoping I won't? What if it's more carnal? What if she really does just like to look? I'm accustomed to the attention of women. Hell, Nate convinced me to cash in on that charm for the past two summers. Oh shit, what if she recognized me from one of my shows?

My foot starts tapping anxiously beneath my desk. She couldn't, right? No, Nate and I were careful to stay away from trendy spots where our worlds might collide. Then again, is my boss remembering me naked on a stage really worse than knowing I'm holding incriminating documents on a flash drive in my pocket?

"Of course it can't be a peanut. Duh," Chad hisses under his breath. I glance over, watching as he sketches something on a notepad. Doesn't appear to be a peanut. More like—is that a blimp? "Cashews, cashews, cashews," he mutters to himself. "What would cashew pants look like?"

What *would* cashew pants look like? I stare back at my screen, doing everything I can to ignore the blistering gaze I feel from the neighboring office.

5—MARISYA

MARCOS

I look like shit today. After poring over the stolen files all night, I finally talked it over with Nate this morning. His advice was to pretend I have no clue what these files are and ask for the nut folder like I just realized I hadn't been researching nuts all along. No point sabotaging my career before it even starts. He also says there's no way she knows about my stripper career and found the thought way too amusing for my taste. But Nate's a go-with-the-flow kind of guy, while I'm more of a throw-shit-at-every-fan-I-can-find type. The result? I look like shit today.

Eva must notice when she calls me into her office ten seconds after I arrive. I haven't finished my coffee and wonder if this is the kind of meeting where one is permitted to bring refreshments. Her expression when I enter makes me glad I left it on my desk.

"Good morning, Marcos. How are you today?"

I force a tight smile. "Fine."

Her look screams *skeptical* as she waves me to one of the chairs in front of her desk. "How's the nut research going?"

"Pretty good. Turns out there's a wide variety of nuts in the nut family. Almonds, macadamia, walnuts, and of course, pine nuts…"

Her gaze narrows. "You're not actually doing the market research on nuts, are you? You understand the campaign is streaming quality. Zero relation to the nut kingdom."

"Is it? Damn. Peanuts are my jam."

Silence.

"You know, because peanut butter and jam… right."

News flash: I'm not as hilarious when I'm exhausted. By the arch of her brow, she wholeheartedly agrees.

"Late night?" she asks after another pause.

"Yeah. Researching."

"Nuts?"

"No?"

"Is that a question?"

"No?"

Her lips press together, and I wonder about the record for an intern getting fired. "So what were you researching?"

"Well…"

"Marcos."

"Satellites."

Boom. Dust mites and desk residue sprinkle around us in imaginary fallout as I read her reaction in the silence. Surprise to curiosity to… relief?

"Satellites, really." That is most definitely *not* a question. "Can you elab—"

"Evangeline! Oh. Em. Gee!"

My boss's door crashes open to reveal a runway-ready scorcher of a woman. Tall, chic, and all manner of gorgeous, she stalks forward on four-inch heels like she's confused about what separates an office from a place that displays weird clothing. Yeah, I'm totally cool with that.

"Marisya. What are you doing here?" Eva squeaks out, flustered for the first time since I've met her. And this is a woman who spends her days surrounded by Reed-weathers and Chads.

"Hey you, baby doll. Had to pop in before I jet. Literally! Ha ha. Milan this week. Remember?"

Marisya's legs are the longest appendages I've ever seen. In those tiny fashionable shorts, it's pretty much criminal. I try so, so hard not to stare at the miles of smooth, shiny skin but holy mother of—

"Marcos. This is my roommate, Marisya. Marisya, this is... but again, why are you here?" Eva clears her throat, obviously not thrilled with the way her goddess room-mate leans on the desk and juts her ass in my direction. Well, not exactly in my direction. It's more of a suggestion. Just enough to have to look, and then feel like a creeper for doing it.

"It's a pleasure, Marcos," she croons over to me. *Croons* is the only word for when a woman like that flashes perfect white teeth and majestic cheekbones at you. Piercing light brown irises strike at me from almond-shaped orbs and... oh shit. We're back to almonds. The universe totally loves me right now.

"Nice to meet you too," I say. "Milan, huh? That's quite a trip."

"I'm a model."

Duh.

She turns and leans against the desk to face me. Just to be sure I have no chance of focusing on anything else, her index finger runs along her full bottom lip. "You ever do any modeling, Marcos?"

"Me? Not really." Well, I mean, define *modeling*.

"Hmm..." Her gaze scours my face before drifting to my shirt. Somehow I think it's not the tie that got her attention, and yeah, come to think of it, today's button-down is a bit snug. I kind of shrunk it in the wash and didn't have time to forage through Nate's closet in my mad dash out the door after our conversation this morning. "You could you know. Don't you think, Eva? He's got the bone structure. And those eyes? Damn. You'd devour a camera."

Her gaze travels over me with innuendo I don't mind even a little.

"Marisya, he's—"

"His hair is just so… tuggable. Don't you think? You single, Marcos?"

The only thing better than this beautiful woman's interest is the look on Eva's face right now. I should definitely shut this down but…

Shit, meet fan.

"Very."

Marisya's grin widens in direct correlation to Eva's frown.

"Okay. Thanks for stopping by," Eva says, hurrying around her desk. We still don't know why she did. I get the sense her *roommate* operates by very different life standards. I'm dying to know how this odd pairing happened. In two seconds flat Eva becomes a beautiful, no-nonsense screen between her roommate and me. "Have a *fantastic* time in Milan."

What happens next is quite possibly the most awkward hug I've ever seen.

"I will, hon," Marisya says before peeking around her to scan me again. I'm pretty sure I'm still wearing clothes but find myself checking just to be sure based on her scalding stare. This is officially the best day ever.

She straightens to leave, and I rise like the gentleman I am.

"It was great meeting you, Marcos." She tugs my hand to pull me in for one of those cheek-brush kisses. "Look me up," she whispers in my ear. She smells like oranges. God, I love oranges right now.

"Great meeting you too," I say, releasing her hand when she steps back. Her eyes lock on mine for another lingering suggestion before she turns back to her roommate.

"Ciao, bella," she sings on her way out, wriggling her fingers at Eva. I get a blown kiss and a wink.

The door crashes closed with the same violence with which it opened. Hurricane Marisya. Hmm.

I drop to my chair, drained and exhilarated. "Your roommate, huh?"

"Kind of. Long story."

"You two are practically twins. Be honest. How often are you swapping power-suits and mini-shorts?"

Her glare might be even cuter than her smile. I certainly have an easier time earning those.

"Our relationship is… complicated."

"By the fact that you're polar opposites?"

"By the fact that we're sisters."

Sisters? I curb my surprise.

"Stepsisters."

Oh.

"Ex-stepsisters, actually."

"And now you're roommates?"

She shrugs. "Well, she needed a place to crash while she figured things out, and I had a spare room. That was two years ago, so here we are."

Interesting. So corporate queen Eva Reedweather also has quite the soft spot beneath that professional severity. Now I'm really intrigued. Enough to make me want to push further and see what else I can find.

"When does Marisya get back from Milan? A week from now?"

"Don't even think about it," she warns, pointing at me.

"Not thinking, just—"

"No."

I shrug. "She seemed interested."

"She's interested in everyone. The fact that you're unusually attractive actually had no bearing on that interaction."

Unusually attractive? Bingo. I don't even have to acknowledge the slip. Her sudden flush takes care of that all on its own. She stalks back behind her desk, her glare deepening into a scowl. So the composed iron commander wasn't just annoyed by the interruption; she was *jealous*. Like I said. Best. Day. Ever.

"Satellites, Marcos."

Damn. Worst day ever.

I swallow, studying my hands in my lap. Game time. Save my career or save my conscience? I'm too decaffeinated for this decision.

"Why would a marketing subsidiary of Sandeke Telecom have detailed operational drawings of a competitor's proprietary systems?" I ask, lifting my gaze in a direct challenge.

She stares back with a stony expression. Not cold, just unreadable. My fingers tingle from the urge to twist into strange shapes on my thighs, and I clench them into fists. Eva's gaze travels over my face, down to my too-tight shirt, and back to my face. Perhaps it's a bit premature to count myself among the great martyrs of human history, but *goodbye* permanent position.

"Why do you think?" she responds after a long silence. Her tone isn't rhetorical but inquisitive.

"I don't have a flattering answer to that question."

"What's your unflattering answer?"

"I wasn't supposed to see that folder. You were supposed to send me the nuts."

Her lips tick up in the slightest curve. It's creepy watching a statue try not to smile. "Maybe. You're deflecting."

"Can you blame me?"

"No."

"Is this one of those tests you were talking about?"

"Maybe. You're still deflecting."

"Chad only got the nuts."

"Chad can only handle the nuts." Definitely a line from *Two Interns, One Job Opening.*

"So it *was* a test."

"Kind of."

"Did I pass?"

"I don't know yet." She leans back in her chair, narrowing razor-sharp eyes at me. I draw in a deep breath and stare back at my fists.

Industrial espionage. The words stream through my head, barreling toward my tongue. *It looked like corporate spying.* For some reason, I sense she's fishing for those very words, but is that a thing you can say to your boss of twenty-four hours? What weird intern wormhole is this? I squirm under the weight of her strange evaluation.

There's a twenty-percent chance Marisya would take me to Milan if I ran after her right now. We'd live the highlife on whatever private jet she has access to. Dance in some posh night clubs. Make out in picturesque locations that make better selfies than make-out locations. Pretty much do anything but sit here talking about—

"I read your thesis," she continues, finally. "On ethics and the clandestine monopolization of big business."

"Wait. Yesterday?"

"A month ago, when I found it on your department website."

W. T. F.

"I found it fascinating. Insightful and inspiring. Quite frankly, after reading your paper, I was surprised you'd even want to work for a company like Sandeke Telecom."

"I work for Reedweather Media."

She smirks. "Right. Don't play ignorant, Marcos. You can't pull it off."

"I'm here for the industry experience."

"So we're just résumé fodder for you?"

"I didn't say that."

Her gaze bores into me, scours my soul. I stare back, happy to let her look and prove my innocence. I'm a kid who had nothing, earned something, and was handed a ticket to everything. What was I supposed to do when Reedweather called with this opportunity? Or did they call?

"Why was I *recruited* for this internship? Don't most candidates apply on their own?"

"Yes. All of them."

My heart rate picks up at the implication, launches into a fury when she casts a wary glance around the room. Pulling out a notepad, she scribbles an address and rips off the page.

"Meet me here on your lunch break. Alone."

I take the paper and stare at it for a moment before shoving it into my pocket. A secret meeting with my gorgeous, intelligent boss? Hell. Yes.

6—J-DAWG

MARCOS

For the love of allergists everywhere, Chad and his nuts need to take it down at least seven notches. Dude is intense. And not the good kind of intense that gets shit done with two-finger salutes. This is the kind of intense that believes bigger is more, louder is more, and more is just *more*. I'm pretty sure his artistic vision is now an actor jumping from a plane in a giant pistachio suit. Also, there might be a white Bengal tiger involved, but I wasn't entirely clear on that part. Because... snow? Yep, there's snow too.

"So once Parachute Pistachio lands, this army of pecans comes storming in like —*bam, bam, bam!*" He makes a shooting motion that tells me the pecans will be armed. I surmise their lack of actual arms to hold the weapons isn't a concern.

"What if the pecan army was more of a medieval conception," I suggest, mostly to watch his face contort into the shape it is now. "Like crossbows and spears and stuff. They could wear chain-mail armor or even the classic villager getup."

His eyes ignite into the wonderest of wonder. "Oh! There could be a Cashew Queen and maybe..." He taps his chin. "A Brazil Nut King!" He winces. "Shit. I mean, the actual nut because it's a badass nut. No offense. I've got nothing against your people."

I lift a brow, now incredibly curious about how everyone in this place pictures Pennsylvania. "Okay? So, good luck with your... nuts."

Staring back at my screen, I check the time again. Only five more minutes until I can sneak away under the auspices of lunch. Eva's note is burning all kinds of holes in my pocket. More specifically, the look in her eyes when she gave it to me. What exactly is going on? All I know for sure is that nothing is as it seems, and whatever intern competition I'm in is in a completely different dimension than Chad the Nut King. For the record, there will be no pistachios jumping out of planes on my watch. In fact, I'm almost positive that nuts won't play any role in my future at this company.

"You have plans for lunch?"

I glance up to see Mark and his kick-ass mug hovering beside my desk.

"Crap, yeah. Tomorrow?"

He nods. "Sure." Leaning close, he casts a conspiratorial look around the room. "We need to debrief after yesterday's breakroom encounter."

I smirk. "You inviting me to play *racquetball,* Mark?"

"You interested?" he returns with a glint.

"Racquetball? I fucking love racquetball," Chad interrupts.

Mark and I stare over at him. Chad's expression is all swagger and zero awareness. I couldn't have asked for a better combination in this scenario.

"Dude, I was the racquetball *king* in college," he continues as Mark and I fight not to look at each other. "That's right. Pimped that shit like an animal."

I bite my lip. I feel Mark's delight beside me.

"I'm sure," I force out.

"Yeah, I would've gone pro, but my partner ditched me."

"No way," Mark says, somehow with a straight face.

I close my eyes and pull in a steadying breath.

"Yeah, that bastard. Hooked up with Jamison Henry. Our suitemate! Worst part, they did it right under me. Can you believe it?"

"I do, actually. Totally believe it," Mark replies, this time with less control of his snicker. When I make the mistake of meeting his gaze, I have to cover my snort with a cough. "Well, hang in there, man. Plenty of fish in the sea, right?"

Chad grunts, a scowl descending over his features. "Yeah, but fish have fins. I need good hands that can handle a stick and balls, ya know?"

Mark blinks, his lips wrestling hard against a response. Looks painful, actually. With a deep breath, he forces his attention back to me. "Tomorrow, man. Lunch." Then he's gone, leaving me alone with pouty, racquet pimp Chad. I watch Mark's shoulders jerk with laughter as he walks way.

"Coulda gone pro," Chad mutters.

* * *

I FOLLOW the address to Midtown East, certain I've misunderstood something. Far from a stuffy members-only lunch spot, this building looks more like a nightclub. Oh wait. It *is* a nightclub, I learn, when I duck through the industrial-looking entrance. The door isn't manned at this hour, and I squint through tacky purple lighting for a sign that I haven't gotten lost.

Eva spots me and waves me toward a booth at the back of the club. If it were ten hours later and four drinks past sober, I'd think she intended to seduce me. This is definitely a booth that requires condoms.

"What are we doing here?" I ask, sliding in beside her. It's a curved monstrosity, spongier than I expect, and I find myself sinking into the massive silver cushion. A table sits at an uncomfortable distance for eating, but plenty comfortable for entwining legs and laps.

"Sorry for the clandestine meeting, but I had to be sure we could talk freely."

"I'd say we're pretty safe."

I scan the space, empty except for a few employees bustling around. Eva draws my attention with the scrape of a container on the distant tabletop.

"Hope you like Cobb. All guys like Cobb salad, right?" She sounds nervous. Because I might not like Cobb salad? Probably not.

I shrug. "Weird stereotype, but I'm one guy who does."

She twists a faint smile.

Admittedly not my best material but then I'm in a purple vomit nightclub at noon on a Wednesday with my boss. Another situation business school doesn't prepare you for. Oh yeah. Also, with a Cobb salad I can't reach.

I stare awkwardly at the container. Do I pull it onto my lap? Squat closer to the table?

"This is my brother's club," she explains.

"Your brother?"

"Kyle. Well, stepbrother. *Ex*-stepbrother."

"Ah. Marisya's brother?"

"No. He doesn't know Marisya. She belongs to Shauna Lee, wife number three. Kyle is Trina June's son from her first marriage."

"And Trina June is… your current stepmother?"

"Nope. She was number two. Anyway, Kyle's club doesn't open until late, so I come here when I need to escape."

"Escape?"

Her jaw tightens as if she slipped. "Sorry. Maybe 'escape' wasn't the right word."

"Maybe it was."

Her eyes search mine, probing in the sultry glow of stripper-violet. She wants to say more. I see the words crest on her lips, then disappear when she sucks in a breath. Her fingers clench in her lap like they're rebelling as well. Are they itching to touch me or push me out of the booth? I lift my gaze from her white knuckles to brown eyes that dart suspiciously away from my lips.

"Sorry. This was probably a bad idea," she mutters.

"Eva, I—"

"Reno?" a booming voice interrupts from across the club. "Oh *hell* no!"

Huh?

I turn to find a giant tattooed man stalking toward us. His stern expression melts into a grin that proves he's way happier to see me than I am him. *Shit!* How in the…? I cast an anxious glance at Eva before plastering a smile on my face. Have I mentioned: *shit, shit, shit*?

"Um… hey, man."

"You know J-Dawg?" Eva asks, unpleasant surprise all over her face. At least her anxiety is gone—packaged and transferred to me, thank you very much. "Wait, who's Reno?"

I shake my head. Then nod. Then shake it again. This can't be happening. J-Dawg was a bouncer at two of the clubs where Nate and I performed. He works here too? Is this more reality show drama? I frantically search for cameras.

"My boy Reno here? We go way back," J-Dawg says, all teddy-bear smiles from that badass biker behemoth. "You snagged a good one, Ms. Eva. This is—damn, kid! How you been? Lookin' good, as always." He adds a wink that adds nothing but more panic.

I try to breathe as Eva raises a brow.

"Oh shit. You here to audition for ladies' night?" he asks before I can get my brain and tongue on board with any of this. "Auditions were last week, but I'll totally put in a word with the boss. You ever seen your man dance, Ms. Eva? I ain't exactly into dudes, but this kid's got moves that'll make a guy think." He taps his bald head and adds a low whistle that makes me pray to the cushion gods for a swift burial in a plush, silver grave. "But I probably don't need to tell you that, Ms. Eva. Sly fox." And now he winks at my boss. That's right. My boss. Who is almost one hundred percent thinking about me naked right now. Well, thinking of *Reno* naked.

I knew I should've stayed in bed this morning.

"Wait… You…" More words try to push past Eva's perfect lips, but as is so often the case, get stuck in my bewildering presence. I have that effect on her apparently.

"Eva is my boss," I say evenly to J-Dawg.

His eyes widen about three sizes—first in shock, then confusion. "Aren't you some bigwig boss lady in marketing?" he asks her.

Eva's lips twitch but she suppresses the smile as she nods. J-Dawg's puzzled gaze snaps back to me. Then to her. Then…

"Ahhh, gotcha. You need strippers for a commercial or something?"

Oh god. I bury my face in my hands, tugging madly at my hairline.

"Pardon me?" Eva asks.

"Unless... wait, you don't have them on staff there, right? I mean... because..."

When I dare a look back at his face, J-Dawg is definitely preparing to quit this club and apply at the marketing firm that staffs full-time strippers. Or part-time... do we work shifts? Oh god.

"Marcos?" Eva asks, focusing a laser stare on me.

"Marcos?" J-Dawg echoes, confused.

"My name," I force out. "My actual legal name I use for actual professional jobs."

J-Dawg stares in utter perplexity until—

"Oh shiiiiiit!" he whispers, pressing his fist to his mouth. "She's your *boss* boss. She doesn't know about your club time! Fuck."

"Not on my résumé, dude," I mutter.

"Sorry!" he mouths six minutes and one-hundred-eight words too late. With a sheepish smile, he backs away from the table, waving as if our business lunch can now proceed as planned. Right.

"Ahh," I groan, scrubbing a hand over my face.

"You're a stripper?" Eva asks, just in case that wasn't already the biggest, fattest elephant in the room.

I heave a sigh and settle back against the cushion. *"Was,"* I say finally.

"Reno," she murmurs quietly, as if testing the name. Her eyes change the longer she studies me, scanning my face, my chest, up to my hair. Back to my eyes. I can't read her expression.

"Books are expensive," I explain, mostly to fill the silence. Seriously, what's going through that overactive brain? The absence of a freak-out is somehow more alarming. "Room, board. My scholarship covered a lot of the tuition but..." I shake my head and rest my elbows on my knees. "Anyway, I tried waiting tables and all that, but time is expensive too. In one night I could make the equivalent of two weeks at the restaurant."

"Wow."

Finally, a response, and I tilt my head for another read of her face. Wait… is she smiling? I squint, certain I must be missing something.

"I just… I'm sorry. I'm just surprised, I guess," she says, clearly working to regain her composure.

"So am I fired?"

She flinches. "Fired? Why would you be fired?"

"Um, because… *Reno*." I wave my hand up and down my torso.

"You think I care how you got yourself through school?"

I shrug. "I'm sure *Chad* doesn't have 'successful stripper' on his résumé."

"Definitely not *successful*." Her grin widens when mine slips out.

Maybe I'm starting to breathe again.

"Relax, Marcos. Of course you're not fired. If anything…" Shaking off a thought, she clears her throat and straightens. "Never mind. Just one more question, and then we drop it. Did you really earn two weeks' worth of waiting tables in one night?"

I shrug. "Sometimes more."

She crosses her arms and blisters a look that lands sparks all over my body. "If that's true, then I stand by my initial response. '*Wow.*'"

BELIEVE IT OR NOT, Eva didn't invite me to lunch to discuss my skill at removing clothing for money. Soon her expression settles back into the severe mask I'm more accustomed to.

"You were correct, Marcos. Those satellite files I sent you were a test."

My stomach drops. "And I failed?"

"What? No. You passed."

She slides toward me until our legs hover dangerously close. I try to ignore how warm and firm her thigh feels when she leans for her messenger bag. It doesn't help that she's one hundred percent going to think about me naked at least a dozen times over the next hour. Her gaze a second ago made that clear. Hell, maybe she is now. Maybe she's imagining me on the stage to our left, unbuttoning my shirt in slow, deliberate movements. Tossing devilish smirks like they're candy at a parade. Am I performing a solo show for her, or is she a voyeur in a packed house, watching me seduce a room of guests, high on the awareness that she's the one who will take me home? She'll get to touch, while they can only drool. Because she could. Take me home. Touch. I'd be putty in her hands with her penetrating stare and more penetrating brain that stimulates my blood in illicit, confusing ways. *Challenging.* That's what has my capillaries pumping toward forbidden parts that have no business at this meeting with my boss.

I swallow and concentrate on also ignoring how amazing she smells.

"Look at this," she says, shoving a tablet into my hands. "The folder I sent you yesterday had the same type of information but contained dummy files. This is the real stuff."

I force away all thoughts of nakedness to study the screen. Scrolling through drawing after drawing, I release a heavy breath. Damn. This has to be SAT Systems' entire operational protocol. I spent a lot of time studying quality management systems for large companies as part of my research. Paging through these files, I recognize confidential SOPs, proprietary hardware design drawings, financial records, and all manner of potentially damaging information if this stuff fell into the wrong hands. Wait, is that a year-to-date profit and loss report?

What I still don't know… is this stuff *in* the wrong hands? Whose side is Eva on? She's Reedweather's daughter, and *he's* clearly a right-hand henchman of demon-mogul Denver Sandeke. And yet, if she read my thesis, she has to know I wouldn't be okay with this. I'm certainly not going to *help* a goliath corporation take down its upstart competition.

"You must have a lot of questions," she says while I continue scanning the documents.

"So many."

"Good. Shoot."

I glance over, and she shrugs.

Lowering the tablet, I shift to face her. "Fine. How'd you get these?"

"I found them on the server when I was cleaning up old files."

"When?"

"Three weeks ago."

"Who else knows about this?"

"I don't know. That's what I need to find out."

"Who put them there?"

"Also a question."

"What is Sandeke Telecom planning to do with them?"

She shakes her head. "Don't know yet."

"What are *you* planning on doing with it?"

"Depends on the answer to the other questions."

I draw in a deep breath, inspecting her face for hidden clues. She seems honest, transparent. Time to ask? "Are you investigating to encourage this spying or stop it?"

Doubt flickers in her eyes. Disappointment, maybe. "You're not sure of the answer to that?"

I shrug, searching her face. "We just met yesterday, and so far, my experience at Reedweather Media has been a freaking circus. I have no idea what to think about any of it. Plus, you're the owner's daughter. Don't you have as much to gain or lose as Reedweather does? Wouldn't you want your parent company's competition to fail?"

Yep, she looks hurt. Not angry, though. She sighs and presses her lips together. I see her brain working behind those dark eyes, evaluating, strategizing as much as I am. Can she trust the stripper intern she barely knows? I have nothing to lose except a day and a half of questionable employment. Her next statement risks her entire career, maybe more.

She takes a long draught of water from her bottle and squeezes it violently in her hands.

"Yes, I'm the boss's daughter. But *the boss* is also a pompous, misogynistic bigot, in case you haven't noticed."

I bite back a smile. "I may have noticed."

She clears her throat. "Reedweather Media is successful in spite of my father, not because of him. I've been working my ass off since I was a teenager to compensate for his inadequacy. I used to think one day he'd recognize that. That it was *my* company I was building because one day he'd appreciate my role in keeping him afloat and reward me by turning over the reins. And you know what he did?"

"Hired a clone of himself to take over?"

"Bingo." She waves her hand with a grunt. "*Grant Worthington.* Then to add insult to injury, he gives me some stupid title he made up as a consolation. Probably because he thinks I'm clueless enough to be appeased by that." She quiets, glancing around the room before leaning close. "The truth is I was cleaning up the server because I was planning to resign. I had an incredible opportunity at another firm, but when I stumbled across that folder, I knew I had to stay. I'd never be able to live with myself if I walked away. My dad is a bumbling idiot, but Denver Sandeke is an omnipotent monster—Sandeke likes my dad because he's easy to control. I didn't really have a choice once I found the folder. Even if I can't win a war, I have to fight this battle."

She draws in a deep breath. "Thing is, I can't do it alone. I'm too embedded in management and the DNA of the Sandeke Empire to have a prayer at investigating what's going on. I needed an ally. A fresh face no one would suspect. Someone extremely bright, intuitive, street smart, and most importantly, ethical. Dad was already drooling over *Chad* for his stupid internship program; I found you for mine. Once I read your work and reviewed your interview notes, I knew you were exactly what I was looking for." She quiets, handing the conversation over to me with her gaze.

Well.

Fuck.

"You're risking a lot in telling me this," I say finally.

"I risked everything to tell you this. Sorry for the test, but you can understand why I had to be sure." She leans back, somehow looking relieved and anxious at the same time. "So what do you say, Marcos? Did I make a huge mistake or did my prayer work?"

I pull in a deep breath, staring at the distant faux marble tabletop. I was fourteen during my third year at Bellevue when I got slapped with full restrictions. Golden boy Billy Stanton framed me for stealing meds from the infirmary to save his own ass. Wasn't even narcotics. Something silly like ibuprofen. For a month I was denied rec time, visitors, even separated from my peers—I was a virtual prisoner, treated like a convict in juvie instead of an abandoned kid whose only crime was having shitty parents. No one would listen to my defense when I said it wasn't me. No one even cared that I had one. You know why? Because it was Billy Stanton's word against mine, and Billy Stanton was fucking *Chad*-Something, and Reed Reedweather, and Denver Sandeke, and whoever Grant Worthington is. Billy Stanton was the prince, and I was the write-off. That was my moment of enlightenment, when I accepted the truth:

1. The world is different for each of us.
2. I'm in the group that will have to work harder, smarter, and sacrificially.
3. I can resign to injustice or fight it.

At age fourteen, I chose to fight. Ten years later, I've not only experienced the blood and pain of battle, but also the sweet taste of a hard-fought victory.

My ass is almost completely engulfed in tacky silver stuffing at this point. I'll need a crane to pull me out of this booth. One could even say I'm currently the victim of *Dogmatic Positioning*. So is SAT Systems if I choose to do nothing.

I cross my arms and meet Eva's gaze. "I'm in. What do I need to do?"

7—BEVERLY HARRIS

MARCOS

I return from lunch with a clear directive but no clear direction.

What: Uncover the root and scope of Sandeke Telecom's industrial espionage against rival SAT Systems.

Who: ?

When: ?

Where: ?

How: ?

To that end, I have a follow-up non-date planning session with Eva at her condo tonight. For convenience only, this meeting will also include the strictly platonic consumption of food, and perhaps, wine. Her excessive use of the word "platonic" throughout the instructions has me questioning the definition.

I approach my work area to find Chad squatting on the floor. His chair is pushed back several feet as he crouches near the opening of his desk, posed suspiciously like a walnut in its shell. The fact that his head is where his knees should be isn't even in the top five of my questions as I study him. Tongue shoved between his lips, brow scrunched in utter confusion, Chad is the picture of a man possessed by the great mysteries of the universe.

"What do you suppose the most efficient geometric footprint of a pine nut is?" he asks, squinting up at me. "Extrapolating for a population of, say, five thousand?"

"A *population* of pine nuts?"

Because the personification of said pine nuts is the biggest problem with this scenario...

"You know what I mean. I'm thinking hexagonal, but then I'm afraid I'm only biased by honeycomb geometrics." His face contorts into what I interpret as a healthy fear of honeybee bias as he rocks back on his heels.

"Honeybees *are* very efficient," I offer, dropping to my chair. "You could be influenced by worse biases."

I've just fired up my laptop when a crash draws my attention back to Chad's weird math problem. He's now flopped to his back, his arms and legs spread wide and moving in rapid arcs as if indoor office snow-angel-making is now a thing.

"Chad?"

We snap our gazes toward the voice—Chad from the floor with a brief look of panic. Eva stares down in confusion, then concern. But when her glance skims over to me, her slight flush makes me wonder if she's suddenly thinking of me on stage, sans tie, button-down, and slacks. It's just a flash, however, before she's bending down to inspect the other, less-naked intern on the floor.

"Hey, Ms. Reedweather," he says, twisting a smile.

"You okay?"

His eyes trace a convenient perpendicular line to Eva's ass, which is now straining against the fabric of her pencil skirt. It's amazing how quickly an experienced sleaze-ball's face can change from confused (best pine nut shape?), to lecherous (Eva's ass), to opportunistic.

"I think so," he says, suddenly rubbing the back of his head. "That damn chair."

"Oh no. Did you fall?"

"Yeah, but no big deal."

Hang on. No fucking way.

I watch in slow motion as Eva kneels on the floor and reaches for the duplicitous liar's hand. Worst part, she doesn't see the triumphant grin he shoots me as their palms connect and she pulls him to a sitting position.

"Thanks," he hums in a sickly sweet voice. "Marcos wanted to help but I told him not to. Guess it hurt more than I thought."

Bastard. I glare at him, which only seems to encourage his bad acting.

"Am I bleeding?" he asks, brushing the side of his head that gently rested on a carpet for twelve seconds.

"Doesn't look like it."

"Whew," he says with a chuckle. "That would not have been good for the fundraiser tonight!"

"Fundraiser?"

"Oh yeah. My parents are board members on The MBF Project. Tonight is the annual gala. I'm supposed to introduce the keynote speaker."

"Is that so?"

He doesn't seem to notice her bored tone as he exhibits more exultant grinning.

"It's black tie of course. Champagne, heavy hors d'oeuvres. Pretty sure the mayor will be there."

"I see." She clears her throat and pushes to her feet. "Well, if you're okay, I'm going to get back to work."

"I think I am. Is there medical assistance on site should I need more attention?"

A fresh wave of concern washes over her face, but somehow I suspect it's not for Chad's head. "Do you think medical assistance will be necessary?"

"No," I interrupt, finished with this nonsense. "I saw the *incident*. I highly doubt he's been seriously injured. Isn't that right, Chad?"

There is *zero* triumph on his face when he glares at me this time. "I'll probably be fine," he mumbles.

"Okay, glad to hear it." Her gaze shifts between us, landing on mine for an extra beat. I nod discreetly, hoping she can read my reassurance, and breathe a sigh of relief when she disappears into her office.

"Way to kill my game, man," Chad hisses, inching his chair back to his desk with jerky leg movements while seated.

"*That* was your game? Acting like a manic starfish?"

"Chicks dig broken dudes. They wanna fix that shit. She was *this* close to riding my train."

Gross. And no. Pretty sure she wasn't even in the station.

"Whatever, man," I mutter, focusing back on my screen.

I sense the heat emanating from his side of the workspace in the silence that follows. If our rivalry was coldly civil before, it's open warfare now. And you know what? Fine. Bring it. I once took on the entire east wing of Bellevue when they bullied my best friend, Nash. This pansy-ass wouldn't last three seconds in a street fight.

I try to keep my snicker to myself at the thought of his manicured fingers balled in a fist, while his thin, scaly lips scream nut-related obscenities.

"What's so funny?" he hisses.

"Nothing," I say with a smirk.

"Obviously you find something amusing."

I look up from my screen and level a stare at him. "You ever been in a fight, Chad?"

"Of course," he snaps, eyes narrowing into an unconvincing scowl.

"Yeah? Okay," I snort, my attention back on my screen. I'm being petty. Immature. Definitely more Bellevue thug than Ivy League prodigy, but my patience for bullshit over the last two days is wearing thin.

"I have!" His face blossoms into a deep shade of indignation. "Junior year. A server insulted my sister for not tipping. So I hit him. *And* made sure he was fired." He leans back and crosses his arms with a self-satisfied smirk.

My god, he's serious.

I lift a brow, staring at him in disbelief. Yep, I take back my generous assessment that he'd last three seconds in a real fight. My new visual is Chad running down a sidewalk, flailing his arms. Maybe throwing a child or old lady behind him to block the threat. I shake my head and pick up the desk phone when it rings.

* * *

MY PHONE INTERVIEW was conducted by an HR assistant named Meredith, my in-person interview by another named Geena, and my orientation by a third named Roland. I have yet to meet the Director of Human Resources and was beginning to wonder if the entire department consisted of new grads who weren't sure what else to do with their degrees. None of them seemed particularly impassioned about their jobs. Then again, Reedweather doesn't seem to inspire much enthusiasm at any level of the organization—except maybe in their *exceedingly* ambitious intern department.

I approach HR Queen Beverly Harris' office with some measure of concern for what crisis would draw her out. Have I been written up already? I run a mental list of my encounters so far. All bizarre, some disturbing, but most involved me being the victim, not the perpetrator. Unless… did Reedweather finally figure out that racquetball isn't the sport he thought? Unlikely.

"Mr. Oliver, come in, come in."

Two things:

1. Mr. Oliver?
2. This woman has spiders on her cheeks.

I hesitate in the doorway, studying her red, watery eyes that have given way to disturbing mascara tarantulas.

"Are you okay?" I ask on instinct. Crap. Am I allowed to ask personal questions? So many hours of academic instruction, and I don't recall a single course that covered sobbing HR directors.

"I'm fine. Why would you say that?" She swipes a handful of tissues from the box on her desk and blots at her face, smearing the spider legs into panda smudges. She then blows her nose into another handful of tissues. After sanitizing her hands from a dispenser beside the tissue box, she clears her throat and stares at a folder in front of her. Blankly.

"Ms. Harris?"

Liquid floods her eyes again. "There's a... problem with—with... your... paper... wooooork." A sob breaks up the last word, and she reaches for another fistful of tissues.

I swallow, balancing awkwardly on the edge of my chair as she wails into her tissue pillow. Should I leave? Wait this out? Offer condolences?

"Um..."

"He used our Bordeaux!"

"The wine?"

"Of course the wine! From our anniversary trip."

"To France?"

"Of course to France!"

"Right." I bite my lip and lean back.

"And you know what she said?"

"Who? About you?"

"No! The wine!"

"The Bordeaux from France."

"Exactly! She said it was sour and not as good as the boxed stuff!"

"Wow." Still not sure who *she* is, but I, too, find her pedestrian palate offensive. "That is... um..."

"And she can't be more than twenty. Look at her! Just look!"

Beverly pounds her phone screen, long acrylic nails tapping out a complementary soundtrack for her wrath. She harrumphs with a strange mix of satisfaction and disgust, then flips the display toward me. Grinning back is a tan, bikini-clad coed who definitely looks like boxed wine is her jam. Probably frozen with a straw.

"Twenty seems like a reasonable estimate," I say for lack of *anything* else. I clear my throat and stare longingly at the folder on her desk. "Um, so the paperwork problem?"

Confusion pokes through her panda-mask of devastation. That is, until she also spots the folder on her desk. "Oh! Right. Yes." She opens the folder and scans the top page. "It appears we were unable to verify your immigration status, which is a requirement for employment at Reedweather. Laws, you know!"

"My immigration status?"

"Yes. You must be a U.S. citizen or have the necessary visas to be employed at this firm."

"I know that, but—"

"So, you see, as much as we work to foster a climate of *Rapid Inclusivity* here at Reedweather Media, it would be unethical—not to mention, illegal—for you to continue employment."

"But I—"

"Here is a list of resources to help you navigate this difficult and confusing time."

She hands me a brochure of a smiling woman in a business suit shaking hands with an older couple of ambiguous ethnic heritage.

"Ms. Harris, I'm a U.S. citizen."

Her hand stalls mid-transfer. Her eyes sink to the glossy photo with some measure of confusion—and maybe disappointment—that I won't need her brochure.

"I was born in Pennsylvania."

"Pardon?" She opens the folder again, squinting at the contents. "According to our records, the social security number listed in your file isn't registered to your name."

What? How...? Wait... "Does my *file* also say 'Mark Oliver'?"

"Yes, of course."

"Well, that must be the problem. That's not my name."

"It's the name on all of your paperwork." Her tone is less sympathetic now that I'm not an undocumented alien and just an imposter.

"Maybe, but that's not my name. It's Marcos Oliveira."

"So why does your paperwork say Mark Oliver?"

I shrug. "Everything I filled out said Marcos Oliveira. It's on my résumé and the transcripts I submitted as well."

She spins the folder around and smacks it on the surface in front of me. "See? Mark Oliver."

I shrug again. "Yes, I see that, but that's not my name. I didn't fill this out."

"So how am I supposed to verify your immigration status if your file has the wrong name?"

I shrug once more, not sure that's a talking point for my department. "I don't know, but that's not even my handwriting."

"Well, that's what's in my system. See?"

She tries to turn her computer screen toward me, but there are too many tchotchkes on her desk to allow such a maneuver. After a unicorn lands on the floor, two cats fall in the trash can, and a snow globe gets caught on the lower left corner of the monitor, she waves me around so I can look over her shoulder. I lean dutifully, and yes, her screen proves that which I never doubted.

"It definitely says Mark Oliver," I say.

"Exactly!"

"That's still not my name."

"Well, it's what's in the system."

"Okay… so how do we change the system?"

She fires a look I haven't seen since I told Sister Catherine there's no way tigers wouldn't have eaten the chickens on Noah's Ark. "You can't just *change* the system, Mr. Oliver."

"Oliveira."

"Mark."

"Marcos."

Her eyes narrow suspiciously, but at least she seems to be considering the fact that I might know my own name.

"I'm not sure what other possibility there is, Ms. Harris. My name is my name, and that's not it."

"Well, we'll just have to put your employment on hold until this gets sorted out."

I stare at her in disbelief. "Are you serious?"

"I'm sorry. My hands are tied." She doesn't sound sorry.

"But it's just a glitch and—"

"You're undocumented, sir."

"What?! I'm not undocumented! I presented all my *documents* yesterday to… to…" Damn, what was his name again? "Roland! He even copied them!"

"Yes, but those weren't for Mark Oliver."

"Because there *is* no Mark Oliver!"

"Well, that's not true, just not one with that social security number."

"Because that's not me!"

"Exactly."

"So of course it doesn't match my social!"

"Exactly. Now you understand."

"Oh my god! Just—just—" I lock my hands on my head, pacing in front of her desk. This can't be real. More intern initiation tests? More hidden cameras for the Oligarch Entertainment Channel? Ratings must be soaring right now.

"Mr. Oliveira, I'm going to have to ask you to calm down."

"You're firing me because *you* spelled my name wrong!"

She shrinks against the back of her chair, aghast. "*I* did no such thing."

"Okay, not *you* you, but your department."

"Pointing fingers is not productive, young man."

Breathe, Marcos. Breathe. I can't breathe. I drop to the chair, gripping the fancy armrests until my fingertips go numb.

"My hands are tied." She holds up her wrists to demonstrate since clearly I'm not getting it. "There's nothing I can do. No papers, no job."

"But I *have* papers! It's not my fault your *department* can't process them!"

Her arms cross over her flower-patterned chest; her panda eyes squint a furious stare of one who is trying to stay calm in the face of pressure. *This is what you've trained for, Bev.* I see the mantra running through her head. A hundred bucks says she has a brochure for this. Maybe an entire video series. Then again, maybe none of this would have happened if I'd just accepted the stupid pamphlet in the first place. Damn that happy old couple.

"Look, we're going to figure this out. I just need you to stay calm."

"I *am* calm," I seethe out. I don't sound calm. Probably don't look it either. Her lips press together in a thin line that tells me she agrees.

"I think it's best if you go back to your desk, pack your things, and take the rest of the day off while we try to figure this out."

"You're sending me home?"

"You can't work here until your paperwork is in order."

"But it's not my fault my paperwork isn't in order!"

"I understand your point of view, but I only know what the system tells me."

"But the *system* is wrong!"

"I understand you think that."

"I don't *think* that. It's not an opinion! That's not my name!"

"You're getting riled up again."

"Because—ahh!" I jump up and march to the door. "You know what, you're right. It's time for me to leave."

"Wise decision, Mr. Oliveira. We'll be in touch."

Somehow I manage not to slam the door on my way out.

Note to future CEO self: All of this. Transcribe every detail of this scene to add to the "Not" section of the manager training manual.

* * *

I FEEL no compulsion to make my exit seamless and discreet. I've had enough with this strange company. Enough with Reedweather and his hot air, Chad and his nut aggression, Beverly and... whatever the hell that was. Enough with it all, and especially—

"Marcos?"

I freeze mid-shove of my charger into my zip-portfolio.

Eva.

The mission.

The quest for the greater good.

Shit.

Chad's face is an invitation for a fist right now, but I ignore it in favor of the one reason I might not go storming out.

"Hey, Eva. Just packing up my desk."

"What? Why?"

I hear the alarm in her voice and avoid her eyes so I don't have to see it too.

"Ask Bev. Apparently, since your HR Department can't spell my name, I'm not allowed to work here."

"Huh? That doesn't make sense."

"Correct."

I shove my personal pen in the portfolio. Should've brought provenance for the pen as well to prove it's mine. I'll probably have to fight security at the door.

The door. Just a few steps and a short elevator ride to freedom. In an hour I can be on my couch, tossing back a beer and applying for another position.

Except, Eva's stare is in the way. Deep, searching, it impales me with a hint of desperation that plunges straight through my anger. But I'm no saint. I'm not. I have limits. Standards. Expectations. I deserve better than...

She chews on her lip and nods toward her door. "A word?"

No. No *words*. Because those lips are deadly, and right now I could still walk. Hell, I have the official corporate blessing to leave. I can wash my hands of this entire shit-storm and choose any one of the long list of opportunities vying for a Grade-A résumé like mine. I don't owe this place anything. In fact, *I'd* be remiss to stay, right? Right?!

Dark brown eyes plead with me, doing exactly what I knew they would when I fought so hard to avoid them. My feet, already positioned for retreat, suddenly won't move. My lungs, primed for a bitter F-U, feel heavy as I grip my portfolio in rebellious fists. Her penetrating stare doubles down through my defenses, piercing hard and low, threatening to haunt me. Can I walk right now and quit? Leave her to fight Sandeke alone? What would Nate do? Leave. And I usually do the opposite of Nate.

Sighing, I drop my portfolio on the desk and follow Eva into her office. She shuts the door and motions to her small conference table.

"What happened?" she asks.

"Short version or long version?" I shake off my own question. "Actually, never mind. The long version should also be the short version. They spelled my name wrong, which means they can't verify my social security number."

Her look is about what you'd expect when someone says a sentence like that.

"Okay…" She squints at the door, considering, until her expression changes sharply. "Wait. Beverly wasn't crying when you got to her office, was she?"

"Yeah. Freaking black widows under her eyes and everything."

"Crap. That's why." Eva groans and massages her forehead. "Okay, look. I'll handle Beverly. Just, Marcos, please don't quit. We need you. *I* need you." Her pleading gaze holds much more as she bores it into me.

Do pretty lashes and pouty lips work on me? No. Do pretty lashes and pouty lips on *this* woman work on me? Apparently, because suddenly I'm sighing my *resigned* sigh.

"I can't believe I'm doing this," I mutter. "Fine. But I don't know what you want me to do. I'm literally not allowed to work here."

"Thank you!" She lunges forward on instinct and freezes just before the collision. Shit, was she going to hug me? She's so close I can smell her expensive perfume as she hovers awkwardly, barely an inch away. Just the slightest shift, an accidental movement, and our bodies would make contact. My pulse picks up at the look in her eyes, the way her tongue slips over her lips as she ponders. Is she thinking the same? Hoping for a tectonic shift that would force her into my arms? With a nervous laugh, she pulls back, patting my arm on the return to her seat.

"Very good. I'm, uh, sorry about the confusion. And the way Bev treated you. I'll take care of it. Just hang out at your desk while I talk to her."

I nod, my gaze still locked on her full, red lips. Hers is fixed on mine.

* * *

"Mr. Oliveira?"

"Yes?"

"It's Beverly from HR."

"Hi, Beverly."

"Great news! We discovered the source of the issue. It turns out your name was entered incorrectly into our system."

"Really? Huh."

"I know. Hard to believe, but alas, here we are. Anyway, we corrected the error, and it appears everything is in order. Welcome to Reedweather Media, Marcos."

"Fantastic..."

PART II
DISCOVER

EVA

8—MARCOS OLIVEIRA

EVA

148: My IQ.

3.93: My final GPA from Columbia.

4: The number of MBA programs that accepted me. This was also the number to which I applied.

All of these facts support one irrefutable point: I, Evangeline Marigold Reedweather, am smart.

Well, it should have been an irrefutable point. Clearly, there's plenty to refute as I pace my foyer with the manic grace of an elephant in a 'roid rage. Darcy, my tortie kitten, watches in confusion as her person stalks the grounds in a manner suspiciously similar to her protest against needless food delays.

"Stop judging me," I snap at her. Her tiny kitten face tilts to the right as if to say, *"judge not, lest ye be judged."* Also, *"how stinking adorable am I?"*

She's not wrong.

"Stop being so adorable," I add, because obviously bullying a kitten is going to make it totally okay that I invited my ridiculously hot subordinate to my condo tonight. Alone.

Just to be clear, that fact in itself is not the basis for this current rash of self-recrimination.

Two points to consider here:

1. We have a legitimate, time-sensitive mission that must be addressed in a private location—like a personal residence.
2. His attractiveness, in theory, is completely irrelevant to said time-sensitive covert mission.

In fact, attractiveness in a male is not a factor I'm accustomed to considering in my daily interactions. As a female executive in a male-dominated world, my day is packed with men of all types, some attractive, some not, some competent, some not. Some have bad breath, some smell like mint fields, some attempt smarmy charm, others stick to aloof detachment. Some respect me, many don't, so yes, I'm also accustomed to working twice as hard, twice as smart, and twice as dedicated to filtering out potential distractions like how attractive a man may or may not be. Attractiveness is just one detail of many that shape the rainbow of male suits that color my day.

Until Marcos Oliveira.

Until cyan eyes, and sun-kissed, tousled hair, and that smile. Oh gosh, that smile that makes you certain there's wry humor simmering behind it you'd pay to experience from the front row. Box seats, season tickets, the full VIP experience.

And just when you can't keep your grubby brain off him, the universe plays the cruelest of all jokes. Pretty sure I heard cosmic cackling this afternoon when it paired that bright, sexy, irresistible representation of *every* archetype of a human male with the word stripper. S-T-R-I-P-P-E-R. So yes, now I not only have to manage his scalding hot brain teasing me with flashes of brilliance, I also have to blink away flashes of him *flashing*. Because ever since J-Dawg's careless revelation, my head has been a non-stop dirty-old-man reel of forbidden intern porn.

Yes, Marcos Oliveira, hired for his incredible intellect, is now naked in my head—always. Toned and slick and flaunting and being so, so inappropriate with those aqua eyes and deadly smile.

Which brings us to my pacing. See, what did I do with this potentially hazardous situation? Did I abandon my original plan and recalculate in light of unforeseen variables? Did I allow this paragon of forbidden crushes to walk away unscathed when Beverly inadvertently solved my ethical dilemma with her inability to spell? No. I begged him to stay and doubled down on what might possibly be the most foolish thing I've ever done. And this includes the time I passed on Stanford's PhD program to work for my father.

A knock at the door sends my heart rate into disarray, just as my pacing stalls mid-stomp. I'd wondered how long it would take for him to make the trek from the lobby to my door on the fifth floor after I buzzed him in. Not long enough.

Maybe he'll show up in a bear costume or something equally unappealing like the ill-fitting polos Chad wears every day. Can a shirt *be* ill-fitting on a torso like Marcos'? Because he definitely works out. Like *works* out works out. Not that I've noticed—frequently—over the last couple of days. For the record, this information *is*, in fact, relevant because a healthy employee is more likely to experience job satisfaction and increased productivity. Never mind that the secret job I hired him for requires neither of these things and—

"Stop judging me!" I hiss at Darcy, whose head tilts to the identical angle on the other side. "Gah, you're so adorable. Come here."

I scoop her up with a slight detour on my way to the door and realize her adorableness was only one justification for the last second cuddle. The bigger reason: Marcos is not wearing a bear costume or ill-fitted polo when I open the door. In fact, he's wearing a perfectly fitted button-down, no tie, sleeves rolled up to the elbows. His dark-wash jeans are equally well-suited in a cut I'm almost positive is called "Forbidden Intern Ass Cut." And his hair—slightly damp. Yep, there's that wave of clean man smell that means he's been naked in a shower in the last half hour or so.

F. M. L.

"Hey, you found me. Come in," I say, stroking my kitten like the cat-lady and/or criminal mastermind I'm clearly aiming for.

"Aww, what's her name?" he asks, reaching for my feline shield. Alarms blare in the masculine-scented, suddenly thick air around me. *Abort! Do not allow Marcos Oliveira to snuggle a kitten in your presence. Do. Not.*

But he's quick and determined, and soon those aqua eyes and fatal smile are dedicating sweet nothings to a smug ball of fur. And smug she is. I swear she's gloating as she stretches her skinny neck back to fire a victorious look at me.

"Her name is Darcy." I try to remove any bitterness from my voice, deciding open jealousy over a kitten is probably not how I want to start this encounter.

"Darcy. Like, from *Pride and Prejudice*?"

Be still my heart. "Yes, exactly. I'm a big Jane Austen fan."

"She's cool. Aren't you precious?" he murmurs, rewarding Darcy's sweetness with extra chin scratches. And, man, does that beast soak it up. She splays out in his large hands with zero shame or sense of decorum. Geez, at least make him work for it.

"Looks like someone has a crush," I say, again, with an admirable lack of resentment.

"Me or the kitten?" he teases, administering one last tickle before flipping her upright and setting her gently on the floor. Am I surprised she immediately grinds against his leg in a plea for more? How would I react after an encounter with those hands on my skin and those lips murmuring affection a mere breath from my face? *Stop it, Eva.*

"You hungry?" I ask, leading him toward the kitchen.

Thankfully, we have actual tasks and an actual mission to occupy us tonight, and in another fortuitous development, I realize that as long as I'm always *leading* our movement around the apartment, I never have to face the temptation of ogling his ass. Unless, of course, he turns to inspect the open floor plan once we pass through the foyer. Crap. And double crap. Were those clothes designed for the sole purpose of displaying his perfect body?

You're being ridiculous.

Inappropriate.

Shallow.

Infantile.

Ogle. His. Brain.

I force my gaze up his defined back, past broad, athletic shoulders, to dark, longish hair that's littered with natural highlights. His hair always makes me picture him waterskiing.

"Have you ever waterskied?" I ask, shifting my focus to the takeout containers on the island as if that makes my question less random.

"A few times. You?"

"No."

Because… random.

"Oh."

I clear my throat and hand him a plate. "Well, just help yourself. I hope you like Thai food."

"Love it."

"Great. No peanut allergies, right?"

"Nope. Just cats."

"Oh no, really?"

He shrugs, flashing that magical grin. "It's not severe. With the hardwood floors, I should be fine. Just can't touch my face."

Well, there you go, Eva. He's allergic to cats. You could never live together.

Also.

What?!

I clear my throat again and reverse course toward the wine glasses. "Red or white?"

"I'm kind of in the mood for an expensive Bordeaux if you have it."

I glance back at him, my surprise melting into something more dangerous when his grin breaks.

"Kidding. That was part of the issue that almost got me fired by Beverly today."

My tongue wets my lips at the thought of a rich, full-bodied wine… *nothing* to do with my companion's smile or the way his eyes sparkle—*sparkle!*—at the inside joke we now share. Marcos and I are forever bonded over Beverly's outburst. Yay.

"I have a pinot noir I've been dying to try. That okay?"

"Sounds perfect." He scoops a spoonful of vegetarian prik king onto his plate and lifts the plate for a hefty inhale. "This smells delicious."

"It's one of my favorite places. I wasn't sure what level of spice you like, so I got medium."

"Medium is fine. I like it hot."

I swallow. Force a nod. Focus with laser precision on the corkscrew in my hand.

"And sorry I'm a little late," he continues. "Nate wanted to hit the gym after work, and I had to clean up before coming over."

"It's fine." It is. So fine. Too fine. Why won't this stupid corkscrew work properly?

"Need help with that?"

No. Because I'm Evangeline Freaking Reedweather and I can open a bottle of wine. Also, I don't need that ocean stare and intoxicating man scent anywhere near me right now. But I'm too late at communicating any of that, and soon he and his smell and his curious, playful eyes are *right* there, waiting to do my bidding. Just waiting, though, because he doesn't snatch the corkscrew from my hand like so many men would have done. He doesn't even look bored or condescending as he watches me struggle with the bottle. His expression is, strangely, *helpful.*

"That's a really cool design." He leans his elbows on the counter to inspect the tool while I work.

I glance over at his disturbing adjustment that puts him in breach of my protective bubble. *Alarm!* I can now smell, see, *and* feel the heat of his body that's mere centimeters from mine. He doesn't seem to notice how the bulge of his bicep keeps bumping against my hip. How when he tilts a grin up from that distance, it's easy to imagine him looking up at me from another, more intimate piece of furniture in the room down the hall.

"It's from Norway. Picked it up on a trip a few years ago."

There! Victory!

Marcos straightens at the *pop* of the cork, and I yank it out, way too proud of myself for something I've done a million times.

But never under the influence of Marcos Oliveira.

No, and I'm learning his presence makes everything more challenging for me. Also, I've always been addicted to challenges.

I pour the wine, careful to slide his glass toward him instead of passing it and risking a direct hand collision. I then fill my plate with several scoops of food and make my way to the table. Marcos follows, and we position ourselves across from each other like mature, rational coworking adults.

"Thanks for coming. I'm sure you have a bunch of other things you'd rather be doing tonight."

"What could be more fun than investigating industrial espionage with my boss?" His fork pauses at his mouth so he can flash a smile before completing the food transfer. I watch his lips curve gently around the tines.

His smile falters, and I shake my head. Shit. What was the question? Never mind.

"I've collected almost a terabyte of files so we have a lot to sort through." My dry tone removes all remaining humor from his face. Good. Or bad if this were a date and my awkwardness just ruined what could have been a potent flirtatious connection. But definitely good if you're me right now, trying to avoid exactly that.

"Okay. Do you have any leads?" He takes another bite, and this one proves much less hazardous to my mental state now that I'm back in my corporate wheelhouse.

"Honestly, no. I'm still in step one of the action plan: define. Step two, discover, is where you come in."

"I love a good action plan."

"Me too." I can't tell if he's joking. My internal radiator suspects he's not, and I pull in a soothing draught of air. There's nothing hotter than a man who loves a good action plan. "I've been focusing primarily on data collection, so I haven't done much in the way of analysis yet."

"Data analysis is my jam."

"I'm aware." We exchange another long, saturated look. I shift my stare back to my uneaten food. "Let's finish dinner and get to work."

* * *

WITH OUR FOOD ADEQUATELY CONSUMED, we've relocated to the couch to be more comfortable as we sift through the volumes of files. Marcos places his wine glass on the end table and takes the laptop I hand him.

"The folder that's open contains the bulk of the data, so maybe start there."

He nods, balancing the computer on his thighs as he leans forward to study the screen.

The initial draft of my plan for tonight consisted of me waiting helpfully on the other end of the couch while Marcos reviewed the files. I've already given them several passes and look forward to the perspective of another set of eyes. I'd sip my wine patiently, ready and available should he have questions or ideas to workshop. That was Plan A.

But I overlooked one critical variable. Sipping my wine patiently also means I have to watch Marcos do something sexier than stripping: Use his brain. With each passing second of studying his dark brows furrow in concentration and the rapid arc of his irises over the screen, the temperature in the room becomes increasingly uncomfortable. I can practically see the neurons firing through that sexy mind, the barrage of data sifting through his brilliant filter at dizzying speed. I've read his work. I know his brain operates on a level most couldn't even comprehend, so when his straight white teeth sink into a full bottom lip, I'm done. Time for Plan B.

"Anything?" I ask, sounding the opposite of patient and helpful.

He squints at the display for another second before darting a look at me. "Actually, yeah. See this?"

He flips the screen to show a complex spreadsheet. I scoot to the neighboring cushion and lean in just enough to view it. I've seen this document before, but it was just a muddle of data points to me. My pulse picks up at the excitement on his face.

"You know what this is?" I ask.

His lips turn up and the matching spark in his eyes make them hypnotic. I can't look away.

"I think so." He navigates the screen and pulls up another file. This appears to be some kind of formal standard operating procedure. "You see?" he asks.

I don't, and his expression drops slightly at my lack of corresponding excitement.

"This is an SOP for a test script. It's what they'd use to test their software applications and make sure they're functioning as expected. Now, look at the title of the document. '7.1 Test Scripts Procedure and Guidelines.'"

"Okay…"

He clicks back to the spreadsheet. "Look here."

I follow the curser, which lands on a cell halfway down the screen. *"7.1 Test Scripts Procedure and Guidelines."* The cell to the left has *"7-Engineering,"* and several cells to the right contain more descriptive information.

Oh my god. "The spreadsheet is an index of their Quality Management System," I say in a low voice.

He offers a corroborative look. "If I had to guess, the folder we're looking at is SAT Systems' entire QMS. You'd be able to recreate the whole company from the contents of this folder."

"Or destroy it."

He nods. "Or destroy it."

He highlights a column to the right and shakes his head. "And it looks like it's still in development. See these status designations for each item in the index? *Complete, pending approval, in development, scheduled...* Damn, they even have the initials of the employee tasked with developing the protocol."

"A lot of M.S. and G.W.," I say.

"M.S. must be Martin Sandeke. So who's G.W.?"

G.W....

Hang on...

My blood thumps in my veins.

"Can I see that?" I grab the laptop from him and start clicking through the files. *G.W.... G.W....* it can't be. It *can't.* But then, doesn't that make perfect sense? Well, if Marcos' theory is correct, I'm bound to find evidence either way.

I glance up at a shift in the cushion and notice we've now switched roles. Marcos has leaned back against the armrest with his glass of wine to wait while I dig for clues. A smile creeps over my lips as I wonder if he's as turned on by intelligent, productive women as I am by intelligent, productive men. When I dare another glimpse at that devastating gaze, I make a pact with myself never to look at his eyes again. Ever. For any reason.

"This is nuts," I mumble to myself, and Marcos snickers. My attention shifts his way, ignoring my pact. "What?"

"Nothing. Just reminded me of Chad."

"Intern Chad?"

He nods. "He's obsessed with nuts."

"Edible nuts?"

Our gazes collide, and a violent rush of heat spreads through me. Of course *edible nuts*. Marcos wouldn't have suggested any other kind of nut. To his boss. A woman. Right? Oh wait, there are also tool-related nuts. Bolts, wrenches... in other words, I could have been differentiating from those and not the ones in his—*stop!*

My eyes flicker back to the screen with a renewed determination not to acknowledge anything related to that side of the couch for the duration of the evening.

G.W....

G.W....

"Shit!" Marcos jumps up from the couch just as Darcy flies several feet through the air to land on the area rug with a yelp. He shoves his glass on the table, ignoring his red-soaked shirt to leap toward her. "Oh no. I'm so sorry. Darcy—"

His pretty eyes are flooded with all levels of *distraught* as he hovers over the kitten, evaluating her welfare. For the record, she's fine. Smug as always. I see the triumphant glimmer in her eyes after successfully stealing his attention from me. So that's how we're playing this?

I push up as well, closing the laptop and moving toward the kitchen for towels.

"She's fine. Trust me. She does that a lot. It's like a sneak attack."

"She came out of nowhere and landed right in my lap," he says, still in shock.

Duh. She's a vixen.

"Oh no, your couch."

When I return, he's inspecting the cushions for damage.

"It's no big deal, really."

I hand him a pile of paper towels so we can tag team the spill. His brows that were scrunched in concentration a moment ago are now knitted in con*stern*ation, and my chest tightens. Weird how much his distress affects me. Disconcerting. Full-on distressing, actually.

"Really, it's fine." I add a laugh, which comes across as more eerie than playful, since I'm not great at that stuff. His gaze crosses to me, shifting from concerned to downright frightened.

"God, I'm so sorry, Eva. Really. I'll pay for this. I promise it's—"

"Marcos, stop." I reach for his arm in another gross miscalculation. Because not only is the contact that follows awkward as hell, it's also mystifying. So mysterious the way my fingers curve around his solid bicep on their own. How he freezes his beautiful stare on mine, searching... and confused. So confused. Shit. I let go and step back. "Go clean up. I got this."

Not surprisingly, my awkward stab at reassurance does little to reassure him. I force another smile that probably falls into the weird category. "Seriously, it's fine. You're a mess."

He follows my gaze to his shirt where he probably also notices how the red, wet fabric has molded to his skin. He may even become aware of the stark outline of defined pecs and abdominals, though I doubt it has the same effect on his internal radiator as it does on mine. A violent rush of heat probably doesn't surge from his chest to his thighs where it stalls with a heady pulse at the apex. And even if he *is* thinking about stripping off that sticky, useless shirt, it's probably not with smooth, intentional movements. Certainly not in a torturous loop of slow-motion replays.

I clench the towels in my fist and snap a glare at the demonic kitten responsible for this disaster.

"Where's the bathroom?" he asks, crossing toward the hallway. "Again, I'm so sorry about this."

"First door on the right." I turn in a safer direction toward the couch. "And stop apologizing. It's not your fault. It was the work of the devil." I wince. "The cat, I mean. Not the actual devil. As in the cat is the devil. As in..."

Crap.

I peek over to verify he's already left the room and was spared that explosion of word vomit, but I get no such relief. Nope, just a killer smile, and aqua eyes, and a now unbuttoned button-down that reveals an equally wet (and stained) undershirt. Of unequal proportion is the outline of muscle beneath it. What had been a hint of physical perfection a second ago is now a full-on congressional testimony as I stare in horrified wonder. He needs to leave. Now. I need to clean. Now.

G.W. be damned.

I spin back to the couch, relieved at the sound of the bathroom door a second later. Crisis averted. He'll clean up, decide to leave, and tomorrow we'll chuckle jovially about this entire incident in passing. Even more impressive is that somehow, despite everything, we still made a measurable breakthrough. Marcos' discovery about the QMS and my hunch about G.W. gives me plenty of direction to push forward in phase two of the action plan. Yes, *Discovery* is well on its way, and a different kind of warmth ignites in my chest at how much we accomplished together in such a brief period. *Imagine if you actually had a fully functioning brain in his presence...* His intuition, my experience, our combined intellect? Damn, we'd be unstoppable.

And we will. I decide right then, by the spy gods, we *will!*

This crush is ridiculous, and from now on it will have no impact on my professional relationship with Marcos Oliveira or my ability to do my job. Since when was I a bumbling coed? Never. Not even when I *was* a coed, so this idiocy ends here. Tonight. Now.

"Eva, do you have a towel I can use?" Marcos ducks his head through a crack in the door, and I don't even flinch when I call back, "Of course. One sec."

Straightening like a champ, I march toward the linen closet with summa-cum-laude-departmental-honors-level determination. One-hundred-forty-eight IQ. Three-point-nine-three GPA. Independent. My bank account dwarfs most of my peers'. My 401k is already stacked at age twenty-eight, and the letters before and after my name speak for themselves. I am a goddess, a badass businesswoman, a fucking *warrior* as I yank a towel from the shelf in the closet. A maroon one instead of white because I'm smart and strategic and think about details like that. Because I. Am. Woman.

Until I open the bathroom door.

Marcos glances over from the sink, stripped to the waist, skin glistening like there should be a rainforest waterfall behind him. Lingering droplets descend through deep, defined ridges down his torso, slithering over taut skin to collect in the band of the jeans hanging low on his hips.

You are woman... a small voice whimpers in the back of my brain as my mouth goes dry. The towel hangs limply at my side, forgotten and no longer impressive in its suitable color.

Because slowly Marcos straightens. His long, thick lashes blink over cyan eyes that darken into teal as he watches me watch him. Study him. *Scour* and explore him. Molest him with the most inappropriate of gazes that I will absolutely write myself up for later. But right now, his hard swallow is mesmerizing; his sculpted, glistening chest rises and falls in increasingly rapid breaths that keep pace with mine.

"You have tattoos," I breathe out.

"A few, yeah."

"Are they recent?" Random. Again.

His brow lifts, widening one teal eye and narrowing the other. I pull in a heavy inhale. I confuse him. I challenge him. I suspect he likes being challenged as much as I do.

"Not really. Well, I guess this one is." He twists to the left so I can see a line of script on his ribs. "From just over a year ago."

I have to tear my attention from the effect of this position on his many well-defined torso muscles in order to read it.

"'*Never will I lose this spark that darkness forged.*' Wow. Is that from a poem?"

"A song."

"You love?"

"I wrote."

Huh?

"You're a musician?"

"Not a serious one. But my best friend, Nash, is."

"So you write with him?"

"Only when he ropes me into it. *Therapy*, he calls it."

"So you needed therapy?"

He looks away. "Once."

"A year ago?"

He nods.

"Is that for me?" He gestures toward the towel, but I can tell his mind isn't on drying off. No, it's back to a year ago when he needed beautiful words to heal a darkness that created sparks.

"Yes, sorry. Here." I shove the towel toward him, and he accepts it with a weak smile.

"Thanks. I'll be out in a minute."

His gorgeous eyes flicker away, and the blistering flame from a moment ago cools into a chill.

"I'll wash and dry those for you," I say, motioning toward the clump of fabric in the sink.

"Thanks, but it's probably not worth it."

"At least so you won't have to wear wet clothes home."

His eyes soften back to cyan. His uncertain smile tugs at my heart. His strong shoulders hunch into themselves, screaming for a foreign embrace to shelter around them. He's not used to compassion. To being cared for. He's his own rock, his own fortress against *darkness that forges sparks*.

Like me. Have I met a person as detached and determined as I am?

I'm far from the nurturing type, but in this moment, protecting this man is the only thing I want. It fuels the gentle smile on my lips, the lingering stare that doesn't want to leave him alone in this cold bathroom.

And that's when I do, because the tenderness turns to panic, the warmth to alarm. That's the moment when my harmless crush explodes into danger.

* * *

I TOSS MARCOS' clothes in the washer, annoyed that this eliminates any chance of him leaving right away. Even on the fastest setting, the laundry cycle will take at least an hour and a half. The presence of his shirt in the machine also means it cannot be used as a covering on his person. I briefly consider searching my wardrobe for something he can borrow, but even my oversized sleepshirts would look comical stretched over his broad shoulders.

I return to the couch and chew on my lip as I absently stare at the laptop on the coffee table. Maybe we can pretend he's not half naked for the rest of the evening. Really, it's on me to stop gawking at him. And it's definitely on me to stop turning our professional relationship into a male escort fantasy.

"This is *your* fault," I hiss at Darcy, who stares unabashedly from the far end of the couch. She doesn't look the least bit contrite as she blinks twice and licks her teeny-tiny adorable kitten paws. "You *wanted* him naked, didn't you? This was all part of your evil plan. I knew you were the devil," I say, pointing at her.

"You could have just asked," a deep, male, non-kitten voice interrupts. Heat spreads through me as our shirtless guest saunters out of the hallway.

"Asked?"

"Me to remove my shirt if you wanted to see me naked. It would have saved a perfectly good shirt."

His grin. Damn his grin. The heat blazes into an inferno. "I did *not* want to see you naked. If you were eavesdropping properly, you would have heard that I was accusing Darcy of that debauchery."

"Ah. So your cat wanted to see me naked." Skeptical would be a good word to describe his tone.

"Precisely. Obviously. *I'm* not the one who jumped on your lap and spilled wine all over your shirt."

"That's true." His eyes darken to that deep teal color that makes my insides warm and quivery. It's a color that tells me maybe he wishes I *had* been the one to jump in his lap. Maybe he *does* wish I'd asked him to remove his shirt so I could see him naked. Maybe he wishes I were naked too. The night is young. There's plenty more wine to get spilled on things.

With Darcy on one side of the couch and me in the middle, he lowers himself to the space beside me—the scene of the crime. The black leather has been wiped clean and is perhaps the most unscathed party in this whole debacle. He settles in, his humor shifting into solemnity as he reaches for the laptop.

"I had a thought about the QMS index in the bathroom. Let me look at it again."

It's a strange sight watching a shirtless man work. It sends my mind to lazy Saturday mornings. Waking up to find Marcos Oliveira beside me with a cup of coffee, laptop, and no shirt because it's our routine to relax on Saturday mornings. He'd smile over at me as I blink awake and make some smart-ass crack about sleeping in. I'd roll my eyes, secretly warmed by the easy, familiar exchange.

I clear my throat and push up from the couch. "You need more wine?"

He lifts his gaze from the screen. A quick smile brushes his lips. "I think I'm good."

9—GRANT WORTHINGTON, ET AL

EVA

I typically despise the weekly executive planning meetings. The last time anything was accomplished at one of these hot air marathons was 2003 when Quentin Thomlison, then CFO, suggested daily stipends for traveling employees so they didn't break the bank at steakhouses every night. He's been hailed as a legend ever since, even entering corporate lore with sayings like, "it's a good step, but it's no Tightwad Thomlison" and "have you used all of your Quentin Quota?" For the record, the daily stipend doesn't apply to management.

Today, though, I have a mission and Marcos by my side.

Sneaking an intern into a top-level strategic planning meeting should have been a difficult task. But everything's possible when egos are involved, and we met little resistance once I fluttered my lashes and insisted my intern could gain valuable knowledge from these Paragons of Industrial Enterprise. You know, important business skills like talking in circles and falling in love with the sound of your own voice. If he plays his cards right, he may even learn the art of shouting over people and making suggestions that were already covered and discarded in previous meetings.

Unfortunately, my justification also means Chad got a ticket to the table. I've placed him strategically beside my father, who nearly passed out at the prospect of directly mentoring a young, eager mind. Currently, Reed Reedweather, III is showing his MBA grad how to read an agenda. Fine with me. As long as I have Marcos to myself. You know, for business stuff. Like using that perceptive brain of his to absorb everything he can about Sandeke Telecom's inner circle. Top of the list, the man at the head of the table, COO Grant Worthington.

Despite hours of searching since our G.W. discovery last night, we never found the name "Grant Worthington" explicitly spelled out in the files. I suppose it makes sense he'd wash his name from stolen data, so this fact doesn't mean G.W. *doesn't* stand for Grant Worthington. But it could also be George Washington, so for now we have to cross that off as an optimistic dead end.

I tap Marcos' shoe with mine and nod subtly in Grant's direction. He nods back, his eyes narrowing on the other man's glib features. Marcos' brain is already evaluating and planning, an obvious fact since his gaze is just *extra* when it probes its surroundings. But he isn't important to anyone except me, so Grant will never see him coming. Slick Grant with his slick hair and his slick smile that never matches his eyes.

Marcos taps something into his phone, and mine buzzes a second later.

His coffee cup is clean.

Confused, I follow his stare to Grant's light blue Reedweather Media company mug. Sure enough, the man is nursing an empty cup. Although his hand is wrapped around the base like it's full, there are no lip stains or drops to indicate there was ever coffee inside. That means Grant Worthington brought an empty, unused mug to this meeting. Why?

My phone buzzes again.

20 bucks says he leaves to fill it at some point in the meeting.

I'm not a great spy, which is probably why I shoot a startled look at Marcos who raises a brow and shrugs. Damn, he's good. What if he's right? I think back to last week's meeting. Did Worthington leave that one too? What would he be doing during that time? And why not say he has to use the restroom if he needs an excuse to leave? Why an empty coffee cup?

I would also like to note that I have not once been distracted by Marcos' pale green shirt that makes his eyes glow at radioactive levels. I have definitely not imagined it sliding off his shoulders or thought about him half naked on my couch. Nor have I considered how his hair falls in waves that are particularly rogue today and draw even more attention to his stunning features. Not once.

Okay, once.

Now twice.

Now three times.

Stop it, brain!

I glare at my agenda.

"Okay, if everyone's here, let's begin," Grant calls out. The chatter fades; phones slowly stop scrolling, tapping, and beeping as they're lowered to the table. "Martha, will you dial in Mr. Sandeke?"

I sense Marcos stiffen beside me and exchange a discreet glance with him.

Yep, that's right. *All* the big guns attend these meetings. I can't even wrap my brain around the amount of money wasted each week with the salaries represented here. Across the table, Chad points triumphantly to the first item on the agenda, and my father pats his arm.

"Are we connected?" Grant asks, squinting at the blurry image on the wall screen.

A staticky response returns from the blur.

"Mr. Sandeke, are you with us?"

Static, static. "…Yacht… I'm…" Static, static.

"Martha, can you get a clearer picture? We can't see or hear him," my father points out.

Martha draws in a deep, calming breath I recognize well.

"Martha, is there a problem with the connection?" Grant. Also helpful.

"He must be out of range," Martha mutters, fiddling with a computer on a stand near the wall.

Probably. Like every other week when we go through this exercise. I pull out my phone and type: **FYI this is the first 25 minutes of every meeting. That should be item one on the agenda. "Troubleshoot conference call."**

Marcos smirks when he reads my message and types back: **We should let Martha know there's a problem with the connection. Maybe she's not aware.**

"Martha, how's it coming?" Grant.

"Maybe if you jiggle the wires?" Reed.

"He's probably out of range." Grant.

"I heard magnets can interfere with Wi-Fi signals. Did anyone accidentally bring a high-powered magnet?" Steve from Accounting.

My phone buzzes.

Marcos: **My fault. I thought you said we were SUPPOSED to bring our high-powered magnets to this meeting.**

I bite down on my lip to avoid a snort.

Me: **Noooo. I said leave all your high-powered magnets at HOME.**

Marcos: **Damn. Maybe if we had two high-powered magnets we could polarize them and reverse the bad connection. Also, that computer is wired into the wall. It's not on wifi.**

Me: **Yup.**

Marcos: **Why don't they just call him? Isn't that a conference speaker in the middle of the table?**

Me: **It is, and they will. We still have seven minutes of troubleshooting.**

I feel him deflate beside me. His closed pen traces absent lines over the agenda page in front of him, and I realize I did a poor job preparing him for this. He won't make it if he's already in the bored doodling phase. With proper conditioning, a skilled executive should be able to reach agenda item four before succumbing to the bored doodling phase.

"Martha, perhaps we should dial him in through the phone." Grant.

"We're sure no one has a magnet?" Steve from Accounting.

"Technology is great when it works, isn't it?" Reed. We could add that joke to the agenda as well. Also the polite chuckles.

Chad points to the conference speaker on the table and whispers something to my father. I can tell by the older man's expression that he has no idea how to respond.

Doesn't stop him from responding, though, and Chad nods reverently. I can only guess what misinformation just transferred heads on that side of the table.

The meeting itself is unremarkable once it finally gets underway. As usual, each presentation is a volleyball match between the presenter trying to impress the field with their accomplishment or idea of the week, and another department head trying to impress the field with their ability to interject. A typical agenda item might go something like this:

Steve from Accounting. "First quarter closeout is complete. We're compiling the report now and should have it to you by next week's meeting."

Bill from Sales. "How do the numbers look?"

Steve from Accounting. "We're compiling the report now."

Bill from Sales. "But initially, how are the numbers looking?"

Steve from Accounting. "We will have that information once we compile the report. We're doing that now."

Bill from Sales. "So they're good, right? They must be good because my numbers were way up in Q4 last year."

Steve from Accounting, now convinced Bill from Sales is the delinquent who ruined the Wi-Fi with his high-powered magnet. "We will have that information once we compile the report."

Bill from Sales. "If you recall, I landed that huge Whitewater account in Q4."

We recall. This also leads to a lengthy recall by other department heads on their Q4 achievements that should be reflected in the first quarter numbers.

My phone buzzes.

Marcos: **This can't be real.**

Me: **Fun, right? What were your Q4 numbers?**

Marcos (with a half-grin that hits me way too hot and heavy for a boardroom): **You really want to know?**

Crap. Apparently, my blood really, really does by the way it's surging through my veins.

Me: **Why? Are they stripper numbers?**

Marcos: **Does it make it more or less hot to know that I could print a detailed P&L of my numbers if you wanted?**

More. Gosh, so much more.

Me: **You kept formal accounting books for your stripping?**

Marcos: **Of course. Income, expenses, assets, liabilities… a full chart of accounts. Some assets were easier to track than others, though… *winky face***

Winky face! Shit. My blood is in full-on rebellion now. The thought of Marcos at a desk in his underwear, entering transactions into the ledgers, reviewing the balance sheet… Ah, I'm dying to see that profit and loss report. What accounts are above the line in the Cost of Goods Sold section?

Me: **I'd pay money to see that P&L. What does the COGS section look like?**

Marcos (chewing on his lip, probably to avoid a laugh): **You'd be surprised what passes above the line for a stripper.**

Me, now chewing *my* lip to avoid a host of responses. Also, I have no idea what's going on in the actual meeting and glance up to check. We're still reminiscing about the fourth quarter, so nothing missed there, but while Bill, Steve, et al. continue their irrelevant volleying, Grant picks up his mug and slips out. I stiffen, just as Marcos pushes back his chair.

"Bathroom," he says for the benefit of the few who aren't participating in the Q4 chest-thumping. We exchange a look, and he follows Grant from the room. I try to tune back into the discussion, but that's impossible now that I'm thinking about Grant's sneaking, Marcos' spying, and what level of human can pull off successful stripper *and* CPA-quality financial records to prove it. I squeeze my thighs together against the new fire in my nether regions.

"Perhaps we can save this discussion for another time," Sandeke finally chimes in from his end of the line. I have zero faith that he's been listening this whole time. My guess, he just came back from slicing a lime for his margarita.

Steve from Accounting. "Yes, agreed. The numbers will be available shortly. We're compiling the report now."

"Great," Sandeke says. "Is Grant back yet?"

"Not yet, Mr. Sandeke," Martha says.

"Okay. Then Beverly, any updates from HR?"

While Beverly launches into her presentation, I cast a confused glance at Grant's empty chair. Sandeke is on a voice call. How did he know Grant left? Half the employees who are actually present probably didn't notice.

Just as I pick up my phone to text Marcos, I get one from him.

Marcos: **Breakroom is next to the server room. That's why he "needed coffee." Our snake took a detour.**

Me: **The Sand Eagle knows the snake is not in the conference room. Just made a reference.**

Marcos: **Interesting. The snake is moving. Must be finished. Headed to the breakroom now.**

Me: **We need to find out what happened in the server room. Have you met Jules from IT yet?**

10—JULES CASSIDY

EVA

Do I condone flirting for the purposes of manipulation? Of course not, so I strictly instruct Marcos *not* to flirt with the shy twenty-three-year-old IT manager. I do *not* ask him to flash that heart-stopping smile or blink his dark lashes over devastating sparks in blue-green eyes. I do *not* suggest he crack witty one-liners or ease into her good graces with his effortless charm. Heck, I wasn't even aware he knew so much about nerdy space shows, so I definitely didn't ask him to flaunt his opinion on *Starfighters* or whatever to make her face glow. However, it would be unethical for me to ask him to be anything other than himself, so when all of those things happen after the initial introduction, well, not my fault. The fact that Jules Cassidy is in love with Marcos Oliveira in two minutes flat is not on me.

"So this is, what, a maintenance log?" Marcos hovers behind her, leaning low so his lips nearly brush her ear as the two of them study her screen. I sense the shiver that runs through her, see the way her chest jerks as if oxygen just got siphoned out. I know that feeling well. She'd be able to smell him too. That clean, musky scent that makes you picture him toweling off after a vigorous swim. Hair wet, streaks of water skimming over his chiseled body, teal stare saturated with an explosive challenge you're dying to accept.

And by *you*, I mean *me*. And by *picture*, I mean *remember* because I've seen that. Once in person, hundreds of times in mental replay. Tattoos, new and old, glistening in the light. *"Never will I lose this spark that darkness forged."* And…

Focus, Eva.

"Um, yeah, so any time one of our techs works on a piece of equipment in the building, it gets logged here. See?" Jules points at the screen, and I can tell she's trying very hard to distract herself from the impossible distraction to her right. She keeps reaching back and twirling her blond ponytail, absently tugging the end while they talk. *Girl, it won't help. Trust me.*

"Wow, that's awesome. So, this is what happened, say, this morning?" Marcos waves at the screen, and Jules nods.

"Yep. As you can see, Lars rebooted Kevin's machine in Copy, Rita cleared a toner error on a printer in the Art Department, and I recovered a deleted file for Accounting."

"Huh. So interesting. Bet you're in the server room all the time then. Those places are so cool. They remind me of the lab on *Star Legions*." I totally buy his casual laugh, so I'm sure she does.

"For sure! But actually, no, not as much as you'd think." Jules adjusts her glasses, settling into her role as gatekeeper for this disgustingly hot IT novice. "As you can see, I only went in once today."

"Oh yeah?"

It's uncanny how Marcos is able to appear supremely interested in anything at any given second. Is the fact that the IT Department has a maintenance log the most interesting thing he's ever heard? I can't tell you it's not, based on his expression.

"Yep. See here? I went in at 11:37 AM, right after the executive planning meeting. I had to check on a drive fault error."

Most. Interesting. Thing. He's. Ever. Heard. "Wow. That sounds serious."

Jules shrugs off the catastrophe like the jaded superhero she is. "Can be, but this one turned out to be nothing. It happened while we were in the meeting but corrected itself by the time we got out and I could check on it."

"Huh. So what would cause a drive fault error?"

I can almost sense Marcos fighting not to look at me. My attention is also rapt on our IT manager from the other side of the desk.

"Well, typically we see that kind of error when something happens with the backup drive. Like, if it fails."

"Or if it were swapped out?" Marcos adds a late smile to cover the specificness of the question. Jules literally sighs into it.

"Yeah, I guess. But I'm sure no one was in the server room swapping out backup drives this morning at 9:48."

Laughter all around. Of course not. No one. Because that would be never happen. Especially not a COO with an empty coffee mug.

This time, Marcos *does* cross an intense gaze to me, and I nod in return. Next stop, server room.

* * *

"WHAT ARE WE LOOKING FOR?" I whisper after using my top-level clearance badge to get us inside. I'm pretty good with computers, but this place scares the hell out of me. I'm not a fan of things I don't understand—things like giant racks of flashing lights and wires.

"Not sure yet," he says, but he's clearly less intimidated by the flashing light and wire jungle than I am. "Grant was obviously doing something with the backup drive. Swapping it out would be my guess. I didn't see him enter or leave with anything except the mug, so he must have it hidden somewhere—"

We straighten in alarm at the click of the lock on the main door. *Crap!* On instinct, I yank his shirt to pull him to the far end of the closet-like room and shove him behind one of the giant racks. Here's to hoping whoever this person is doesn't need to access whatever this thing is.

The clatter of the door closing, followed by the squeak of sneakers on the floor tell us someone entered, but we can't see them through the wall of computer junk obstructing our view. This also means they can't see us, so yay for that.

Initially, adrenaline keeps my attention fixed on the action at the other side of the room. Soon, though, hormones interrupt our regularly scheduled caper to parade neon signs of awareness that I'm pressed tightly against Marcos Oliveira. Yes, my brilliant, urgent spy maneuver was to crush him into the wall. To press my body against his in an invisible cocoon of stealth. Except this cocoon is suddenly hot. And hard. And electrified with the current of a thousand server racks. It's inhabited by a sun god who stares down at me with blistering, intelligent eyes and full, tempting lips. Those lips spread into a smile—nay—a challenge, when they catch me gawking. An I-dare-you-not-to-touch-me-right-now message. His hard chest joins the taunt, molding solid muscle to my soft curves. His hips, gah, I can't decline that invitation. It's not my fault. They just—react, aligning with his of their own accord. And when his chest swells with a labored inhale at the friction, a shudder runs through me. My hands don't know what to do either, and soon they're exploring belt loops at his lower back. Fingers coil around fabric, hooking in until they have no choice but to pull our hips into a firmer embrace. His eyes clench shut, his breathing rapid like mine. His heart—I can feel the raging pulse, or maybe that's mine. Where does he end and I begin right now? We're not ourselves. We've melded into that new entity—that throbbing, scorching cocoon. My lips burn with a hunger to explore his neck. I grip the belt loops tighter, needing to breathe soon so I don't lose control of a gasp and give us away.

Somehow, I manage to break one hand away, but it gets sidetracked on the return journey. Instead of safety, it seeks his chest, palm opening wide for a full, greedy experience as it slides from his waist up solid, mouth-watering planes. My touch absorbs his heat as it travels, tingling from the contrast of the soft fabric of his shirt and the hard angles of muscle beneath. I take extra time exploring his pecs, sinking in and enjoying the way his breathing changes as I rake his skin with my nails. My hand should stop when it reaches his collar, but it doesn't. No, it keeps moving, skimming over his neck and curving behind until my fingers tangle in his hair. My thumb glides over light stubble, locking below his jaw and angling his perfect face right where I want it. Where I need it as I lick my lips and stare at his mouth. My genius stripper intern, who couldn't be more accessible and forbidden in this moment.

"No freaking way," a voice echoes through the room.

Marcos and I snap our gazes toward the sound. Neither of us move as we wait, our breaths coming heavy from fear now, in addition to desire. Gosh, this is pretty much the most addicting sensation I've ever experienced. No wonder James Bond is a thing.

"What the hell?" The voice clearly belongs to Jules and she's clearly muttering to herself, not at the two super-charged intruders, which comes as some relief. Some.

There's no such thing as a full reprieve when you have Marcos Oliveira in your hands and can't do anything about it.

More indistinct muttering follows, along with rapid tapping and clicking. Marcos and I hold our breaths, trying not to move and risk our position—a position which, coincidentally, makes every muscle in our bodies want to move at once.

"Hey, Lars. It's Jules. Hey, weird question. Did you happen to swap out the backup drive this morning? … No, I know, just wanted to make sure. What about Rita? … Yeah, I know, but maybe after that? … Hmm… okay. Yeah, I got a drive fault error this morning, and now the current backup drive has a different serial number than what we have on file. Nah, I'm sure it's nothing. We probably forgot to update the log last time we swapped it out. Thanks."

"Shit," Jules mumbles. "Probably another Tim mistake." A few more taps, clicks, and bangs, and the door to the server room clatters closed again.

Marcos and I exchange a long look once we're alone. His gaze lowers to my mouth, then rests back on my eyes. At some point, my thumb had begun smoothing small arcs over his jaw. Now it continues in the scorching silence. I enjoy the chafe of his day-old scruff. Is this what it'd be like to reach over the morning after? Sucking in a deep breath, I soak in oxygen for what feels like the first time in hours.

"Can you come over again tonight?" My voice sounds strained. I swallow, hoping to reset it. "We need to talk about this." I realize as I say it that I don't know if *this* refers to the swapped backup drive or the thousand-degree encounter in the back corner of a server room. All I know: I need to see him tonight. But not touch. *Never* touch, because oh-em-gee as Marisya would say.

I step back and drop my hands. He remains inclined against the wall, watching me. His shirt is ruffled where I teased it. His pants… I blink and force my gaze back to his face. I don't know which view is more dangerous right now.

"I'll bring food this time," he says. "And wine."

* * *

THE FIRST THING I notice when I open my door: Marcos has abandoned the office button-downs in favor of a soft, aqua tee that should be illegal for humans with irises like his. No joke, I'm calling my congresswoman. Second: his criminal tee is also too thin for his build if the goal of clothing is to hide the body beneath it. Because lines. Angles. Ridges. Everywhere muscles that make shirts irrelevant. And his jeans. I add those jeans to the meeting agenda with my congresswoman. My attire skews more casual as well, but I doubt anyone will be calling the cops on my khakis and pink sweater.

"I brought Mexican and a cabernet sauvignon," he says, holding up his offerings.

Pretty sure I'm the first person to look at a nice cabernet sauvignon and think: *That wine would look excellent on you.*

He clears his throat, arching a dark brow.

"Can I come in?"

Of course. But instead of that, I step to the side and motion like the world's most inept butler. Because lines. Angles. Ridges. Fluorescent eyes.

148 IQ, Eva. Come on now.

"How much do you know about competitive advantage theory?" is what my mouth considers a suitable recovery.

Crap.

His gaze flashes with surprise, then amusement. "Quite a bit. So that's a yes to Mexican food?"

"Of course. I love Mexican food."

"Good. This place has the best mole."

"I've never had mole."

"What?! Oh man, just wait."

I lick my lips as I follow him into the kitchen, clearly due to the prospect of mole, which I've never tasted, and not the way his shirt tapers from ripped shoulders to a slim waist and soon-to-be-banned jeans.

"My thought was that we try to ascertain Sandeke's objective for the stolen data by talking through the precepts of competitive advantage theory." My mouth continues its assault on *awkward* while Marcos unloads our food from the bag. Also, I don't totally hate its direction this time. For once I sound like my competent, badass self in his presence. "Then we look for evidence in the documents to support each principle.

Whichever is most logical and supported would be our answer, and we focus the investigation from there."

Marcos' hand stalls with a container as he considers my plan. Have I mentioned how much I love watching his brain work?

"Makes sense. So we should start by looking at the comparative advantage and then the differential advantage of Sandeke Telecom and SAT Systems relative to each other?"

"Exactly."

"Do we know enough about the functional areas of both companies to do that?"

"Sandeke, yes. SAT, no. But we have their QMS, so with some elbow grease, we can fill in the gaps... What?"

His smile flickers toward me in a cocktail of surprise, teasing, and shyness. Also, that too should be illegal.

"Nothing. Just... elbow grease?"

I narrow my eyes at him. "Yeah, it means working hard to—"

"I know what it means, I've just never heard anyone under the age of fifty use it before."

I double down on my glare, which amuses him more. "Well, excuse me if I'm not a young, hip intern like you."

"Whatever, grandma," he says, focusing back on a container of rice.

"Excuse me?"

"You're what, a year older than I am?"

"Twenty-eight."

"Hmm... four years. Okay. Guess grandma-language makes sense then."

That smile. Makes my chest burn. Triggers tiny buzzing cicadas in my belly. I blame the surge of blood for launching my palm into his bicep for a playful shove. His smile turns deadly at the contact, and soon I can't remember what we were talking about. Or anything else. Why is he here again? How do I prevent him from ever leaving? I'm pretty sure I'm not allowed to tie him up in my bedroom. Oh wow, I really want to tie him up in my bedroom.

What?!

I'll attribute that to hunger.

"This looks so good. Is that the mole?" I ask, pointing to the dark sauce. *Pointing*: homo sapiens' oldest, most proven diversion tactic.

He nods. "They aren't the best enchiladas I've ever had but definitely up there. Here." He grabs a fork from a drawer and sections a small bite.

Captivated, I watch in slow motion as he lifts the fork toward me all romance-movie like with his cocky grin and smoldering stare. The music would be swelling now, the film editor cuing up the bedroom montage that follows. Zoom in on Marcos' alluring expression; cut to Eva's starry-eyed response. And—

"Oh shit, that's hot!" I cough out, jumping back and waving my hand in front of my mouth. "Oh my god." My legs start pumping until I'm bouncing in place with the grace of an agitated Easter Bunny.

Marcos looks equal parts horrified and amused as he rushes toward the cabinet for a glass. He fills it with water and slides it down the island in an impressive bartender maneuver. I gulp down a few swallows, gargle another, and leave the rest in my mouth to soothe the burn.

"Are you okay?" he asks on a chuckle. "Sorry, I didn't think it would still be so hot. I'll be sure to blow it off next time."

Blow it off?

Next time?

Wait, what are words again?

"Thanks," I say. "Yeah, it definitely could have used a hard blow."

Huh? Oh god, his face right now.

"I mean, for the heat," I rush out. "Of the… enchilada. Um." *Words, Eva. You know so many.* "It was delicious, though... From what I could taste."

His mouth crooks up at one corner as he studies me. "You'll love it once your taste buds grow back."

"I'm sure." I draw in a deep breath and clap my hands together. "Well, that's one way to kill the mood, right?" I add a late laugh to show how much I'm joking about said "mood," which clearly we didn't kill because, obviously, the two of us couldn't have something resembling a *mood* together. Obviously. I laugh again, and he stares in bewilderment before shaking his head with another surprised/amused/shy blast of facial art.

"You ready to eat so we can work?" he asks.

* * *

"Wait, it's gone," I say, squinting at my screen.

Marcos scoots closer on the couch to look, and Darcy whines a protest at his betrayal. She had just secured a prime location on his lap when he gently placed her to his right. She seems to forgive him and curls up in the warm, vacated spot. His wine glass is also noticeably absent since he left it in the kitchen this time. Darn.

"What's gone?" he asks.

"The folder. See? This is where the stolen files were located on the server. Now they're gone."

"Shit. You still have copies, right?"

"Of course," I say, waving off that concern. "But this means someone removed them from the server."

"Probably because they were never supposed to be there in the first place." He shoots me a look, and I wait patiently for the thought I see running through his brain. "That must be why Worthington swapped out the backup drive. They just realized the files were on the server by accident and deleted them, but still have to erase their tracks."

Hmm, makes sense. Good thing I copied them first.

"So there it is," I say, my adrenaline spiking. "Proof that Grant is involved."

Marcos nods. "He has to be. And didn't you say Sandeke knew he left the meeting this morning? That means he knew what Grant was doing, which confirms he's in on it as well."

I swallow, my stomach cramping at the thought. "So this goes all the way to the top."

"Looks like it." His expression turns grave. "Eva, when do we bring SAT Systems in on this?"

Excitement flares into alarm. This spy game just got real.

Yeah, Eva. When do you officially betray your father and kill your career? It's a fair question, and one I'll have to answer, but *now* doesn't feel right. What do we really know about this plot? Should we explode our lives and the chance to learn more over a glimpse of the tip of the iceberg? Once we blow the whistle, there's no going back.

"Not yet," I say. "We need more information first."

Marcos leans forward and rests his chin on a clenched fist. I imagine this same earnest expression on his face while he typed his paper railing against the evils of ruthless, cheating corporations like Sandeke Telecom. I hate the flicker of doubt in his gaze when it searches mine, but this decision can't be made by passion. We have to be strategic and patient—even when confronted by gorgeous blue-green irises that disagree.

"How can we not? Their entire business has been compromised. They need to know. Plus, they'll be able to help us. Or go to the feds if that's what they want."

"Go to the feds?"

Right. Of course there'd be fallout. Repercussions. You know, "feds" and the like. I'd been so focused on *doing the right thing*, I hadn't even thought about what happens when we do.

He shrugs. "I don't know Martin Sandeke. How would he play this?"

I only know him by reputation, but: "Smart. He'd play it smart."

Marcos leans back, stretching his arms above his head. A good spy notices their surroundings, the subtle things. Like how his aqua shirt rides up his stomach when he stretches to expose a line of taught ridges above the waistband of his jeans. And how his pecs and biceps bulge in perfect proportion when he clasps his hands behind his head to rest against the back of the couch. He stares at the ceiling, thinking, and I glare at Darcy, who's eyeing him greedily as well.

Don't even think about disturbing him, you beast.

"The question is, how?" Marcos says finally. "How do we approach SAT Systems without sounding ridiculous or throwing suspicion on ourselves?"

How indeed?

Darcy chooses that moment to reach out an adorable tiny paw and rest it on his exposed stomach. His expression immediately softens as he straightens and lifts her off the cushion.

"You have any ideas, princess?" he asks, holding her up to eye level. I know that view well. Sensory memory fires sparks at the flashback of staring into those volcanic eyes from an inch away. Of being pressed against that marble-sculpted body behind a server rack. Of running my thumb over the rough hair on his chin and longing for a taste of his lips. I look around for a glass of wine to dump on him. Or me. I don't care which of us gets wet at this point.

"You okay?" he asks.

"Fine, why?" I don't sound fine.

He lowers the cat back to the cushion.

"You're staring at me."

"I'm thinking."

"About?"

"The server room."

Now *he's* staring at *me*. "That was… intense."

"We almost got caught."

"But we didn't."

"No."

He shifts closer, and my gaze falls to the flex of his arm as it supports his weight. I know what that feels like too. I study the rise and fall of his chest beneath his soft, thin shirt. Also that. My gaze falls to the zipper of his jeans. The tiny cicadas in my stomach launch into a full-on rampage. I even know what that feels like.

"I'm your boss," I say, but my voice doesn't sound certain of that fact.

"Kind of." His tone is low and strained.

Kind. Of. My two favorite words right now.

"You didn't hire me as a real employee," he continues. "We both know I won't be at Reedweather for long."

"Yeah, but no one else knows that," I manage. "There'd be consequences if we were caught."

"Caught where? In your apartment?"

Right. My mouth goes dry when he shifts again, his thigh brushing against mine. He's finally where I've wanted him: within reach, willing and open. His argument is even valid. It's just... complicated. More so than he even knows in his young career. We'd be playing with fire, and I'd be the one bearing the brunt of the burn.

It's hard enough being taken seriously as a female executive. An affair with a subordinate not only breaks a handbook rule. It could ruin my reputation and career. Then again, he's right. He's not *really* my intern, so ethically maybe we're solidly in the gray on this?

"Look, I get it, Eva. I do. But as long as we're not caught before we finish this spy thing, is it really wrong?"

His eyes. So hard to resist—and so kind of right. There it is again: Kind Of. When did *Kind Of* become my personal mantra? This guy seriously messes with my wiring.

"I'm four years older," I blurt in a weird Hail Mary before my brain can adjust. When it does: stupid.

A brief smile flashes over his perfect lips. "Seriously? Do you know the average age of our clients when I was performing?"

I swallow, my gaze reflexively falling to the shirt that is no longer on him in my head. "Thirty?"

"Forty-one."

I swallow again. "How do you even know that?"

"Want to see the spreadsheet?"

Oh god, he wasn't joking. There really is a spreadsheet. Bet it has sophisticated formatting and formulas and *All. The. Things.*

He leans closer, waiting, willing me to say the words I want so desperately to say. They're right on the tip of my tongue, screaming through my brain. *Yes. Yes, I want you too. So, so much.*

But.

"Marcos." His name is a breath on my lips. Probably why there's no air in my lungs after I say it. He's stolen it all with his illicit offer, because we both know my protest isn't about age. What we're seeing here is pure, unadulterated fear about how much I want him and how little the consequences are starting to matter—yes, we've just tripped into the dangerous gray national symposium of *Kind Of.*

Agenda item one: Touch.

Two: Taste.

Three: Explore.

Just…

One kiss. Only one, and I promise…

His gaze finds mine, hot and imploring, tempting me with all the forbidden fruit in the entire Garden of Eden. Eva who? I'm Eve.

I stare back, shaking from the hum of those electric cicadas. They rush through my body from limb to limb until finally settling low in my belly. *Just one touch.* Catalogues of ethical constructs flow through my head and disintegrate into a confusing, fiery mass. I'm not really his boss. I'm not. And it would just be one touch. Just one simple glide over his chest, down his ribs, along his waist. Maybe a trace of the button on his jeans. A zipper. One generous handful that hardens into more—and yeah, there would be no *one* anything when it comes to him. One touch would become all the touches. So, so many touches that still wouldn't be enough. Because I. Want. Him. Badly and entirely.

Thanks, brain. Welcome to the party.

I push myself up from the couch and move toward the kitchen. "I could use a glass of ice water. You want some?"

11—CARTER HOLLIS

EVA

Yes, I'm late. What of it? I'm in no mood for either of my interns as I step off the elevator and march toward my office. Nope, not Chad and his nut fixation, and especially not Marcos and the general confusion he brings. Marcos seems to get the hint when our eyes connect for one searing second before he lowers his gaze to his screen. Chad—not so much.

"Ms. Reedweather! Do you have a second to review some notes on the campaign? I'd love to make sure I'm on the right track."

He's not. One hundred percent certain based on the fact that I found him flailing on the floor the other day. Unfortunately, he's still a professional responsibility, and secret spy missions require one to maintain a façade of normalcy. For the record, defining "normalcy" at Reedweather Media is a complex exercise.

"Sure. Give me a few minutes to settle in," I say, brushing past their desks.

It's an extra thirty degrees hotter on Marcos' half, even though he still won't look at me. Good. I don't allow myself to indulge in an evaluation of him either. Who cares how his button-down fits or if his tie makes his eyes glow today? I certainly don't. Maybe he buzzed off all his gorgeous locks to sport a bald look. If he did, so what? (He didn't. I caught that much in my peripheral—can't help optical physiology.)

Anyway, it's not like I suffered the burn of frustrated longing all night after he left. (I did.) But I made the right choice in rebuffing him. No regrets. (Some.) (A lot.) And we can still keep things professional, as proven by the fifteen (awkward) minutes we tried to work after the tense moment on the couch. He left very cordially at that point, but really, what else was there to do once we decided mole was delicious, if too hot, and Martin Sandeke should be informed of the plot against his company? (Quite a bit. Pretty much everything.) Still…

Martin Sandeke.

After much consideration, I've decided not to contact the younger Sandeke at this time. I'm not against involving him. In fact, I fully support it, I just disagree with Marcos on the timing. We don't know enough yet—the scope, the players, the plan—to present a clear, actionable picture. One thing working at this firm has taught me is the danger of incomplete information. Marcos won't like my decision to wait, but I have to trust my gut and the instincts that got me this far. Besides, he wasn't here when we had to shut down for two days because Marge in Copy sent out a company-wide e-mail claiming she was bringing several varieties of bombs on Monday for anyone who was interested. They'd be in the breakroom. After a thorough investigation, it came out that she thought it'd be self-evident she was referring to *bath* bombs, since real bombs don't come in flavors like "soothing lavender mist" and "honeysuckle amber."

Incomplete information can be dangerous.

Speaking of…

"Knock, knock."

I glance up from my morning e-mail purge to find intern Chad's big-toothed grin poking through the crack in my door. *Cheshire Cat* comes to mind. If Marcos is the polar opposite of an oily sycophant, Chad is the prototype—i.e., he fits in perfectly here at Reedweather Media. Each day he resembles my father more and more. First the hair that went from slicking left to slicking back. Then began the overuse of hand motions to compensate for lack of words. And now the smile, apparently. Overly sweet and grossly condescending, with expectations that it actually holds power.

I am in no mood for *Chad* right now. Heaven help him if he insists on this conference.

"Hi, Chad. I'm still working on a few things. Can we meet this afternoon?"

"Oh, right! I'm sure you're *exceedingly* busy. But I promise it will only take a second."

"I get that, but—"

"It just seems like Marcos has had a lot of opportunities to review his portion of the project with you, and I want to make sure you have no concerns about mine."

Do I contain my eye-roll? It feels like I do. I blink to be sure. "I'm not concerned."

"Oh good. So just a second, then."

He moves into my office and shuts the door. With his back turned, I free the eye-roll so it doesn't cause permanent nerve damage. The only thing worse than the use of passive-aggressive manipulations like Chad's are when they come with a patronizing Cheshire Cat grin. *Oh golly gee, Chad. Here I thought you just wanted to flaunt your work in my face since you're concerned Marcos is being shown favoritism. But now that I know you're really here for* my *benefit, do come in...*

It's going to be a long day. Maybe Marge is hosting another bomb party in the breakroom.

He places his laptop on the table near my desk, and I let out an exhale. I've just risen to join him when he darts back to the center of the office.

"Okay, picture this. It's winter in the North."

Great. He's prepared a skit. Of course he has. I drop back to my chair. "Like in *Game of Thrones*?"

"Exactly! Snow everywhere. Maybe a wolf."

"This is for print? Broadcast? Internet?"

He's clearly annoyed by the interruption. "Doesn't matter," he says, waving me off.

It does. A lot.

"Okay, so it's winter. There's the wall, right?"

"Which wall?"

"You know, *the* wall."

I lift a brow, but he waves that off as well.

"Anyway, so the wall is in the background, and you have this army of White Walkers gathered at the bottom, but instead of zombie ghosts they're cashews."

He says this with a straight face. In fact, he's not finished.

"So they're standing there with their Brazil Nut King on a horse, right? And there's these two guards on the wall, talking to each other and—"

"Are they nuts too?"

Chad looks vaguely annoyed. "Yeah, pine nuts. But human pine nuts."

"Human pine nuts?"

"Right. Not zombie nuts."

"Right."

He waves his hand again. "Anyway, so Pine Nut Guard One looks down at his tablet and is watching this same scene in the actual show and says, 'Shit, it keeps breaking up. I can't see how it ends.'"

"We can't say 'shit.'"

"Oh shit. I meant, 'crap.' '*Crap*, it keeps breaking up. I can't see how it ends.' And the other Pine Nut Guard shows him *his* tablet with a crystal-clear picture and says, 'Oh, you need Sandeke Telecom's new Warp Speed connection. Look, you get industry-leading streaming quality at an affordable price.'"

"Is that the campaign copy included in the proposal I sent?"

"Oh. I don't know. Probably not."

"Because you really need to use what Copy sent over. It's already been researched and vetted."

"Sure. Yeah. So, anyway, now both guards are watching the screen as the White Walker King attacks and takes down the wall in the TV version. Then they look at each other and go, 'Uh-oh.'"

He stops talking, the grin frozen on his face. His eyes have widened into full circles that show white all around the irises. I fear for his sockets. Can eyeballs pop out from overextension? It's a better question than anything that just came out of Chad's mouth.

Speechless, I swallow and stare back with a cool, even expression. Is it the worst pitch I've ever heard? No. Because, once, Marge in Copy tried to sell bath products and launched an FBI investigation.

Chad adds a slight head-bob-nodding gesture to his grin face.

"Why nuts, though?" I ask finally.

His grin falters slightly. "Because it's the *Nuts for Speed* campaign."

"Right. But the consumer viewing the ad won't know that. They're just going to wonder why a bunch of cashews are attacking two pine nuts on a wall."

"Because *Game of Thrones*."

"Is *Game of Thrones* known for its portrayal of nuts?"

His grin falters further. "Well, it's a metaphor."

And here we go. When a person can't be wrong, they will say the stupidest stuff. My father invented this game and created an entire language of meaningless corporate jargon. Chad isn't nearly as skilled, though, so I can't wait to see what comes next.

"Oh?" I cross my arms, lean back in my chair, and place a decidedly interested expression on my face. It's not even an act. I'm so, so interested right now.

"Yeah, for... capitalism?"

Does he know what capitalism is? Actually, does he know what human beings and/or nuts are?

"I see. Because...?"

He blinks, which comes as a relief to me. It was hurting my own eyes to watch his unnaturally expose themselves to the elements.

"Um, because the White Walkers are supply and the guards are demand?" He must like this answer, because I see the moment his brain commits and pats itself on the back. "And the wall is Sandeke Telecom, which has overcome its army of competitors to satisfy the small demand."

"You think there's limited demand for broadband connection right now?"

"Oh, no. That's not what I meant. I meant small as in..." I see the wheels turning as he searches for an answer. "As in, a person can only have one telecom company, right? So the demand is small in a home, in that there's only one. Demand. One demand. Which... Is small."

I arch my brow. I could challenge any and all of that, but why? Instead: "And the nuts?" Now I have to know.

"They represent… consumers."

"So we're calling our customers nuts?"

"Oh. No. Not consumers. I meant, competitors."

"Ah. So the White Walkers, which are supply, are nuts because they're our competitors. Sandeke Telecom is the wall that rises above the rest, and the guards are the consumers being elevated due to their embrace of our superior product and service?"

"Right!" He looks relieved, sweat evaporating at his temples.

"Great. So why are the *guards* pine nuts again?"

* * *

CHAD FINALLY CONCEDES that his pitch might need work. Also, after losing at least a hundred brain cells from hearing it, I'm craving something I promised myself I'd stop obsessing over after last night. So, really, it's Chad's fault that I pick up my phone and text Marcos.

Lunch today?

I respond to an e-mail looking for weekly KPI reports for my department and scan another with minutes from yesterday's executive planning meeting. I open a third, launching a new initiative my father is calling "Agile Synergy," which is a lot like regular synergy except it can be formatted into fun logos, when Marcos responds to my text.

Can't. I'm eating with Mark today.

Me: **Mark Oliver?**

Marcos: **Hilarious. No, Mark from Accounting.**

Confused, I blink at my screen.

Me: **Yeah, Mark Oliver.**

Marcos: **Wait, he's actually Mark Oliver?**

Me: **Yes. Carries around the Badass Accountant mug?**

Marcos: **Incoming.**

I'm not sure what that means until my door opens a second later after a brief knock. Marcos closes it behind him, and it's amazing how different my mind and body react to his intrusion than Chad's.

"Can I help you?" I ask, slightly serious and a lot teasing.

"Is Mark's last name really Oliver?"

"How did you not know this? Aren't you besties now?"

"We had lunch once. And no, it's never come up."

"Now twice, apparently."

"Are you jealous?" He shakes his head. "Don't answer that because we're still talking about Mark. You realize that whole mess with HR and my documentation was because they had me in the system as Mark Oliver?"

"Really?" I snort a laugh. "So when we hired you we thought we hired another Mark Oliver?"

He groans and drops to the chair in front of my desk. "That makes it so much worse."

I laugh and shrug. "Welcome to Reedweather. Where are you going for lunch?"

"Mark's boyfriend's restaurant."

"The Hollis House, right? Sounds nice."

Now that he's sitting across from me, there's no way not to notice that he looks as waterskiing-swimsuit-model perfect as ever. Yep, he looks like a *huge* regret. I shake off a shudder from his stare last night. I could know things right now…

"It will be, but that's not the only reason I'm going." He glances around the office and leans forward. "I have a plan."

"You do? For Project Snake?"

He nods. "Well, a plan for a plan. I have to scope things out first."

"The restaurant or the chef?"

"Both."

"Maybe I should go with you." You know, now that there are *plans* involved.

He studies me, his eyes darkening to a dangerous teal. "Isn't that a little too 'double date' for your comfort?"

To be fair, based on the way my heart rate picks up, one could argue I'm uncomfortable with it. One could also argue discomfort isn't always a bad thing and that my pounding pulse is because I'm *too* comfortable with it.

"It's work. Just coworkers sharing a meal," I say, meeting his gaze.

He searches for a moment, and my breathing accelerates to match my pulse in the silence. He must find what he's looking for because soon his expression changes from curious to smug. Bet he learned that expression from Darcy. "I'm sure Mark wouldn't mind if you came with us."

Relief. Sweet, sweet relief. And irritation because—smugness.

"This changes nothing," I warn, even as the cicadas erupt into a buzzing cloud in my stomach.

"Okay," he says, now with a *very* smug grin.

I resist the urge to point at something to distract him. "Get back to work. Stop slacking," I mutter, returning to my computer screen.

"You got it, boss." I don't have to see his face to know the self-satisfaction is still there. I hear it. He pushes up from the chair, and I also resist the urge to watch his body's every move as he walks out. I'm just the queen of restraint today. Bodes well for a lunch non-date.

Funny how I wanted to punch one Cheshire grin this morning and completely devour another...

* * *

THE HOLLIS HOUSE was founded by renown celebrity chef Carter Hollis—or as he's better known at Reedweather Media, "Mark in Accounting's boyfriend." The restaurant itself is an on-trend, upscale exhibition of French fusion cuisine. The atmosphere is classy and sleek, if a little pretentious, with clean lines, sparse greenery, and an attractive, polished staff. In other words, I know exactly what Marcos was thinking when he said he had a "plan": It's the perfect location to host potential business mogul cheats like Denver Sandeke and Grant Worthington. The rest of his plan isn't as clear to me, but I don't miss the way his gaze continuously inspects the décor and structural features.

Mark himself is a delight. I never spent much time with Accounting's resident bad boy, but it doesn't take long to see how his dry wit and subversive awareness would attract a mutual cynic like Marcos. They have a lot in common, and I don't doubt for a second that Marcos' affection for the man is genuine. He may be "plotting" right now, but he's also enjoying lunch with an actual friend. Carter Hollis, however, was called away on a kitchen emergency the second he joined us, so verdict is out on him. He returns toward the end of our meal—which *was* delicious—very apologetic and not nearly as pretentious as his restaurant. I decide after a short conversation that I like him too.

"This place is amazing," Marcos says, flashing that killer smile at Carter as we finish dessert. "How long has it been open?"

Carter beams back. "Thanks. About two years."

Marcos offers an impressed nod. "Bet reservations are tough to get."

"They are if you don't know someone," he says with a glint. "Lucky for you..." He and Mark exchange an amused glance before focusing back on Marcos.

My intern grins back and looks every bit the grateful patron. "Don't you think this would be a great place for Sandeke's visit next week?" he asks me. He fixes his gaze on my eyes, urging me to play along with a slight widening of his own.

"Sandeke? As in Sandeke Telecom? Denver Sandeke?" Carter asks. It must take a lot to impress a man like Chef Carter Hollis, but I suppose multibillionaires who rule multibillion business empires are impressive.

"Denver and Grant would love it," I say. "But we already have that reservation at Pascal East." We don't, but it was the most exclusive reservation I could think of in the moment.

"Wow. I mean, if you wanted to bring them here, I'm sure Carter can find room," Mark interjects, nudging his man.

Carter nods eagerly. "Absolutely. We could move some things around."

"Hmm..." Marcos furrows his brows in thought. He scans the space with an analytical expression. "Do you have a private room or anything? At least a more secluded table?"

"Of course. If you're finished eating, I can show you around."

"Great," Marcos says, putting down his napkin.

We follow Carter through the main dining room toward what looks like Asian-inspired paper doors.

"If you'll give me a moment, I'd like to smooth things over with the current guests before we barge in," Carter says with a smile. We wave him on with more pleasant smiles and hang back while he enters. A moment later he beckons us in, and we offer polite greetings to the occupants of the table inside. Yep, they look exactly like Denver Sandekes and Grant Worthingtons. When I glance over to see if Marcos notices, he's already inspecting the perimeter of the space.

"This is perfect. Don't you think, Eva?"

"I love it," I say, following his lead.

Carter seems relieved. "Fantastic. Then let us know what time you're looking to reserve it, and we'll see what we can do."

"Great," Marcos says. "Oh, one more thing. Would we be able to come by that morning and drop off some materials for the meeting so we don't have to cart them in when things are busy?"

Huh? Now he's really lost me.

Carter looks surprised but covers it quickly with a shrug. "I don't see why not. You can coordinate any logistics with Sheldon, my manager."

"Perfect," Marcos says, holding out his hand. "Carter, it's been a pleasure."

Carter takes it with an expression I see often on people who encounter Marcos Oliveira: Enchantment. "The pleasure is all mine. Make sure Mark brings you around more."

Mark leans in for a quick kiss from Carter, and after paying our bill, we head back to the office. But instead of following Mark into the elevator in the lobby, I drag Marcos around the corner and down another corridor.

* * *

THERE IS no crying in business, so when you lose a hard-fought account or face a misogynistic backlash—or your father humiliates you by giving your well-deserved position to some guy named Grant Worthington—you need a place to purge your frustration free of prying eyes. That's how I found this maintenance closet in the bowels of our building and why I know it will be the perfect (only) place for Marcos and me to debrief.

"Why do I feel like I'm in trouble?" he asks as I shove him into the room and close the door.

"You're not in trouble, but you need to fill me in on what's going through that crafty brain of yours."

"Crafty?" The smug smile returns as if he knows how much I enjoy that crafty brain. Crave it sometimes. Like now. Ugh. I jab my finger into his chest, forcing him back against the door.

"Ow," he winces, still grinning.

"Talk. We now have a critical business meeting with Denver Sandeke at The Hollis House? What's that about, genius?"

"Do you think we can get him and Worthington out to dinner?"

"Maybe. It'll take some finessing and the involvement of my father, but it might be possible. But first, I need to know what you're thinking."

His eyes glint with mischief that triggers a flare in my internal radiator. I need to get that thing serviced. Wait… no. I mean… ugh.

"Did you see the sculpture in the private room?" he asks.

"By the plant?"

He nods. "Perfect place for a hidden camera, don't you think?"

I stare at him.

He stares at me.

My mouth opens to respond, to probe, because… what? But instead: "That's why you asked if you could go in early to drop off supplies. You want to set up a hidden camera?"

"Yes, ma'am. We go in, get the room ready, and then we have our dinner where we get them to say something incriminating. After that, we have evidence we can turn over to SAT Systems, or the feds, or whatever we want."

"Is that legal?"

"Not sure, but we're not looking for court documents at this point. Just proof to add to our findings for SAT Systems, right?"

My nod turns into an absent shake of my head. That's next-level spy shit right there. And he put that together in a blink of an eye, all while cementing one friendship and fostering another. This guy is unbelievable.

"How do we do that? Why would they admit to the stolen information in front of us?"

The glint in his eyes turns downright lethal. Cicadas burst in my stomach, buzzing around like tiny, fluttering henchmen. Yeah, I have to call the exterminator ASAP.

"They wouldn't. Which is why we need a recording device in the room and not *on* us." I must look confused, because he takes a breath. "See, it's kind of like a bluff. We casually drop a comment or two during dinner. Then we see if they panic after we leave. Regardless, the camera will pick up whatever they discuss in response."

Right.

Genius.

And...

I kiss him. Hard.

It's not my fault. It's the cicadas. They lunge forward and shove him into the door. They force my hands into his hair to lock his surprised mouth against mine. They taste him, and touch, and grab in a voracious hunt to satisfy every fantasy that's tortured them for so long through a deafening drone of *Kind Of*. They want the feel of his hard body and soft lips and silky hair. They want the sensation of his labored breath, his skin, his heat—they want to own. To devour. To trap him in this closet and take and give and burn for days on end. Yes. They want everything, but soon it's me who succumbs to the fire. *I'm* the one who lets it consume me when he surrenders to my sneak attack. His mouth anchors to mine, his tongue dipping in for a sample before his young, ravenous drive demands more. I feel the return of his *smugness* when his shock transforms into desire. When the prey becomes the hunter and his blistering touch turns me into the desperate one. I slide along his body in a slow, needy pulse. Up, down, pressing, pushing. My hips hook into his, grinding to the rhythm of our mouths. Agile Synergy. Oh yes, I get it now.

A moan leaks out when he finds my neck, and I rake my fingers in his hair to hold him in place. I want his mouth here forever. No, not just here. Everywhere. I want to feel him everywhere. His power, suppressed and caged and stalking the perimeter of its pen as I taunt him into submission. He's already hard—so hard—and my leg instinctively fastens behind his thigh to scissor us closer. I want to feel him *there*—deep inside—forbidden and hot, evidence that he suffers like I do. He gasps out a curse when I sink down, his body tensing in a delicious statue of muscle and fire.

"Eva," he groans. "What are you doing?"

"You've never thought about this?"

"All the fucking time. But the other night you said we can't," he breathes against my ear. His fingers sink into my hair, gripping hard against the pain of his lust. It's intoxicating. My hips assault his again, this time pleading—*demanding* a response. He hisses in a sharp breath.

"I know. I don't care anymore. Come over tonight," I rasp out, bucking against him again.

His hands curve around my butt and yank me into sweet, painful friction. I reach down between us. Just one touch. Only one. I rub my palm over him, and his eyes clench shut. Okay, two. His head goes back against the door. Maybe three.

He groans again, breathing hard. "We should stop," he roughs out with zero conviction.

"Come over tonight," I repeat, massaging. "We can figure this out."

There's nothing polite about my kiss to round out my argument. Certainly not in his response when I continue to knead him. It's a yes. More accurately, a *hell yes*. Still, I wait for the words.

"Seven?" he growls, gripping my neck to stare into my eyes. An inch away, his irises slay me. Which means… his lips. Heaven help me, they're *right* there.

"I'll get takeout," I pant, finally releasing him.

The cicadas are responsible for the next kiss. I was fine postponing until tonight, but they saw his minty pillows of heaven and reacted on instinct. Animals. Pure, rabid animals, those treacherous little creatures.

Marcos groans again and gently pulls away. He holds me at arm's length, staring at my hands with suspicion until I step back on my own.

"You should go. I'll be up in a few minutes," he says. The lust lingering in his voice keeps my cicadas swarming in a fury.

I watch, trembling, as he leans his head against the wall, clearly trying to reconstruct himself. His breathing is labored, his face flushed. His eyes are wild with need and evidence of his own roaring cloud of angry insects. He's a mess. A gorgeous, hypnotic mess of frustrated want, and when my gaze scales his disheveled state and lands on his tented zipper, a smile curves my lips.

A pretty darn smug one at that.

PART III
MONITOR

MARCOS

12—LUCINDA MAE

MARCOS

I have three minutes to figure out what just happened and how the hell I'm supposed to finish my day at a desk. The dude beside me in the elevator keeps firing suspicious glances like he knows I just made out with my boss in a storage closet. Not my boss. Not really, we decided.

Shit.

Truth is, as much as I argued in favor of giving in to our feelings, she's not the only one risking backlash. I'm pretty sure an affair with my boss wouldn't go over well with my advisor and the university. I'd been arguing with myself as much as her in those debates, trying to convince myself she's not really my supervisor. That our situation *is* temporary and therefore not an ethical construct, just a physical challenge of not getting caught. But now I'm so freaking screwed, because I don't care about any of the technical bullshit anymore. I absolutely want to go to Eva's apartment tonight. Scratch that: now. I want to go to her apartment *now*—potential consequences be damned—and have since that first awkward greeting in her office doorway.

Her return attraction was obvious, or so I thought, but after two visits to her home, both of which involved me in very comprising positions where I practically threw myself at her, I'd started to lose hope. Either I'd completely misread the situation, or her restraint is otherworldly. Regardless, her professionalism is without question. Aside from our little encounter in the server room—which I chalked up to adrenaline

113

over our spy games—I hadn't even been sure she felt the same way until she jumped me in the closet. Now I'm positive.

And completely on fire.

I shoot a glare at the judge-y dude in the elevator as I step off. It's so easy to stand there with your briefcase and to-go coffee when your body isn't a raging bonfire and your entire world hasn't been turned on its head. Besides, it's not like I'm wearing a sign that says, "Guess what scandalous thing I just did." I glance down at a tiny smudge of lipstick on my shirt. Hmm... well...

Instead of heading to my desk, I hook left toward the restrooms. When I meet my reflection in the mirror... perhaps I owe elevator dude an apology. Thanks to Eva's ministrations, my hair's been tossed in eccentric genius disarray. After smoothing the wayward strands, I shove the left side of my shirt back into the waistband of my pants and readjust my belt. There.

My clothes and hair pass as presentable; all I need to work on is my face. Animalistic fire heats my gaze, and a crimson flush stains my cheeks. I lean over the sink and splash several rounds of cold water over my skin, hoping no one enters the bathroom. That's just what I need right now, Chad chanting about nuts or Reedweather making up a story about a time he used a toilet. After patting myself dry, I study the new man in the mirror: I should be able to pull off bored intern... as long as I don't think about what happened in that closet.

Certainly not the way Eva's tight, forbidden body felt pressed against mine. The way she clawed at me. The burn of her fingers exploring my favorite business slacks until I was hard and desperate and completely owned.

"Come over tonight?"

I would have done anything in that moment. *Anything.*

And shit. Here we go again.

I groan and lean over the counter, resting my elbows on the cool surface. Burying my face in my hands, I draw in slow, deep breaths and visualize ice water flowing through my veins. Maybe that will counter the hot, pounding blood? No. Eva thinks her cat is the devil. Wrong. She's the temptress in this situation.

I picture a ceiling fan, spinning its blades in absent monotony. Around. And around. And around. My pulse slows in time with the blades as I reduce their speed. My breathing evens out.

Note to future CEO self: Install fans in strategic locations throughout the office.

After another minute or so, I feel prepared to face Intern Life again and march back to my desk. Except...

"Oh! *Cashew* nuts." A well-dressed middle-aged woman cackles from behind Chad's desk. "I thought you meant, well, *you know.*"

"Ahh, dirty mind," Chad cackles back, pointing at her naughtily. The woman responds with a flirty eyelash flutter I can't unsee, and I decide I need coffee or a photocopy or anything that will send me back the way I came. I glance around for a hidden ceiling fan I might have missed.

"Wait a minute," the woman says, stopping me mid-turn. "You."

"Me?" I ask.

She straightens from behind Chad, who looks downright murderous that I blocked his game again. Her eyes grow round as she nods. "You!"

I look behind me, but there's only Jerry staring at his monitor with his *about to win Solitaire* face. Please let her be a big Jerry and/or Solitaire fan.

"Yes. You. You're Reno! Oh my!"

Shit.

She fans herself. A different kind of heat fires through me.

I shake my head. "No."

"Yes! I could never forget that face. And that hair. And that *body.*"

Oh my god.

The way she says body has Chad leaning past her for a peek. He doesn't even look mad. Just bewildered. Maybe slightly fascinated. I try to think of the most exciting nut-related fact I can shout back to distract him. Hang on, is a cocoa bean a nut? If it is... mind blown.

I shake my head once more. What's happening again?

"No," I repeat, because everything about this moment is a hard *no*.

"No? You're not Reno?"

"No. I'm Marcos?" It comes out as a question. I search the area again but only find a personal fan at Jerry's desk. The violent *whir* of the device merely fuels my agitation.

"Ah. I see. Well, hello, *Marcos*." Her wink makes me positive she thinks I made that up too. "So nice to *meet* you." I don't know what her wink on "meet" means, and I'm not eager to find out.

She holds out her hand, and I take it tentatively. Her gaze runs over me in response to a conversation I'm not a part of. Her forehead wrinkles. She nods slightly. I swallow and try to look not confused as I nod back, thinking that will cover a lot of possibilities.

She scrunches her brows together.

I smile.

She winks.

I squint.

She's still holding my hand. We both stare at that.

"Mom?"

Our attention shoots to the new voice, and... oh *hell* no.

Eva approaches, confusion clouding her gaze as it lands on the woman beside me. *Mom*? No effing way.

"What are you doing here?" Eva asks.

"Just picking up my paycheck, honey."

"Dad's still paying you?"

"I'm his first wife. He'll always be paying me."

Eva's eyes drift down to my hand still mated with her mother's. Damn, could this get any worse?

"What's in Reno?" Chad asks.

At least I know where Eva inherited her shocked expression.

"Reno?" she asks, confusion descending into horror. Is that what I look like right now?

Mom squeezes my hand. "You naughty girl. Strippers at work?"

"Mom!"

"Stripper?" Chad asks, his eyes resembling the Brazil nuts he loves. Also, why is he staring at my ass?

"Oh, sorry. I'm being rude," Eva's mother says to me. "I'm Lucinda Mae. Nice to meet you... again."

"Again?" I croak out. Even though, duh.

For the first time since his employment, Chad seems to have forgotten about nuts. He's definitely, one hundred percent checking me out instead. Mysteries have clearly been revealed, puzzles assembled, secrets exposed. I can't even rank everything wrong with this scene.

"You performed at my girlfriend's office party," Lucinda Mae says, and I shake my head.

Breathe. See?

"You must be mistaken. We didn't do office parties."

Chad's mouth opens.

Wait.

Shit.

Reno, he mouths to himself. *Reno.*

"She runs The Sinful Shelle in Bristol," Lucinda Mae continues. "Her *office* party was quite the hot-topic event. Pretty sure you did." Another wink.

Fuck. I remember that night. Nate said it would be easy money. It was. Then. Not so much now. Because I'm sure I'll be paying dearly for it—with a healthy amount of interest in the form of my reputation.

I blink, hoping this isn't happening. This can't be happening. Why is Chad still mouthing my stage name?

"Lucinda Mae. A pleasure," I say when I can't think of anything else. I even add a bow. I guess that's what you do when you speak like an eighteenth-century landowner. Except, I'm not sure what to do next besides circle around her and pretend none of this happened. All three of them are staring at me when I look up from my desk. Four, actually. Even Jerry's taking an intermission from his daily three-card-draw marathon.

"What?" I ask, passing my gaze over each of them. I hope I look innocent. Just a working man working. Nothing to see here. I resist the urge to blurt something about cocoa beans.

Lucinda Mae snaps a look between her daughter and me. "You work here. As an employee? With clothes?"

"Yes, Mom," Eva interrupts. "This is *Marcos*. My intern."

"*One* of her interns," Chad clarifies. For no reason. Still, I'm finally grateful for a pointless Chad interjection. "Also, Reno is a city in Nevada." He holds up a finger to accentuate his point. He's not wrong.

When Lucinda Mae winks again, this time at her daughter, I wonder if maybe she doesn't understand how winks are supposed to work.

"Ah, I see," she says, then stops cold. Her eyes grow three sizes as her neck strains to fire suspicious glances between Eva and me again. "Wait. *Marcos*? *The* Marcos?"

Hang on. *The* Marcos? Hell yeah.

Eva jerks forward and grabs her mother's wrist. "Mom." Her glare bores into the older woman, who shrugs. First an innocent one, then a mischievous sequel. Her gaze is definitely saturated with messages for me as Eva drags her backward into her office. Like the other silent messages, I can't read this one either, and decide she's telling me she either approves of her daughter's crush on Reno the Stripper, is jealous of that fact, or she has a kidney stone.

The door closes behind them, and I draw in a long draught of air. Will our date tonight be canceled or hotter than ever after this? I can't begin to sort through the dynamics of what just happened. My only choice now is to try to remain calm.

"Yo, Oliveira."

I glance up to find Chad peering at me.

"You really from Reno? Maybe you know my cousin Greg."

13—AXL RHODES

MARCOS

"You came," Eva says.

She leans against the door to her condo, studying me like I'm studying her. We never resolved what kind of meeting this was going to be. We hardly talked at all after the confrontation with her mom, so I can't begin to guess where we stand. Based on the look in her eyes and what she's wearing, though, we're in decent shape.

"I brought my laptop," I say. Her expression dims slightly. "And wine." It lifts again.

Yep, still don't know.

"Great. We have a lot to *review*."

Her emphasis on *review* doesn't help either. Not when her attention pays equal tribute to the messenger bag at my hip and the neighboring zipper of my jeans. My attention is more dedicated in its focus on the effect of her tight, low-cut sweater. Is this the first time I've seen her in non-office attire? I add that to the growing collection of clues. It cancels out the fact that I'm still in the hall.

"So…" I say, tapping my fingers on my laptop bag.

"So…" She taps hers on the doorjamb.

"Can I come in?"

"Oh. Right." She steps back and waves me in—I think. She swats at something anyway, and I accept that as an invitation.

"I ordered Indian food. Is that okay?" she says from behind me as we walk toward the kitchen.

"Perfect."

"And hot. *So* hot." She clears her throat. "The food, I mean. Is spicy."

I smirk. Okay, yeah. We're on. "I knew what you meant."

She emits what sounds like a grunt and brushes past me to the cabinets.

"I laid the groundwork for our meeting with Sandeke next week," she continues, handing me a plate. "According to my father, he'll be in town on Monday. They always do an executive dinner while he's here, so we just have to figure out how to get invited to that."

"Great. I'll set up a reservation with Mark and Carter. Eight sound good?"

"That works. So how do we get invited?"

Good question. *An intern and a VP walk into a bar...* We have three days to figure out the rest of that joke. "Do you think you can get me more face time with your father? I should buddy up to him and Grant."

"Agreed. They're more likely to trust a male intern than a female executive."

Ouch. Also, I hate that she's right. Even worse is her *mild* irritation, which demonstrates how often she faces that reality. She should be livid. Probably was at one point, and an ember of anger ignites from my Bellevue days. Those fucking ghosts of injustice are always sneaking around, wreaking havoc in the shadows of society. Every so often, inequality takes zombie form, lurching down main street in raucous parades. Everyone runs and screams and raises arms to take it down in the name of justice. Mostly, though, it's a personal haunting. Disturbing to those experiencing it, invisible to those who don't. So we swallow it, brush it off with *mild irritation* so as not to be the delusional person who sees ghosts.

It makes me want to stomp this spy shit out even more.

"You know you're smarter and more competent than both of them combined, right?" I say.

She looks over, surprised. "Maybe. Not that it matters."

"Of course it matters."

"Yeah, well, tell that to the industry." Her eyes narrow at the island; her fists clench around the plate in her hands. Yep, her ghosts are screaming much louder than her voice right now. "How are you supposed to get ahead as a young female when the same behaviors that are glorified as strategic business qualities in men—like confidence and assertiveness— are labeled as defiant and bitchy in women? I'm damned if I do and damned if I don't."

"It freaking sucks."

"Do you know how many times they've taken credit for *my* work? How many times I've been asked to get coffee and order food for meetings I'm attending as a department head? If I let it slide, I'm perpetuating the bias. If I stand up for myself, I'm petty, at best—insolent, at worst. Sometimes, I just..." Her words fade out, and I fight the urge to drive my fist through a wall.

"You just want to punch something?"

A slight smile twists the corner of her mouth. "Yeah. But after that, then what? Sometimes it feels pointless to fight a war you know you'll lose."

"Doesn't mean you can't win a battle here and there. Sometimes right is just right, and you fight for the sake of the means, not just the end."

"Okay. And when you challenge the system and still lose?"

"Then you keep working your ass off. You absorb as much information and experience as you can, and one day you run your own company that doesn't tolerate that bullshit. You learn their world so you can break it."

Note to future CEO self: No. Bullshit.

She studies me. Curious at first, then with something else: awareness. "That's what you're doing, isn't it? That's why you agreed to take this job. You *wanted* to see the dark side. You've experienced what I'm talking about."

"Bias based on things I can't control? Yeah. All the time. And yes, that's why I'm taking in everything I can. The good, the bad, and the repugnant. One day I'm going to be a CEO and show everyone how things *should* be. I have to study the beast to defeat it."

She sets her plate on the counter and pulls mine from my hands. "You're amazing. You know that?" she says, sliding her hands around my waist.

I grin, loving the pressure of her hips against me. "I thought we were talking about how amazing *you* are."

Her eyes search mine before landing on my mouth. "Is this conversation going to get sappy?"

"Do you want it to?"

She reaches up and traces a finger over my lower lip, studying it intently. That action alone has me hardening into the danger zone. She must have noticed when she smiles and settles closer. Her hands descend over my ass to cinch us together. She sighs, the sound of relief. Like if she didn't touch me, the pent-up lust would burst arteries. I know that feeling well.

She tilts her head up, staring into my eyes with an invitation I feel throughout my body.

"You know what we need?" she breathes out.

"What?" My voice is hoarse.

Her eyes ignite: "A killer pitch."

* * *

SHE'S NOT WRONG. In fact, she's absolutely right. The best way to secure a meeting with the Sandeke empire bigwigs is to lure them with the only thing they love more than themselves: money. An intriguing proposal for how they can acquire more of it is the perfect bait.

Except there's that sweater. And those thick lashes fluttering over brown eyes that beg to see me naked. We haven't touched the food since our fingers became more interested in exploring skin.

She tugs at my collar, slipping open the buttons one by one. Her eyes darken with each freed inch. I shudder from the brush of her nails as she works.

"For the record, *I* love your confidence and assertiveness," I say as she fans the fabric open and shoves it over my shoulders. *And how she licks her lips when she stares at my body.* I let the shirt slide off my arms and sail to the floor, then grip the hem of her sweater.

"And I love your intuition," she says, shrugging out of her top when I pull.

"It's survival," I murmur against her neck. Damn, she tastes like strawberries. I go in for another bite, and her moan sends my blood directly south.

"From your foster care days?" she gasps out, tangling her fingers in my hair.

"From all my days." I move up to sample her jaw. Also strawberries. Yum. She shivers beneath me.

"I want to know everything." Her breathing accelerates into short pants as my palms skim over her curves.

"One day." I taste her lips while slipping my hand between her thighs. She groans into the kiss, releasing my hair to find my zipper. I probe deeper with my tongue as our bodies begin an instinctive, complementary rhythm. She unhooks the button on my jeans, shoving them open with the force of her wrist. I hiss in a breath at her grip.

"Living room or bedroom?" she breathes, massaging slowly, deeply. Her eyes flare with hunger; she must like what she's found. I certainly do.

"Eva..."

She strokes harder, and I groan against the current. "Living. Room. Or. Bed. Room?" she repeats. I'm not sure how she expects me to speak when her other hand threads into my hair and draws my mouth to hers. "Now, Marcos. Please," she gasps out.

Please? I'm the one who's begging at this point.

"Living—"

My response is cut off by the clatter of the front door. Eva jumps back with a gasp and lunges for her sweater. She's just stuffed her head in the wrong hole when a familiar woman and an unfamiliar man stop cold at the entrance to the kitchen. Marisya, I think? The other woman's shock spreads into a grin while she observes me casually zip my jeans. Then she swings her gaze to her frantic roommate. I return a sly smile, but Eva isn't nearly as amused as she struggles with her sweater. Her head is buried inside the fabric, and I gently tug it off to free her. She fires a glare at me, followed by a wince when I flip the shirt around so she can slide it on the human way.

"Thanks," she mutters, yanking it down her chest. She shoves her arms in the sleeves and smooths out the wrinkles. "I thought you were going away for a week," she hisses at her roommate-sister.

"I was, but Axl had to come back for a gig."

"Axl?"

The stranger lifts his hand. "Hi." His gaze crosses to me, and I smile back.

"Hey, man. I'm Marcos."

"Hey. I'm Axl."

"Yep. Um… cool."

"Ahh. *Marcos, Marcos*," Marisya repeats to herself, scanning me in slow, obvious appraisal. "Damn, girl. Didn't I tell you he was model material?"

"Yes, well, he's also intern material," Eva quips, crossing her arms.

Marisya's grin widens. "I bet. I'd be working after-hours too, sweetie."

"Not a word about this, Mari," Eva grunts and swipes my shirt off the floor. She slings it into my chest as she marches past, and I capture the fabric against me.

"Guess we're finished," I say to the other couple. "Welcome home."

Marisya offers a thumbs-up of approval while Axl snickers.

"Intern, huh? Way to go, dude," he says, clapping my shoulder as they pass. "Aw, food! Hell yeah. I'm starving. You mind?" He's already piling chicken tikka masala and the entire order of naan on his plate.

I shrug and slide my shirt back on. "Go for it. So you're a musician?" I ask while he eats and I button.

Marisya squeals. "A musician? You don't recognize him?"

I toss an apologetic look. "Sorry. You're in a band, obviously."

"Marcos! This is Axl Rhodes, lead singer of Unicorn Magpie!"

Yeah, that doesn't help me at all. "Oh, cool. Good to meet you."

Axl nods a *we can do autographs later* from his seat at the table. Marisya claps and hops in place.

"They're playing Eva's brother's club tonight," she informs me.

"Kyle's place?" Translation: you flew home for *that*? I played bigger venues stripping.

"I know, right?!" Marisya claps again. "We met in Milan."

"Oh yeah? You there for a show?" I ask him.

Axl nods. "Yep. A fucking big-ass stadium show."

Huh. Unibrow Maglite. Who knew?

"A stadium concert, wow."

"Hell yeah. Once in a lifetime, dude. It was lit. Man, this shit is spicy. You got water or something, babe?"

"I'll get it, babe," Marisya sings, leaning down to kiss the back of his head.

"Thanks, babe."

"I bet," I say, stepping aside so Marisya can scoot past me. Anything to stop the *babes*. "Was it just the one show or part of a tour?"

I wait as Axl swallows his bite. He shoves another in anyway. "Just the one show," he garbles out. "Funds are a little tight right now."

"Really?" I say. "Even though you played a stadium?"

"Played?" Axl snorts. "Nah, man. We saw Night Shifts Black. They were awesome."

I swallow my initial response. And the next. Finally, I manage a tight smile, which seems safe. "I've heard they're great live."

Marisya bends down to place his water on the table and loop her arms around his neck from behind. "But Unicorn Magpie is so good too. Right, babe?"

Axl nods, maneuvering the glass around his new girlfriend's elbow. "Sure, babe."

"Their music is just…" She twists toward me and presses a hand to her heart. Her lashes flutter with the magic of such indescribable music.

"Wow," I say. Yeah, that's all I got. I suppose I could escape to the bathroom to do a quick search for more on his band, but why?

Speaking of search, where's Eva?

"And Axl knows *everyone*. Luke Craven, Jesse Everett, Mason West…"

I tune out the name-drop as I scan the space for my kind-of-boss. Is she hiding in her room? After what we started, how it stopped, and whatever I find myself in now, is it better or worse for us to reconvene within spitting distance of her bed?

"Oh, plus Abram Fletcher and Kaitlyn Parker."

I freeze and focus back on Marisya. "Kaitlyn Parker?" Why do I know that name? "The… musician?" I guess.

They look at me like I just asked the fourth stupidest question of all time.

"Uh yeah. Kaitlyn Parker is one of the biggest songwriters in the industry right now." Marisya crosses her arms like she's personally offended by my ignorance.

That may be true, but her songwriting isn't the reason her name is haunting my brain.

Kaitlyn Parker…

Wait. I remember reading it recently. What was I researching again? "She's connected to someone, right? Romantically?"

Apparently, I just asked the third stupidest question of all time.

"Duh. Only Martin Sandeke, your boss's boss's boss's son."

I pass on doing that math and concentrate instead on the first part. I must have read it when I was looking up Martin and SAT Systems.

Axl Rhodes, lead singer of Unicorn Magnet or whatever, is suddenly way more interesting to me.

"So you're friends with her?" I ask, grabbing a plate. Maybe I am hungry after all. Axl left us two small cubes of chicken and a teaspoon of rice, which I transfer to my plate. Should be enough to admit me into his universe for a minute or two.

"Oh yeah, man. We're tight," he says through another mouthful. I even get a demonstration of "tight" with his non-fork hand.

"Like, how tight? You hang out?"

Well, there's my second stupidest question, apparently.

"I mean, we don't *hang out*, per se..." He shovels a fresh mound of chicken into his face.

"Okay. So you...?" I pause to leave room for his verbal explanation of "tight," since it doesn't seem to coincide with the visual. His fingers were definitely "hanging out" in that demonstration.

He shrugs, and my optimism officially takes a nosedive.

"I have her number."

"Yeah? You call each other and stuff?"

"I mean, not *call*, per se."

"Text?"

"What's *texting*, though, really?"

The bare minimum of "tight."

"So, by *have* her number, you mean you *know* her number."

He shrugs again. "Same thing."

It's not. Guess I didn't need that chicken after all.

"Okay, man. Well, hey, it was great meeting you." I push up from the table. "Good luck with Unicycle Magician."

"Unicorn Magpie," Marisya corrects, narrowing her eyes at me. Playfully, I think, but now I've lost confidence in any of their social cues. Still, she's Eva's roommate-slash-ex-stepsister, which means I need her on my side.

I manage a quick smile. "Right. Sorry. So, um, you have tracks or something I can check out?"

He snorts at what was clearly the silliest question of them all.

"Nah, man. We're *real* artists."

Right.

He shakes his head and exchanges an eye-roll with Marisya. "Tracks," he huffs and returns to his food.

I nod and set off in search of Eva.

* * *

IT'S NOT hard to find Eva's room. There are two doors in the condo I haven't explored yet. One is open and leads to a dark space that looks like the splintered remains of a fashion institute. The other door is closed with light streaking out from underneath. I knock on that one.

"Eva?"

"In here," she answers.

I swallow a snarky reply and push it open.

Not sure what I expected when I finally encountered the enchanted realm of Evangeline Reedweather's bedroom. Maybe a choir of angels. A gathering of the Tooth Fairy, Easter Bunny, and all manner of mythical beings. Perhaps even a rare Unicorn Magpie, whatever that is. But no. Instead, I enter a sparsely furnished, severe chamber that looks eerily similar to mine. Clean lines, zero clutter, neutral industrial tones and materials. Yep, pretty sure I have that same dresser.

"Wow," I say, inspecting the room.

"I like simple." She's seated at a desk with a laptop open in front of her. I should have guessed she'd recover from an embarrassing situation by working.

"Me too. Does your dresser have the extra divider for the sock drawer?" I ask, tapping the top of the gray wardrobe.

Her eyes widen in surprise. Possibly alarm. "How did you know?" Okay, maybe I hear the stalker vibe in that statement now.

"I have the same one." I make an obvious appraisal of the rest of the space. "In fact, my room looks a lot like this. Except for that." I point to the throw pillow on her expertly made bed.

Her expression changes as something flashes behind her dark irises. I can't tell what she's thinking, but I recognize that look as one that typically fares well for me.

"I'd like to see your room sometime," she says, then blushes. "I mean, since it's close to mine. I'd like to see the similarities."

I bite back a smile. "Right. For comparative study purposes."

"Exactly. Strictly out of observational interest." Her gaze is definitely observing me standing near her bed right now. Is she grateful or disappointed that I'm more clothed than the last time she saw me?

She clears her throat and spins back to her laptop. "Anyway, I've been working on a pitch to get Sandeke's attention. I have some broad concepts to discuss if you have a minute."

"Interesting, because I've been working on your roommate's new boyfriend for a tie to Martin Sandeke."

She stiffens and swivels toward me. "Axl knows Martin?"

"No. Martin's girlfriend or wife or whatever." I cringe. "Well, he knows who she *is*. Her name's Kaitlyn Parker and she's a songwriter or something."

"And you think he can hook us up with her?"

"No. I have zero faith that can happen. But..." I pull out my phone. "My roommate who actually *is* connected to industry influencers might be able to."

Eva watches as I fire off a text to Nash.

"He's the musician who makes you write therapeutic songs?"

I look up, surprised. "You remember that?"

"Of course." Her gaze intensifies, blazing from across the room. What did we trigger this time? By the fire in her eyes, it's more than just a memory of me naked in her bathroom.

"He's one of my oldest friends," I add, suddenly anxious. "We grew up together at Bellevue."

"The group home?"

I nod. "There's... history. A lot of it."

"I'd love to meet him."

I pull in a breath, my heart racing. Things got heavy—fast—which tends to happen when my past pokes its ugly head into my present. She thinks she wants to know everything, but we're still working on some things. Sock drawers. Cat allergies. Only one person knows everything, and he saves me now with a timely response to my text.

Nash: **Kaitlyn? Yeah. She's great. What do you need?**

I smile and glance back at Eva.

"You want to meet Nash Ellis? How about now?"

14—MARY LOU BARR-REEDWEATHER

MARCOS

Never mind. Nash is running front-of-house for a gig tonight, so Eva talks me into heading to Pascal East for cocktails with her parents instead. For the record, it wasn't so much of a discussion as a command, and I try to check my attitude on the ride over. I can get damn cranky when things don't go my way, and I'm already crabby about postponing the Kaitlyn Parker line of inquiry—also that I'm underdressed and "meeting the parents" before we've had our first date.

"You sure about this?" I mutter under my breath as the host leads us to the table.

"You said you wanted more face time with my father."

"As a colleague, not your date for a meet-the-parents scenario."

"This isn't a date," she quips, but her smug smile suggests differently. The woman can do *smug*, I'll give her that.

"I'm wearing jeans."

"And a button-down."

"No tie."

"Will you relax? He already loves you," she hisses as we approach.

I force a smile when they spot us.

"Mark-O!" Reedweather belts out, rising to take my hand. *Loves me? He can't even pronounce my name.* "What an *expected* surprise." He winks at Eva, who returns a tight lip-twist at the joke. "Eva," he says in a serious tone as a greeting, I think. Then to me, "She said you two were working late and could use a nightcap. I knew I had a feeling about you. Didn't I tell you I had a feeling about him?" he asks the elderly woman to his right. His mother, maybe? Also, he's still holding my hand. His grip tightens when he turns back to me, his eyes narrowing on mine.

Oh shit. It's happening. *The Handshake.* I try to suppress my shudder and narrow my eyes right back. Not sure how long we're supposed to narrow-stare, though.

"Okay, Dad. How about you introduce Marcos to Mary Lou," Eva interrupts. When he doesn't let go, she grips our wrists and forces our hands apart. Reedweather's face cracks with a grin that's infinitely creepier.

"And who is this handsome chap?" the woman asks. I pull my gaze away from my boss's serial killer leer and rest it on a prim matron who was enjoying her seventies quite a while ago. She adjusts the fur boa around her shoulders and flashes a bright red lipstick smile at me. The woman screams wealth. Old wealth that still has—and *flaunts*—heirlooms like fur boas and the rock-candy diamonds dangling from her ears. Her hair is professionally coifed into a bun with a small pin twist in the front. Her nails are short and perfectly manicured. She was a showstopper sixty years ago, no question.

"Hello, ma'am. I'm Marcos."

I take the hand she extends to me, not sure if I'm supposed to kiss it. Maybe? She lifts it higher toward my face when I hesitate. I cast a quick look at Eva, but she only returns the most amused of amused looks. No help at all.

"Go ahead, handsome. I won't stop a good smooch," the older woman croons.

Oh my god.

I suck in a breath and press my lips to her hand, careful to avoid the ginormous gem mountain ridge on her fingers. Seriously, how is she able to function with that much bling in the way?

"It's a pleasure, *Marcos*." She rolls the "R" like an old Broadway star.

"The pleasure is mine, assuredly, ma'am," I say and cringe. I've never said that sentence in my life. Probably no one has. She just has an air that transports you back a hundred years. I ignore Eva's pure delight beside me.

"Oh, please call me Mary Lou. I simply couldn't stand to have such a handsome young man call me *ma'am*." She repeats the word with such disdain, I believe her. "He's divine, Eva," she informs my boss in front of my other boss.

Eva clears her throat, now scowling. "He's an intern, Mary Lou. We're just coworkers."

"Right," Mary Lou says with a cackle. "Just like your father and I are *business partners*."

Panic flashes across Eva's face before she steps forward as if blocking the flow of information to her father. I'd be more concerned if I thought the man paid attention to anything that didn't involve him. "Marcos, this is my stepmother, Mary Lou Barr-Reedweather," Eva says, clearly redirecting the conversation.

Wait. Stepmother? I fight to maintain my smile against every instinct that wants to choke on air right now. It can't be. This woman must be twenty or thirty years older than Reedweather!

"Don't worry, my dear. You can talk shop in front of me. My Reed-y and I have no secrets from each other. Isn't that right, pumpkin face?" Her voice goes up an octave on the last sentence, and I swear the hard man melts right in front me.

Okay, yep. There's no doubt. Corporate mogul Reed Reedweather, III is a trophy husband.

I don't even know what to do with that as Eva takes my arm and drags me to the chair across from her father. Once she's convinced I'm stable and seated, she takes the empty one next to me.

"It's so nice we could do this. Thanks for having us," she says.

"It's our pleasure, my darling," Mary Lou replies. I can't help but notice the tinge of disapproval in her tone. "You work entirely too hard, you know." Ah, there it is. Less tinge and more deluge in that one. I swallow my retort, knowing Eva wouldn't want me stepping in right now.

I'm glad I don't when she quips back, "Well, sadly, I'm not qualified for a career in Rich Dead Husbands. I'll just have to keep using my MBA to forge my own destiny."

Mary Lou's bright red lips press together in an even thinner line. Any more and they'd be transparent. "I understand that, dear. Perhaps one day you will meet a man who can overlook such things."

Eva's expression hardens into a glower all living organisms should fear. Even Mary Lou stirs a bit in her seat before pretending to inspect the wine list. Apparently, she can read upside down. Good for her.

"What are you drinking, Mark-O, my man?" Reedweather asks. "Wait, I know. Scotch, am I right?" His corresponding finger gun is one of the best I've ever seen.

"Sounds great, sir," I say, resisting the urge to finger-gun back.

Note to future CEO self: Commit to thorough training in hand-gesture protocol.

"Excellent! A Bay Breeze for you, my butterfly nose?"

"I don't know, sugar fingers. It's not a *Tuesday*." By the look they exchange, I have no interest in knowing what happens on Tuesdays. My phone buzzes in my pocket, and I pull it out for a discreet glance while our hosts smarm across the table.

Eva: **Having fun, my little tapeworm butt?**

I bite my lip to block a snort.

Me: **Just wish I could find a woman who's skilled at balancing giant rocks on her knuckles. I seem to get stuck with smart, successful ones.**

Her teeth sink into her lower lip as well.

Eva: **Every man's dream girl.**

Me: **I'd be happy to help you train later. Although, personally, I think your "gems" are already flawless.**

A blush spreads over her cheeks as she shifts in her chair. Did she just squeeze her legs together? I smile to myself and focus back on the awkwardness across the table.

Reedweather lifts two fingers, and sure enough, a server appears as if he'd been waiting for this very moment. The guy nods encouragingly while Reedweather rattles off an order for everyone at the table, including Eva, who never asked for anything. She's getting a White Russian and seared scallops with some sauce that probably isn't *car engine juice,* but that's what I heard. The older couple also must've decided Bay Breezes on non-Tuesdays are fine after all, especially when paired with a shellfish tower, cheese tray, and some other thing I didn't understand. I'm getting a scotch that sounds as old and expensive as Reedweather's wife.

Rude, Marcos. I cast her an apologetic look. Mary Lou smiles back.

"So, *Marcos*." Still rolling the "R." "Tell me something shocking about yourself."

Eva chokes on a sip of water.

"How about that he's a damn good intern," Reedweather interjects with an emphatic nod. No finger gun this time, but the serial killer sneer is back. I'm about ninety-seven percent sure that's supposed to be his *we-have-fun-don't-we* face.

"Wow. Thank you, sir." I'm flattered but have no idea how I earned that title. I've basically spent my entire employment trying to thwart him.

"I said *shocking,* rose bonnet," Mary Lou chides, tapping her beau lightly on the nose. It's amazing. I can't look away.

"I know, Easter flower."

"Good. Marcos?" Her finger twitches on the table, and I wonder if she'd tap my nose if she could reach it.

"Shocking… hmm…" I say before she can try.

Eva squirms next to me, and I allow a quick smile to flash across my lips. *Don't say stripper!* she's silently screaming. I continue to hesitate, staring at the ceiling as if I'm having trouble finding a scandalous secret, even though my entire existence is basically one hulking scandal.

Her hand flies over to squeeze my thigh under the table, and my muscles tense. The explosion in my body completely ignores her intended warning, interpreting it instead as a forbidden sequel to the heated contact in her kitchen just an hour ago. In fact, my body is downright stubborn in its refusal to accept any other explanation, but then, so is hers when she doesn't remove her touch after making her point. Instead, her fingers sink further into my leg and start climbing.

Shit.

Something scandalous, Ms. Barr-Reedweather? Look under the table.

I pull in a steadying breath. Her hand keeps moving, and I reach down to trap it in place before it does irreparable damage. I sense her delight at successfully arousing me. Distracting me too, and now my jeans are incredibly uncomfortable. I gently return her hand to her side of the table, but not before my fingers linger with a soft caress. She shudders, and I try to recall what I'm supposed to be contemplating.

"Come now, Marcos. You don't look like a boring man. There must be a delicious secret."

Right. That.

I clear my throat and shoot Mary Lou what I think is a *delicious* grin. "But do I have one I can share? That's the question."

"Oh you," she replies, swatting her blinding rocks in my direction.

"Okay."

Eva stiffens when I lean forward with a glint, and I block her hand mid-dart this time. "Don't you dare tell a soul about this, but I was a damn good gin rummy player back in the day."

I could have said I'm descended from royalty and her face probably would have lit up the same way.

"Gin rummy! Oh my. Heavens, that's my favorite. Isn't it, pookie breath?" she asks her husband.

"Hmm?" Reedweather responds, staring at his phone. "Absolutely, honey hen."

Yeah, he has no clue what she said, but that doesn't deter her excitement. "Oh you *must* come to rummy night with the ladies tomorrow. They will *love* you."

I was hoping to score some points with my confession, but a direct invitation into the inner sanctum? Even Eva seems impressed beside me.

"We'll be there," she says before I can respond.

Mary Lou's smile falters. "Oh, do you play, dear?"

"Not really, but Marcos can teach me. Right, Marcos?"

"Of course," I say, exchanging a look with Eva. Also, I may have lied. Am I a damn good gin rummy player? Eh. Do I know *how* to play gin rummy? Sort of. It involves cards... pretty sure.

"Did you hear that, kitten bear? Marcos and Eva are coming over tomorrow!"

"Yeah?"

Reedweather didn't hear that either.

Mary Lou clears her throat. "Really, Reed, you're being rude," she hisses. "Those cellular mobile telephones should be banned, I say."

Reedweather startles a bit and finally looks up from his screen. "Sorry, the stock market," he mumbles, though I'm almost positive I see sports scores not stock prices before he tucks it away.

The server prevents more awkwardness by delivering our drinks, and I study the others for a clue on how this is supposed to go down. "An evening of cocktails" means different things to different people. Sure enough, Mary Lou lifts her glass, and we all follow suit.

"To present company," she says, targeting a grin at me.

I tilt my glass toward her and echo her toast along with the others. When it seems clear that's the end of the festivities, I turn to Reedweather. "So how are the Sandeke financials looking? There seemed to be some concern in the executive planning meeting this week."

"Psh," Reedweather says. "Nothing but some healthy *Competitive Unrest*. You remember *Competitive Unrest* from your Yorkshire days?"

No. Also, technically, I'm still in my Yorkshire days. "Does Sandeke Telecom face a lot of stiff competition?"

Eva tenses beside me. She knows what I'm doing, but I can't tell if her subtle head movements are intended to encourage me or begging me to stop.

He guffaws into his glass. "Stiff? Hardly. In fact, there's really only one player we need to worry about and that's already being handled."

My pulse picks up. "Oh yeah? Handled how?"

He returns a haughty look that tells me his secret is not one he should share, but he will anyway. Perfect.

"Well, I can't get into details about *that*, but I can tell you, you needn't worry. This company isn't even a real telecom company. They deliver the internet via spaceships."

Satellites, actually.

"Can you imagine? What is this? Star Wars Trek? And their financials..."

Are impeccable.

"Psh. They won't last another year."

"How do you figure?"

He shrugs. "They're a non-profit." That alone should answer all my questions, apparently. When I don't seem sufficiently convinced, he continues. "Besides, based on their Q1 numbers, all their money is tied up in assets. They don't have nearly enough cash for overhead and operating costs. They may know how to build spaceships"—they don't—"but they clearly know nothing about running a business. You should see their advertising budget. It's a joke."

I suspect he's referring to their lack of funding for golf and company yachts, not consumer advertising. Because I have seen it, and their financials are no laughing matter if you're Sandeke Telecom. I plaster a contemplative look on my face. "Huh. So interesting. And how do you know all of this?"

He lifts the glass to his lips and sucks down a large gulp to buy time. Based on the price of that scotch, I'm guessing he just stall-guzzled about fifty bucks. "Uh... their annual report... filed with the state."

Nice recovery, I'll give him that. Although, it would have worked better if he'd said the Form 990 filed with the IRS, since state requirements vary, and I guarantee he has no clue where SAT Systems is incorporated. Also, there's the small detail that the public record on file wouldn't contain current quarter numbers. Still, I nod and allow myself to look grateful for his reassurance.

"Well, that's a relief," I say. "I'd hate for all our work on the Nuts for Speed campaign to be for naught." Naught? I squint at the scotch, avoiding Eva's amusement beside me. I blame the magnetic field of Centenarian Mary Lou Barr-Reed-weather for that one. When she beams back at me, I decide to research other old-timey words before tomorrow's rummy date.

"Well, as I said. You needn't be concerned. Keep doing a bang-up job and reaching for the stars. Sandeke Telecom will be around for generations to come." He lifts his glass to Sandeke's longevity and star-reaching. I take another sip from mine. "*Agile Synergy,* Mark-O, my boy. It's all about *Agile Synergy.*"

Right. My brain skids to a memory of his daughter pressed against my groin in perfect alignment, our hips and mouths volleying in harmonic sine waves. Probably not what he means.

I swallow the heat flaring from my jeans to my throat. "I look forward to learning more about it."

* * *

"He practically admitted they're spying, and it only took one drink," Eva whispers outside the restaurant. Reedweather and Mary Lou are safely on their way to *The Brownstone,* as Mary Lou calls their residence, while Eva and I debrief in hushed tones on the sidewalk. It's too late in the evening for a formal relocation to another setting, and yet, neither of us seems eager to flag a cab and end the night. Eva keeps finding excuses to touch me. I don't need any to let her.

"Imagine what we could get after several," I say as she plays with an untucked tail of my shirt. Her slight tug forces me closer.

"Exactly. We have to be at that meeting on Monday." She traces the hem, running her finger along the stitching. Up and down. Every so often I feel the heat of her touch when it brushes too close to my skin. She switches to trailing the inner waistband of my jeans. I like that even more.

"It was so hard not to mention the meeting tonight, but we need to coordinate our plan with your pitch," I say.

Her fingers stall in a sudden clasp on my jeans, her gaze lifting to mine. "*My* pitch?"

"It's your idea, isn't it?"

"Yeah, but—"

"So you should take the lead—*and* the credit."

She slips her fingers further into the denim, achingly close to where I want them. "We should work on it tomorrow then. Before rummy." Her fingers dig in, lower.

Still not low enough. She shudders a sigh as I brace my palms against the stone wall behind us. I hiss in a breath when she teases sensitive skin and coarse hair.

"I need to teach you how to play anyway. Come to my place?" I search her eyes. "For observational purposes. You can see my room and finally meet Nash."

She removes her hands from my jeans with what seems like reluctance and tugs at a wing of my collar. Her gaze burns into mine. "Text me your address."

15—NATE HANOVER

MARCOS

I could strangle Nash when he tells me he's running sound for yet another gig and has to split. Of course Nate, the one I needed gone, informs me his girlfriend Myra cancelled their plans because of a fever. He'd love to meet *Eva,* however. The way he says Eva does nothing to improve my opinion of these developments.

I love Nate, don't get me wrong. He's a friend, mentor, and (at times) an inspirational force in my life. At other times he says things like *"I'd love to meet Eva"* in a way that makes my blood run cold. Usually that tone ends with me agreeing to *prank Billy Stanton* or *audition for a male revue.* Yes, always said with the same titillating tone and slight arch of his brows that he uses now. Also, I always say okay and always regret it the second I do.

"She's my boss," I remind him.

"But she's hot."

"So?"

"So... do you want to see her naked?" he asks, dumping creamer in his mug as if coffee flavors creamer, not the other way around.

"Yes, but that's—"

"Does she want to see you naked?"

"Yes, but it's—"

"Exactly. Dude, she's coming to your house. Your *domicile*." He flicks a finger into my chest as he passes on his way to a stool at the small island.

"To work."

It sounds even more ridiculous out loud.

Nate rolls his eyes. "Uh huh. On a Saturday?"

"We have a rummy date with her stepmother tonight. I have to teach her how to play."

"What the hell is a rummy date?"

"An event where people congregate with other people and play rummy."

He doesn't look impressed. "Please tell me her stepmother is smoking hot and this involves some kind of competitive stripping?"

Competitive stripping? *There's* an underdeveloped concept for later consideration.

I shrug and take a sip from my cup. "She's about ninety, so probably some logistical challenges for stripping, but there might be cold mint tea."

He narrows his eyes.

"Cucumber sandwiches?" I suggest.

He shakes his head.

"Hypoallergenic lap dogs."

He sighs. "Marcos, Marcos, Marcos." It's never good when he says my name more than once in sequence.

"I'm involved in something. Something big," I say, holding up my hand to stop the lecture.

He freezes, his expression hardening the longer he studies me. Yeah, should have gone with the lecture.

"Hang on..." He presses a fist to his mouth, his gaze boring into me. "Hang on just a second."

I clear my throat and pretend to see something really interesting in my coffee cup.

"Oh fu— You didn't back off the satellite shit," he says finally. "You didn't ask for the nuts."

I sigh and shake my head. "No. And it's good I didn't. It turns out that's the whole reason I was hired."

"They hired you to catch them spying?" It doesn't take an Ivy League degree to read his skepticism.

"*They* didn't hire me. *Eva* did." And I realize too late that I used the titillating pronunciation of her name. Great…

Of course Nate notices when his critique-face spreads into an entertained-face. Sometimes it would be awesome if my roommates were clueless.

"So let me get this straight. The owner's daughter stumbled upon some incriminating information and brought you, Mr. I-Hate-Monopolistic-Cheats, on board to help weed it out—until your pants got in the way."

"My pants?"

"I was going to say dick, but I'm guessing since she's willing to come to your place on a Saturday *to work*, her pants are involved as well. I opted for more gender-inclusive terminology."

"The movement thanks you," I mutter.

He smirks. "What is it your boss is always saying? *Rampant Inclusivity?*"

"*Rabid* Inclusivity."

Nate mouths the phrase to himself with a look of delight. I'm just glad we're talking about meaningless buzzwords instead of my relationship with Eva.

"What's his latest anyway? You haven't shared any in a couple of days."

Despite my sour mood, I can't help but crack a smile. "*Agile Synergy.*"

"What now?"

I shrug. "I can show you the e-mail if you want to review the official roll-out package."

"Roll-out *package?*"

"There are logos. Developmental and team-building exercises. Case studies. A Venn diagram."

Interesting. So that's how I looked when the e-mail popped into my inbox.

"Please show me," he says. "In fact, never stop showing me."

* * *

NATE APPROVES OF EVA. Not that I had any doubt about that. Eva is basically a clone of his badass boss-lady girlfriend, Myra. They even kind of look alike—kind of—and a flash of future hangouts and double dates skitters across my brain. Skitters, because then he says, "So how's the industrial spy caper going?" Eva straightens abruptly on the island stool. "Can I get you another tea, Eva?"

"No. I'm fine, thanks," she says stiffly, firing a look at me. I return an apologetic grimace.

"I didn't give him any details, but we talked it through in the beginning when I wasn't sure what to do about the files you sent me. I thought it was an accident then."

Her stare hardens on me as she considers my defense.

"Those weren't the real files, and I haven't said a word since," I continue. "He didn't even know we were still on the case until today."

The slightest of smiles flickers over her lips. Probably because I just said "still on the case" like a ten-year-old playing awesome police detective. Yep, Nate is snickering too. Whatever. She's not mad anymore. I win.

"What do you do again?" she asks Nate.

"He's a junior VP of Finance at Eon Tech," I interject before he can make some snarky comment about being a counter-espionage investigator at Sandeke Telecom. "He's not in our industry and is the second most trustworthy guy I know," I add for Exhibit B.

"Second?" he asks, squinting at me.

"Nash is first. Dude doesn't talk. About anything."

Nate eases back against the counter. "True. Unless it involves music."

I cross my arms. "Exactly. Anyway, my point is Nate won't give us away. He has much worse dirt on me than this."

"Also true," he says.

"Nate doesn't even know anything," I direct to Eva.

"Well, except that Denver Sandeke is an asshole," Nate corrects.

Eva tilts her head. "You know Denver Sandeke?"

"No."

"So how do you know he's an asshole?"

"Doesn't everybody know he's an asshole?"

Now we're all smiling, and yeah. That's Nate, ladies and gents. Intelligent, charming —he sincerely likes people so they sincerely like him back. It's also why he'd probably be a great ally after all. Eva might be thinking the same thing when her stance relaxes.

"Fine," she says, gripping the edge of the island, still in thought. She finally releases her fists and pulls a laptop from her bag. Nate and I exchange a look while she fires it up. Guess he's in.

"There's a dinner with Sandeke, my father, Reed Reedweather, and another guy happening Monday night. We need to get invited," she says, studying her screen and opening files. "We thought a good strategy would be to pitch a marketing idea that would catch their interest but require an in-depth discussion at dinner."

Nate nods. "When's the meeting again?"

"Monday."

"That's not a lot of time. You have any ideas?"

She taps a few more strokes on the keyboard and spins the screen toward us. "This. We partner with a well-known band." She holds up her hand to prevent us from responding. "I'm not talking about using their song in a commercial. I'm talking about a relationship. We sponsor original music, livestream a concert through our platforms, collaborate on social campaigns, merch... whatever our creative minds can invent. We disguise something boring and old—corporate telecom—with something current and fresh." Her hand shifts into a wave. "Okay, now we can discuss."

Wow.

It's perfect.

"Would you be able to find a band willing to sell out to that extent?" Nate asks. "I mean, Nash would gouge out his eyes before selling his soul to the corporate regime."

I snicker at the thought. He totally would. I can see him standing right where Nate is, all drama, a paring knife poised at his cheek. *I'll do it, I swear! I will never dance before your throne of lies!*

Clearing the vision from my head, I focus back on Nate. "First of all, have you seen reality television? Absolutely you'd find musicians willing to bow down at the capitalist throne." I wave off the point. "But second, it doesn't matter. That's the brilliance of this. Hell, the pitch doesn't even have to be viable, just interesting and complicated enough for further discussion. In fact, the more they can shoot down and feel like powerful smarter-than-thou kingpins, the better."

Nate's smile grows. So does Eva's.

"Plus, flashy graphics," she says, clicking open some slides. We lean forward to examine her screen, and I can tell Nate is as impressed as I am.

"You did all of this last night?" I ask.

She shrugs. "Finished up this morning, but yes. Best part, most of the data is accurate. If they fact-check anything, it'll probably come up true."

"*If*," I say, trying to imagine Reedweather doing anything besides wandering aimlessly and making up boring, irrelevant stories to enjoy the sound of his own voice. I don't know Denver, though. By all reports he's a ruthless businessman. He'd have to be to build the empire he has. Bet he fact-checks. Bet he also eats spiders. *Ew.*

I clear that image from my head too.

"Okay, so how and when will you pitch it?" Nate asks, scrolling through the slides.

"That's the question," Eva says, deflating. "It would raise too many flags if we emailed this presentation directly to Sandeke out of the blue. He doesn't know we exist. And yet, we have almost no chance at pitching to him in person. He only does a flyby at the office when he's in town. It's too risky to count on that and wait for Monday to make our move."

My heart rate picks up at the blast of an idea. "Right. So, *we* don't pitch it," I say, drawing their attention. I send a targeted look to Eva. "Your father does. We slip the concept to him tonight at rummy and make him think it's *his* idea. Once he commits, we reinforce it and build his excitement into urgency. Then we offer to work on it tomorrow and present it to Sandeke and Grant at the dinner."

They quiet, reviewing my plan for a flaw. There are several, but any that are too big for our brain trust to overcome? Like the pitch itself, it doesn't need to be flawless, just non-flaw-obvious.

Nate lets out a breath. "Damn. Now I wish I'd been invited to rummy."

* * *

NATE FINALLY LETS me off the hook and remembers something *super important he has to do* at another location. Once the main door clicks, I turn to Eva, fully aware of the charged silence around us.

We're alone.

In my apartment.

Under the acknowledged pretext of her wanting a tour of my bedroom. From there I can extrapolate plenty of other pretexts that have my blood pounding and my body tense. I draw in a deep breath, also aware of the way her gaze keeps darting away when I catch her scanning me in unnecessary places.

"So, you ready to train for Mary Lou's card night?" I ask, clapping my hands on the counter.

Her lips curl in the most adorable smirk. "Do you actually know how to play rummy?"

"Sort of?"

"You told Mary Lou you were, and I quote, 'a *damn good* gin rummy player.'"

"Well, excuse me if I didn't realize she was in a freaking pro league. It got us an invite, didn't it?"

"Yeah, but now she'll know you lied."

"You underestimate my charm." I shoot a grin that lands pretty successfully based on her sudden flush. Her gaze sinks to my mouth, and nothing in her demeanor indicates she's interested in rummy right now.

"What about your room? Maybe you should show me that first." Her tone is low and sultry.

I brace against the heat firing through my chest. "You want to see my sock drawer divider?" Admittedly, a weird pickup line, but it might have worked because she's sliding off the stool.

She takes my hand, running her thumb over mine in suggestive strokes. "Lead the way, rummy god."

"Wait. Is rummy like poker? Do we need player names?" I ask, guiding her down the hall.

"I dare you to wear a visor tonight."

"Hmm…" I lean my back against my closed door and pretend to consider the suggestion. "Not a bad idea. I bet *the ladies* would like it."

"*The ladies* aren't why we're going, Casanova."

"Would *you* like it?"

"Are you stalling? Is your room messy or something?"

"No."

"So?"

I grin as she presses into me to reach the handle. "I just like when you crowd me against doors."

Her eye-roll doesn't match the flicker of a smile on her lips. Or the way she lingers against my body. She's loving this as much as I am. "Except I could be crowding you against something else right now."

Whoa. Sparks flare straight to my groin, bright and hot. Her eyes fuel the burn, settling on my mouth with raw hunger.

"Fine. Your kingdom, my lady." I push open the door and back into the room.

She seems disappointed when a cool rush of air chills the newly vacant space between us. I resist the urge to cough out an *I told you so.* Closed doors make things happen. It's the two-finger salute of foreplay.

She scans the space while I shut the door behind us. We may be alone in the apartment, but with our track record, you can't be too careful.

"Wow. You're right. It does look like mine," she says, her tone introspective. Not sure if I'm winning or losing points for that. "That's my dresser!"

"Told you."

Her amusement fades when she picks up the one framed picture in my room. She studies the smiling teen boys by the lake, then crosses a quick glance to me. "You, Nash, and Nate?"

"Yeah. Nate left a week later. Transferred to a facility for older kids. But that was an awesome day. One of the few good memories of my time at Bellevue." A week later, hell rained down when our protector was taken from us. When angry boys with little minds tried to make themselves big. It's also when I learned to fight and that justice is subjective.

"What happened a year ago, Marcos? What made *the darkness forge a spark*?"

She's in front of me now. When did that happen? I swallow old memories, choke on recent ones. I flinch from sudden pressure on my hand and look down to find it firmly encased in hers.

Clearing my throat, I force a smile. "We only have a few hours until rummy. We should get to work."

"Marcos…"

I close my eyes and pull in a deep breath.

"What happened a year ago?"

Emotion wells in my chest, angry and decayed. It's acid, suddenly burning through neglected walls and hemorrhaging into my blood stream.

Her grip tightens on my hand.

"They've declined."

"Counseling services are available…"

"This isn't a reflection on you."

Isn't it, though? Is it anything but a reflection on the son who wasn't worth anything? Not even a conversation years later?

"Marcos?"

I blink back stubborn tears and shove my arm across my eyes. "Let's just work."

She halts my retreat with a tug on my hand, tightening her hold until I stop resisting. Reaching up, she traces my cheek, catching a rogue tear I missed. Shit, could this get more embarrassing? I clench my jaw, my fists.

"What happened a year ago?"

I take an unsteady breath and focus on the far wall. At least the white builder-grade paint doesn't have dark brown eyes teeming with compassion. Her stare is potent, tangible in this moment. So fucking dangerous.

"I found my birth parents," I say finally. My voice is hard. I don't like how much it gives away, but it's better than sad and weak. "Last year."

Her grip constricts on my hand. I'm not actually going to do this, am I? Tell this story. Make it real again.

"They weren't what you hoped?" she asks softly when I don't continue.

The weight pressing on my chest shifts into my throat. I swallow again, desperate to keep it from my voice. Heaven forbid it reaches my eyes. I blink against the burn.

"I wouldn't know. They refused contact."

I hear her gasp, see it when my eyes lose their battle for the wall and drift to her face. I close them before they do more damage. She can't see the rest. Not now. Not ever.

"Marcos…"

I shake my head. "No, it's fine. I mean, what did I expect, right?" My harsh laugh grates the silence into fractured seconds. How did we even get here? I try to pull away, but she doubles down, sliding her other hand over mine. Now I don't even have a barrier against the emotion boiling behind my eyes. It's too close to setpoint. It's going to burst into visible steam if I can't end this.

Her eyes soften the longer she stares, and I clench my jaw, directing my gaze back to the safer wall. She lets go with one hand only to rest two fingers on my jaw and coax my attention back to her.

"Marcos, you are…" She hesitates, searching.

I press my lips into a firm line. "Nothing. But one day I will be. I *will* be someone special."

Her expression crumbles. A glossy sheen clouds her eyes. "My god, you actually believe that," she whispers.

"That I'll be something one day? I *have* to be. I just…" My throat closes. I just… what? Have to fill the holes. So many broken pieces that have been worn down and no longer fit.

"That you're nothing! Marcos"—she shakes her head—"You're… you're incredible. How can you not see you're already *everything?*"

I stiffen. What?

"Anyone can shine in a spotlight. Show me the person who radiates from the shadows." Her fingers move to my lips. Her smile grows through the tears as she follows the slow outline. She lifts her gaze to mine, probing, begging me to understand.

"Marcos Oliveira, you're going to achieve your dreams not because of who you will be but because of who you already are."

Well, damn. There are no words to follow that. Nothing except my mouth on hers. My hands in her hair. My legs walking her back toward the bed. It's clean and freshly made because that's a habit formed in lonely group-home shadows. She grips the hem of my shirt, ripping it up my chest, and I help shrug it off. Her gaze scours me, covetous and enflamed. I love how her eyes touch me before her fingers, appreciating my powerful body that's also a relic of the boy who never wanted to feel weak again. Does she get it now? Stripping—who doesn't want to be publicly loved and admired? Humor—laugh with me not at me. Charm—make them like you before they can reject you. All of it stems from a past I couldn't control, now driving my quest to own the future.

She's just discovered I'm a walking case study for any psychological textbook, and instead of running, she traps me against a mattress. Instead of pushing me away, she clings with a violence that has my blood hot and my brain short-circuiting into dazed lust. She straddles me, sinking down hard, as if her body is desperate to draw me in.

"No interruptions this time," she breathes, jerking her hips and surging down on my groin in an agonizing plea.

"Door's locked," I gasp out.

"Good."

She pulls off her top, flinging it to the floor. A red lace bra, the absolute last thing I expect to see on Corporate Queen Eva Reedweather, sets fire to her pale skin. Her hips move again as she strips, and I groan at the relentless rush of blood and heat. She's going to kill me. My jeans clench against the pulse of my arousal. She unhooks the button on hers, exposing matching red lace panties. Air stops filtering into my lungs, reducing them to the most useless of organs. She's literally breathtaking.

"You are so fucking perfect," I mutter as she adjusts to slide off her pants. No one deserves her. She should be on a cloud somewhere, sipping honey milk or whatever the hell those Greek goddesses drink. Sucking on grapes and shit. Sucking... I groan again. "You're killing me. Are we really doing this?"

She grins and traces a finger down my chest. "We're doing this. Your turn. Strip," she commands. Her eyes go dark with desire as she watches me reach for my jeans. They flare hot when I lower the zipper. But freeing my erection brings no relief. If anything, the ache sparks into jarring need for her touch. She obliges with zero warning, releasing the sweetest moan when she grasps me in a gluttonous hold.

My body jerks from the flood of arousal. The flames rage. Her palm must be burning right now. Her chest rises and falls with rapid breaths, her expression drenched with longing.

"Do you have any idea how much I want you?" she groans, letting go to lean forward. She tangles her fingers in my hair, angling my face toward hers. "How much I've wanted you since the second you walked into my office?"

"I have an idea," I murmur against her lips. My hands smooth over her thighs, circling around to feather over the firm flesh of her straining backside. Straining because her entire body seems synchronized and dedicated to the sole task of consuming mine in this moment. My grip sinks in, sliding toward her center as our kiss steers us into a slow, deep rhythm.

"It's torture being around you all day." She reaches between her legs to mold her hand over mine, and I oblige with more direct pressure. She bucks into the friction, gasping out the most delicious, angry encouragement.

"Hopefully, it's a different kind of torture than being around Chad all day," I say, my voice labored. "Try sitting... at my...desk."

Her eyes narrow, then close when my fingertips dip a little further. "Ah! Can we... not talk about Chad right now?"

"I mean, if there was ever an appropriate time for nuts..."

"Oh my gosh, Marcos."

"You could call me your king Brazil nut. Chad does."

She snorts a laugh through a moan. It's my new favorite sound. "I'm about to gag you."

"Promise?"

She shuts me up with another kiss, and I guess she doesn't understand operant conditioning in behavioral psychology. Threatening me with kisses?

"Don't reward the behaviors you're trying to stop," I warn against her lips.

"Shut up. Do you have a condom?"

"In my nightstand. I'm just saying, don't kiss me if—umph." She twists her hips, grinding down hard as she reaches for my drawer. I groan against the pain, the pleasure when she does it again, and again—this time with a smug smile.

"Found them."

"My point is B.F. Skinner would—"

She shoves down my underwear and rubs her thumb over my tip in soft, deliberate caresses. "Would what? Tell me more about the father of operant conditioning," she teases when I don't respond.

"He would... ah." My head falls back against the pillow. Her hand accelerates into fuller strokes.

"Come on, babe. I'm dying to hear all about B.F. Skinner and his theories."

"I... hate... you..." I gasp out.

Her grin is not that of a woman who believes she's hated. In fact, she resembles a deeply revered goddess as she releases me to tear open the package with a fiery look. I arch up, claiming her mouth in a ravenous kiss. She falls back onto my chest, and I use the distraction to take the condom and slide it on.

"Still hate me?" she asks, positioning me in place and sinking down. My response lodges in my throat; her teasing transforms into a sharp gasp that ends in a sigh. The rest of my brain fogs when she starts to move. What was the question again?

"Holy Pavlov," I groan, locking my hands on her thighs.

Her chest and face are flushed, her breathing shallow. Her eyes are half-glare, half-hooded when she pants out, "You are not... bringing... salivating dogs... into this." She moans and wrenches her hips in harder, deeper movements.

"But Pavlov... is..." Icy hot flames shoot straight through my blood, flaring into an all-consuming blaze. I clench my fists in the sheets. For leverage or restraint? *Hang on. Hang on.* We're building fast. Who knew behaviorist theory could be such a turn-on?

Her body arches back, giving me the most perfect view of her spectacular form. Her moans become whimpers, her face a mask of desperation. I pull in rapid breaths as our bodies move in a frantic rhythm, instinctively matching each of our surges with reciprocating force. I release the sheets to sink my fingertips into the tense muscle of her thighs again, losing myself in how amazing she feels, how mesmerizing her body looks, writhing over mine. Pure art. Pure ecstasy. Pure *Agile Synergy*.

"Wrong... studies..." she gasps out, leaning back further. She grips my legs for leverage and wrenches down in hard, deep strokes. Stars blister at close range behind my lids.

"Not Skinner... or... Pavlov!" Her words choke into a gasp. Even now, she has to be right. Damn, she's stubborn.

Her hips drive into a flurry of pulses, igniting supercharged air in my lungs. Heating. Expanding. Searing pressure building until...

"Masters and Johnson!" she shrieks, and I let my stars explode into supernovas to the soundtrack of her cries.

Wow. Just.

"The sex studies?" I exhale in a depleted breath.

"Exactly." She collapses on my chest, curling her fingers into my damp hair. "Way more relevant."

"Yeah, I see your point." I tuck my arm around her back, holding her close and teasing the ends of her dark waves as well. We lie like this in silence. Seconds, minutes, I don't know and I don't care. Time feels trivial, an intruder on this perfect moment.

She twirls a lock of my hair around her finger, tugging slightly as she studies it. At least I think she's studying it. I can't see her face with her position on my chest, but she's settled in as if she has no intention of moving. I hate the thought of not having her there.

"That was amazing," she sighs out finally. "But…" She lets go of my hair and pushes up on her elbow to face me.

But? No dude wants to hear "but" after sex. I definitely don't have any *buts* on my end. Just lots and lots of ideas for next time. Is this about the repercussions? Consequences and ethics again? I thought we resolved this.

Her brow furrows as she traces my cheek, my jaw, my lips. She doesn't look guilty or regretful, though. In fact, she looks content and well-sated. And a little mischievous, like maybe she has more ideas too and would prefer another round of this game instead of rummy. But then her eyes narrow. Her nose scrunches in what looks like irritation. "Does Chad really call you a Brazil nut?"

16—THE LADIES... AND GERALD

MARCOS

The Brownstone turns out to be an aptly named townhouse in Manhattan's Upper East Side. Not sure what I expected from a man who drinks expensive scotch at his mahogany desk and a woman who wears dead animals on her shoulders. A chandelier, I guess. A fountain, maybe. A tiny dog that cost more than a year's rent? Okay. But this? No, this is one of those Middle Eastern oil palaces. A place where you hold your breath out of fear your carbon dioxide could damage an artifact worth more than your lifetime income.

"Sixteen point five million," Eva whispers to me as the butler—are they called butlers?—leads us through the white marble wonderland. Olympus. That's what this is. No wonder Eva looks so comfortable here. "Mary Lou lived next door with her third husband until he passed. She and Dad bought this place last year when it went up for sale so they could 'start over.'"

"Start over right next door?"

"Yep. She didn't want to start over with a new parking space, though."

Makes sense?

"And the... that guy?" I ask, nodding toward the severe man several paces in front of us.

"Gerald?" Her brows knit at my beseeching look. "Oh. He's the *household manager.*"

I relax, happy to have one mystery revealed.

"Also, pretty sure his real name is Jim," she adds, ruining it.

"But you call him Gerald?"

"It's his professional name."

"A butler needs a professional name?"

"Household manager."

Right.

"He has a business card." She plucks one from a discreet antique bronze holder on a side table and hands it to me. It says *Gerald.* "Should you need anything."

"I don't understand."

"Yep." She pats my arm with a grin. "Welcome to the home of Reed and Mary Lou."

I stuff the card in my pocket and plaster on a smile as we approach the columned entrance of what can only be described as a parlor.

Although, this is not your mother's parlor, if she had a parlor. Or your grandmother's. Possibly your great-grandmother's, and I'm almost positive that's an original copy of the Declaration of Independence framed above the giant mantle. This is the first time in my life I feel like I should be wearing tights and a wig. I wonder if that's something Gerald can score for me on short notice.

The chatter dies as a circle of permed coifs and ornate dresses shifts to face us. Delicate-looking chairs creak through the silence. Less delicate coughs rasp out.

"Marcos Oliveira and Eva Reedweather," Gerald announces in a formal, brisk tone.

Do I bow? I already know hand-kissing is a thing in this world. I glance at Eva, but she doesn't make any weird gestures, just smiles tightly and advances toward one of two open chairs. Regrettably, they are not adjacent, so there will be no discreet touching between Eva and me at this gathering. After what just happened in my apartment, this fact feels like a deal-breaker. If it were up to me, we would've blown off the event in favor of more pleasurable blowing, but lucky for SAT Systems, cooler heads prevailed. Namely, Eva's, who insisted we needed to follow through on our plan to convince her father of his awesome marketing idea he knows nothing about.

Not sure how that's supposed to happen while we're trapped in a cluster of sequins, hairspray, and dentured grins. Reedweather is nowhere in sight.

"There's my handsome new rummy partner," Mary Lou chirps with a cheeky smile.

Crap. This game is played with partners? I know even less than I thought.

"Ladies, meet Reed's newest acquisition, Marcos Ol… Ol-ee…"

"Marcos is fine," I say with a quick smile. Also, Reed's acquisition? What the hell does that mean?

I must have missed Eva's eye-roll, because she's already glowering at the doily-chic table covering when I find her across the table. In my experience with Eva, glowering usually follows eye-rolls.

"Marcos, these are my dearest lovelies, Mrs. Allen, Mrs. Blakely, Mrs. Crestwood, and Mrs. Danvers."

"It's a pleasure to meet you all," I say, studying them carefully because, wait. While the alphabetical alignment is on point, the math doesn't add up for pairs. Now I'm not sure I actually know what rummy is. For the record, Eva and I ended up doing very little (no) training this afternoon.

Is rummy played in pairs? I tap out to Eva.

You're the shark. You tell me, she types back.

Maybe I earned that, but I still don't understand why she's irritated. After all, she's the one excited to go all James Bond with her surreptitious slide presentation.

Me: **Are you mad?**

Eva: **No. Impatient.**

Me: **To find your father?**

Eva: **To see you naked again.**

Damn. I suck in a breath, blood gushing south. Thank god for lacy tablecloths you can tuck over your lap. I'm not even a little surprised by her smug smile when she notices.

"So, Marcos, Mary Lou tells us you're a big rummy fan," one of the Missuses says. Danvers? No, she's the one with the ginormous peacock around her shoulders. I don't think it's an actual peacock, but then... *shrug.*

"The biggest." I don't look at Eva as I say this.

"Which is your favorite kind?" another asks.

Shit. There are kinds?

"Um..."

"He looks like a *Contract Rummy* player to me," Mrs. Diamond Tiara says in a sultry voice. Not sure if I'm supposed to be flattered or offended, so I settle on a coy smile that could go either way.

"Oh no, darling. Look at those shoulders. Definitely a *Five Hundred* man. He has the stamina for the long haul." Mrs. Peacock's innuendo is easier to interpret, especially when she adds a flirtatious wink.

Also, I hope this isn't *Five Hundred*, whatever that is. It sounds long.

Eva's suppressing an amused smile when I search her out for help. *You dug your own grave. Have fun,* her return look says.

"Come now. Are we here to grill the poor boy or play some cards?" Mary Lou interrupts. "We play first, and then nibble," she explains to me. "Is that acceptable?"

Since I didn't know this event had a food stage, I decide I'm okay with that.

"I heard Myrtle Tindale's league nibbles *first*," Mrs. Peacock says in a low, conspiratorial voice.

"They would, of course," Mrs. Green Tulle replies, waving her hand in disgust. "Have you seen them lately?"

By their snickers, crossing paths with Myrtle Tindale and her friends would be a hilarious encounter. Not to take sides, but nibbling first sounds like the way to go to me.

"Now, ladies. Don't be mean," Mary Lou chides, removing a deck of cards from an antique wooden case. "We all know their league thrives on *the nibble.*"

All five erupt in a cackle, and never mind. Now I'm not sure what "nibble" means either.

Me: **What does "nibble" mean?**

Eva: **No idea.**

Thankfully, we don't have to find out when Reed Reedweather barrels into the room, Gerald close at his heels. "Mark-O, my boy! How good of you to come! And Evangeline," he adds. His gaze flickers to his daughter in a strange cross between stern appraisal and wily collusion. Getting some serious spy vibes from my girl right now. So hot.

"It was kind of you to invite us," I say, flashing a quick smile to distract the others from whatever is going down between Eva and her father. Mrs. Purple Hair melts a little. Maybe Mrs. Peacock, too. I file that away.

"You're not really going to sit here fiddle-faddling with the ladies when I have a Trivello scotch with your name on it," he belts out. But is that name *Marcos* or *Mark-O*? I keep that question to myself.

Still, my smile isn't forced this time. I've got no clue what a Trivello scotch is, but whatever it is will put us light-years closer to our goal than rummy gossip and "nibbling." Plus, now I'm positive I don't know what rummy is.

"Oh, but, my darling wax noodle, we were just about to deal," Mary Lou whines.

"Well, then how very fortunate for my *Dexterous Timing*. You won't have to make adjustments to deal him out. Come, Mark-O. How about we retire to the den, a.k.a. the *male cavern*?" He turns and marches out, confident I'll follow. I offer an apologetic look through the chorus of laments, but it's Eva who has my attention. She wasn't invited, and I'm not about to do this without her.

"You mind showing me where the den is?" I ask her, rising from the table.

"I'd be happy to assist, sir," says Gerald the Thwarter.

I send him an icy look. "Please, I wouldn't want to take you away from overseeing these fine ladies... and their nibbles," I add. Seems like something he'd oversee.

His brow creases in disdain. Clearly he doesn't like being overruled by one of his boss's *acquisitions*.

"Thank you, Gerald, but I have to discuss something with my father anyway," Eva interrupts before we can throw down. He looks ready to smack me with a glove and tell me to meet him at dawn by the water's edge. His stance softens slightly to acknowledge Eva.

"Sorry to abandon you," I say to Mary Lou, offering a slight bow. "Hopefully, we can play another time."

Mary Lou returns a thin smile and mutters something about no one appreciating the sacredness of rummy. I'll take my chances with the card gods; I'm more anxious about Gerald's sinister scowl on our way out.

"He hates me," I whisper to Eva once we're clear.

"Who?"

"Gerald."

A smile flickers over her lips. "He doesn't hate *you*. He hates your poorness."

"My poorness?"

"Well, not your poorness, just the fact that you don't appreciate the class system. You're not appropriately apologetic for being poor."

"Huh?"

She shakes her head. "Don't try to understand it. It'll break your brain and I like that the way it is." Her arm slips around mine, and I forget all about Gerald and his prejudices. "Anyway, thanks for getting me out of there. I should have known when I texted Dad to let him know we're here, he'd only come to rescue you."

I wince, pretty sure I should be the one thanking her. My efforts nearly had us stuck in a card game we know nothing about and a duel with a butler—sorry—*household manager*. She's the one who got us on track.

"If it makes you feel any better, your dad only likes me because he thinks I like scotch."

"Do you not like scotch?"

"I don't not *not* like it." I think. Wait. I squint at the floor as we walk, trying to figure out what I just said.

"I believe that means you don't like it."

"Does it?"

"If you didn't not like it, you would like it. So if you didn't not *not*, you wouldn't."

"Okay?"

She seems confident in that math, so it works for me.

"I don't not not *not* like it," I mumble to myself.

"Also, he's going to want to smoke a cigar. It's what one does in the *male cavern*. Do you smoke cigars?" She asks this like it's a thing Nash, Nate, and I might sit around and do on a Wednesday night. We don't, actually.

"I mean, I've smoked a couple of times," I say as consolation. Not a cigar, though. Well, maybe a cigar? Trying to remember what happened immediately after those times we smoked not-cigars. Seems like we very well could have. I do know Nash bought a live fish once and Nate ended up engaged to a woman whose name he couldn't remember. Technically, they're probably still engaged since he couldn't contact her to call it off. I just have the one scar on my foot. Still don't know what it's from.

"I can smoke a cigar." My voice doesn't sound confident about that, though, and her gaze brushes over me. "I *will* smoke a cigar." That one sounded better.

Eva pulls me to a stop and turns me to face her. "You don't have to, Marcos. You don't have to do anything you don't want to do. You get that, right?"

"Of course."

"Do you, though?" Her eyes search mine. "These people can be bullies. They don't ask, they tell. They may believe their way is the *only* way, but it's not, and you should never do anything you're not comfortable with. I brought you into this because I love what you stand for on paper. The more I get to know you, the more I love the person behind it too, so please. Don't try to be like them. Be you. Be different. Be *better*. Be the person who doesn't 'tolerate that bullshit.'"

She finally takes a breath, and I can't move. Standing here, her cheeks flushed with passion, staring up at me with kind, intelligent eyes, Eva Reedweather is quite simply the most beautiful woman I've ever seen. Also, she used the word *love*. Twice. In light of present circumstances, perhaps I can be forgiven for wanting to forget everything and just kiss her. For wanting to lead her straight out of this Oil Mansion and back to my cramped apartment where we can abandon all "bullshit" and explore each other instead. Because I want to. There's no question in mind that when all of this ends, I only want a new beginning with Eva. I want to grow with her, individually and together. Support her, discover the light and shadows deep within the recesses of her soul. Yes, mold a future where we seek the stars and shoot beyond them. I want everything, so I say, "I really am cool with cigars."

Her eyes widen in surprise, then narrow in amusement. "Oh. Okay... well... uh, good, I guess."

Crap.

She's still smiling as she pulls away to continue our journey. *Well done, Marcos.*

* * *

IF MARY LOU'S card parlor is an anachronistic eighteenth-century marble homage, Reed's *male cavern* is an inexplicable shrine to wood. Wood paneling, wood floors, wood furniture, and plenty of wood artwork to fill in around the wood. Some is shiny and processed, some is rustic and natural, and other pieces are... I dunno. Wood-*ish*? For example, the life-sized bear guarding the fireplace could have been a really cool artisan carving. Instead, it's made of a weird glossy material painted to look like wood. Also, one eye is larger than the other, making it appear as if the bear knows something you don't and desperately wishes he could tell you. The taxidermy fish on the wall also isn't wood, though it's mounted to a wood backboard. The more I study it, the less real it looks, like this piece was designed for someone who wants to give the impression he enjoys fishing but doesn't. I shove away the temptation to ask if it's *reel*. I know... that's why I shoved it away.

"Mark-O, my boy! Evangeline." There's that stern collusive look again for Eva. Have to remember to ask her about it later.

"Hello, Mr. Reedweather. Thank you for inviting us," I say, advancing into the room. I'm ready for *The Handshake* this time and squeeze-eye-narrow with expert precision. His head dips in an impressed, encouraging nod. Hopefully, Eva caught that awesomeness.

"Come, come. I don't bite." He waves us forward with that creepy grin that makes you kind of think he could. Except, he doesn't offer us seats on any of the impractically large wood and leather furniture. Instead, he leads us to a wall near the bear, and it's then that I notice Eva's suppressed amusement. Her lips press together as her eyes dart away to focus on Reedweather's exaggerated number-punching into a padlock. There's no obvious door or opening in the vicinity. Wait, is this a faux wall?

My pulse picks up as we wait. What hidden secrets require such cryptic measures? Are these the treasured cigars that are so rare they must be kept under lock and key? Or is this the resting place of Trivello scotch? Shit, what if it's bigger than that? Secret societies? Exotic pets? Does he have an actual bear? Isn't that a thing eccentric rich people do? Tigers and elephants and shit? A wall seems like an unlikely place to keep an elephant. Oh my god, what if Reedweather's entire clueless disposition is an act? Maybe he's actually a brilliant spy playing a role and this is—

"Take your pick. You look like a large." A panel slides open to reveal a rack of red velvet robes. Eva won't even look at me when I shoot a bewildered stare in her direction.

"Oh, um…"

"Go ahead. Don't be shy." Reedweather's creepy grin is back, and I'd think this was a joke if he wasn't reaching for one himself.

I study his movements in dazed awe, watching as he reverently peels a robe from its hanger and shakes it out in gentle ripples. Eva follows suit, snagging a small one off a hanger on the end. They're organized by size, maybe? Guess that makes sense.

I reach out hesitantly, my fingers brushing the soft fabric. Not sure what porn stars wear between takes, but probably this is close. And suddenly, I know what the plastic-wood bear was trying to warn me about.

"Nothing like a good scotch robe, am I right?" Reedweather says, dusting off invisible lint on his way toward a heavy wood sideboard lined with bottles and decanters.

I stare down at my scotch robe, wondering if I should have gone for the extra-large. The sleeves stop about three inches above my wrists and the hem falls mid-thigh. The fabric itself hangs on me like a tent, though, clearly intended for larger girths. So maybe this is right. Not sure how scotch robes are supposed to fit. But while I look like a cherry ice cream sandwich, Eva somehow manages *adorable*. In fact, my brain quickly jumps to lazy days in a hotel suite. Joint showers, jacuzzi tubs, lots and lots of…

Stuff I don't want to think about while wearing robes with her father.

He hands me a glass, but not before inhaling a healthy whiff from it.

"Heaven," he says, shaking his head like he can't comprehend such divine fragrances. Eva's drink comes with a bonus sniff as well, and we wait while he examines the contents of his own glass.

"To new friends," he says finally. His brows pull together in a severe testament to the authenticity of his declaration. With a determined nod, he pulls the glass to his lips as if fighting the end of the toast. Like words alone, this *moment*, aren't enough to express the magnitude of his appreciation for new friends—of which I'm not positive I'm a member. I'm an *acquisition*, right? Whatever that means. Eva is a long-established daughter, so not her either. Perhaps it's symbolic, an ode to all new friends over the course of human history. I guess that would justify the robe and his strangely introspective expression. We wait again while he composes himself after the emotion of honoring "new friends," relieved when he finally clears his throat and waves us toward the leather furniture.

Reedweather situates himself in a sprawling armchair while Eva and I take seats on opposite ends of a couch. We all kind of face the bear, which now seems more curious than desperate to share a secret. I could see my relationship with this bear getting increasingly complex as the night wears on.

"Do you smoke cigars?"

Game time.

"On occasion," I lie. Well, we've established it might not be a lie.

"We'd love one, Dad," Eva says, tossing me a discreet look to verify. I nod back.

Reedweather's cheeks crinkle into delight—almost on par with his scotch expression —as he pulls out a large humidor.

"The best cigars come from your part of the world, of course," he says as he opens it. "But these are handcrafted by a *friend* and are pretty damn good."

Again, didn't realize Pennsylvania was known for its cigars, but hey. Eva appears to literally be biting her tongue.

"They look great," I say. And by that, I mean they look like how I think cigars should look.

"Smell that, Mark-O," he says, pulling one out and handing it to me.

I do my best impression of every gangster movie I've seen and run it under my nose in a slow, smooth trajectory.

Note to future CEO self: Practice smelling things. Seems to be an important skill at this level.

"It's very…" I sift through a sea of adjectives. "Sensual?"

When in doubt, aim for obscure. Your answer can't be wrong if it's not understood. I guessed correctly when he beams back with the rays of a thousand Pennsylvanian sunsets.

"Sensual, yes!" He brushes another cigar along his nostrils. "Sensual like the bosom of a beautiful woman."

Okay, definitely not what I meant. Now I'm the one cringing and biting my tongue on behalf of Eva and all women everywhere. Do his fantasy ladies really smell like old paper and stale tobacco? I think of Mary Lou and try to recall her scent. I suppose "cigar musk" could've been a popular perfume back in the day, but seems unlikely.

"Oh, here." He hands me a small yet intimidating-looking tool I also recognize from gangster movies, except crap. What do you do with them again?

I study it, rapidly comparing it to the cigar in my hand. Having deciphered SAT Systems' entire QMS in five minutes, I should be able to figure this out. Let's see, long cylindrical shape meets circular openings, one of which has a blade. Which means… Right! Two circles for fingers and one to cut the cigar. Just… which end? Hmm.

"Here, that one can stick. Let me help," Eva says, taking the (cutter?) from me. I send her a grateful look and hand her the cigar as well. She expertly removes the tip I probably would have gotten to eventually, just not fast enough to avoid looking like an idiot.

"Does she cut your meat for you too, Mark-O?" Reedweather says with a snicker.

Eva stiffens. Eye-roll. Glower.

"Actually, she does," I say before she can erupt and blow our cover. "She's a badass with blades." We exchange a look, and something flickers across her face. Warmth, maybe. Admiration. I return a quick smile, wishing I could touch her. Already counting the seconds until we can be alone again.

Lighting a cigar turns out to be a more complicated task than lighting other things, and Eva subtly demonstrates that for me as well. I note the way she holds the end just above the flame instead of directly on it. It's a cool trick, until my gaze gets caught on her lips. Red, glossy, formed around the tip of the cigar, they're going to be a real problem for this mission. Because suddenly, all I can think about is their heat, their soft aggression as they explored my body. I remember the way they tasted, their touch, even the sounds generated by two desperate mouths intent on devouring each other. Okay, so maybe I'm kind of grateful for the awkward robe right now. When it's my turn with the lighter, I manage to gather enough breath to complete the process—after constructing a mental wall around Eva's mouth.

Robes. Check.

Scotch. Check.

Cigars. Check.

Disturbing giant bear. Check.

We settle into our leather cushions like legit 1920s mobsters. Part of me is desperate for my nemesis Gerald right now. If there was ever a time for a two-finger salute... But playtime is over. Time to get down to business.

"So, Mr. Reedweather, I'm sure you'll be pleased to know planning for the Nuts for Speed campaign is going well."

"Hmm?" Reedweather's response contains just the right amount of interest and disinterest to go with the puff of smoke he emits. God, I love this. Lefty Two Eyes is just around the corner with money bags and a machine gun, I know it.

"But it got me thinking, maybe we should go bigger."

"Bigger?" Puff. Sip. Robe adjustment.

I catch Eva's gaze and tilt my head toward Reedweather.

"Yeah, Dad. I saw this livestream of a Redburn concert the other day. Since they don't tour, they get huge numbers when they *broadcast* a show."

Broadcast a show. Damn, she's good. I see the moment Reedweather's brain hears words it can interpret. Livestream, no. Concert, no. Broadcast... yes.

"Redburn is a music group?"

Okay, so this might be harder than we thought. Even Eva flinches a bit and pulls in a steadying breath.

"Yes, a rock band. A very popular one, particularly among our target demographic of young adults."

"Hmm…" Puff. Sip. Robe adjustment.

"Too bad we couldn't team up with them somehow," I say with a laugh.

Eva echoes with a chortle that could use some work. A lot. We'll practice that later. "Right? I mean, can you imagine if Redburn and Sandeke Telecom had some kind of formal partnership? Ha. Ha. Ha."

I squint at Eva and will her to stop attempting the fake laugh. She's so good at everything else. There had to be one thing.

Reedweather taps ashes into a tray beside him. His face contorts in the most curious of shapes. His robe adjustment is a full-on alteration this time as he leans forward and points his cigar at us.

"You know what. Why couldn't we?"

"Why couldn't we what?" Eva and I ask together. Shit. We need to dial it back a notch. Double shit when Eva adds another weird cackle. She needs to stop that.

Thankfully, Reedweather wasn't listening to anything except the genius that is his brain. "Why can't we partner with Redwood?" His question is clearly for the universe at large based on the airy, drawn-out tone and the way he stares off wistfully.

"Well, Redburn… but what do you mean?" I ask, shifting toward him, oh-so-intrigued.

"I mean, my dear boy, why not partner with Redwood? If they are as popular amongst the youngsters as you say, then what better platform for our message?"

I release a slight gasp, my gaze snapping to Eva, who also looks convincingly astounded.

"Do you… do you think that could happen?" she asks, turning her stunned attention back to her father.

"We can make anything happen," he says over the edge of the glass at his lips. His eyes take on a mischievous flair that bodes well for us.

"It's brilliant, Mr. Reedweather. But how would we be able to convince Mr. Sandeke? He's so busy and always on the run," I sigh out.

Reedweather's face lights up. "Actually, he'll be in town on Monday. I can present the idea to him then!"

I? Uh-oh.

"Really? That would be fantastic!" Eva says, ignoring my sincere look of surprise. Can't help it. *We* need to be there, not him. "Let's see, you have all day tomorrow to do the research, brainstorm ideas, put together the presentation, coordinate the meeting…" Her voice trails off as the color drains from Reedweather's face. "Unless, of course, you'd like Marcos and me to help with any of it."

He clears his throat, some color returning. "As much as I'd love to do… all of that… I'm afraid my schedule won't permit it. If you and Mark-O have time, I'd be happy to pass along the opportunity to you."

"Oh? Which parts?" she asks, pulling out her phone to take notes.

"Oh, um… well, if you could help with the research, ideas, presentation, and coordination, I can show it to Sandeke."

Getting closer.

"Of course, Dad. I know how busy you are. We'd be happy to help. Right, Marcos?"

"Absolutely. These types of campaigns can get pretty complex and difficult to present in an effective, coherent way. I'm sure we could arrange a time to get together with you on Monday to review everything so you can present." I smile encouragingly. "What do you think, Eva? Three hours? Four? We'd definitely be able to get you up to speed in five."

"Oh yes. No more than five hours for sure," Eva agrees.

"Right," he says, his face back to greenish. Puff. Sip. Sip. Sip. Siiiiip.

"Although, I guess our schedule is pretty open on Monday night if you think it might make sense for *us* to present your idea to Mr. Sandeke," Eva thinks out loud.

"Actually, I know this amazing restaurant in Midtown," I add. "Maybe we could present over dinner or something. Do you think Mr. Sandeke would enjoy a high-end gourmet meal in an upscale environment?" I ask.

Reedweather's face indicates he thinks he would.

"Wait, you're not talking about The Hollis House, are you?" Eva asks, concerned.

"Yes, it's amazing. Have you been?"

She sighs. "No, because it's impossible to get a reservation there. Especially on such short notice. There's no way we could have it there."

Reedweather's face indicates he's now very, very interested in having it there.

"Is it?" I say, tapping my chin. "I wouldn't know since I'm friends with the owner."

His face really loves that.

"Do you think you could call your friend, Mark-O?" Reedweather asks. "Set something up for Monday night?"

I lean back in my heavy leather chair, scotch in one hand, cigar pinched between two fingers of the other. I lift them smugly. "Consider it done."

17—DENVER SANDEKE

MARCOS

Nash: Redburn? Sure. Kaitlyn writes a lot of their songs. Let me ask.

Great. Nash knows pretty much everyone, I've learned—except Eva. We tried to connect again yesterday, but he stayed over after a late show in Philadelphia and went straight to another gig on Sunday. I swear the dude is the busiest, most well-connected broke musician on the planet.

Now it's Monday, and I told Eva I'd take care of the hidden camera on my way into the office this morning. I tuck my phone back in my pocket and crouch behind the sculpture in the corner of the private room at The Hollis House. Carter said we'd have the room to ourselves, and I promised a big enough dinner check to justify it. Somehow, I don't think buying booze and expensive add-ons will be an issue with this crowd.

After leaving a box of materials with the manager for tonight, I asked to take a quick peek at the room for "AV reasons." The manager didn't question my nebulous cover, no doubt accustomed to eccentric requests from entitled patrons. Hell, he was probably relieved that's all I wanted. With the restaurant currently closed for service, the lighting isn't great, but I manage to get the small camera positioned and tested just before the manager ducks in to check on me.

"Everything okay?" he asks, his brows pulling together at finding me crouched behind a sculpture.

"Great, why?" I straighten casually, deciding it's better to look weird than suspicious. *Don't mind me. Just a dude who likes to squat behind stuff.*

"Well…" He studies me again, as if questioning whether he actually wants to know more about my squatting.

"Just checking for outlets," I explain, rounding the decorative sphere of twisty wires to stand in a less awkward spot.

Relief settles over his face. "There should be several along that wall."

"Yep. I found them. Thanks." I brush off imaginary debris and join him at the entrance. With a final scan, I stuff my hands in my pockets and nod confidently. "Should be all set. Thanks again."

"Excellent. Just let the hostess know you need your box when you arrive."

"Will do."

All systems a go, I type to Eva on my way out of the restaurant.

Eva: **Good. Also got confirmation we're officially good for tonight at 8pm. Just one kink.**

Me: **Uh-oh. What?**

Eva: **Well, two.**

Me: **??**

Eva: **Can you add two more to the reservation? Patrice will be there.**

Me: **Who?**

Eva: **Sandeke's wife. Come see me when you get in.**

Me: **Okay. But that's only one person.**

Eva: **Come see me when you get in.**

* * *

"You have to be kidding me," I grunt, dropping to the chair in front of Eva's desk.

"I know, but there was no way around it. Chad was here when Dad stopped by to confirm everything. You know how he is."

"Weaselly?"

"So weaselly."

I shake my head, groaning out a response that was definitely sexier when it involved Eva in my bed and not Chad right now. Also, why would my brain even go there? *Stop it, brain.* I pull in a long inhale and consider the new developments. We can still make this work. Correction: we *have* to make this work.

"Okay, so how do we get Chad out of the room tonight? You know he's going to want to kiss asses for as long as possible." I lower my voice, still not sure what we can say in her office. "He can't be hovering around if we have any hope of *you-know-what.*"

"Agreed. We have a few hours to figure something out. Also, you need to watch out for Patrice."

"Sandeke's wife?"

"Yes. I met her once and she's…" Her gorgeous eyes narrow in agitation as she searches for the words. I should probably be concerned by her apprehension, but damn she looks good today. I guess to others she'd look the same as every other day, but now I've got the image of her braced on top of me seared into my head. Devastating red lace. Shiny dark hair draped over her bare shoulders. She clearly chose that lingerie just to wreck my subconscious. Joke's on her, though, because this proves I won the study argument with my reference to Pavlov and his trained dogs. In just one trial, she's conditioned my body to shift into sex-drive the second I see her. Visual stimulus—conditioned response. Even now, a distant brain cell recognizes the sound of her voice, but all I comprehend is red lace and red lips. I'd wanted an encore yesterday—maybe it would have helped quell the fire—but with tonight's high stakes, we had to stay focused. So yeah. Here we are, poised for the biggest meeting of our lives, and my mental state has been reduced to: *See Eva. Get naked.*

"Did you follow any of that?" she asks, drawing my attention back to her face.

"What? Yeah. What?" I clear my throat, and a smile creeps over her lips.

"Because it didn't look like you were listening."

"Huh? Of course I was."

"It looked like you were staring at my chest."

"Was I? Um." We are so screwed. "Sorry."

Her smile spreads into a grin. "Just get us back on track for tonight. Also, don't be sorry. I'll be staring at your ass on your way out."

* * *

CHAD HAS A COLLAGE. And a very impatient demeanor because I'm not answering his question about which important dinner shirt looks the importantest.

"The one on the right," I say without looking away from my screen.

He grunts and shoves the phone directly in front of my face. "There are two on the right and you didn't even look."

"The pink one."

"It's salmon!"

"The salmon one."

"You're lying. You didn't even recognize the color."

"Chad, I—"

"Just pick one, Marcos! I have to run home at lunch, which is"—he glances at his fancy gold watch—"now!" Wait, an answer will get him to leave?

"The blue one."

"Powder, sky, or electric blue?"

"I don't know. The light blue one."

"Powder or sky? Or the robin's egg?"

He takes a step back at my glare. "Powder. Okay, powder. Thanks."

I shake my head as he slinks back to his desk and glance down at the buzz of my phone.

Eva: **We need to talk. Storage room. Now.**

Me: **Chad is heading out. Will meet you as soon as he leaves.**

A minute later, Eva exits her office, sunglasses in one hand, purse in the other. She locks the door behind her and brushes me with a quick glance. "Have a nice lunch," she says to both of us on her way past.

Chad stares after her, mouth slightly opened. "She's so fucking hot," he mutters. "Should've asked *her* about the shirt."

Hell yeah, she is. Also, he needs to keep his stupid opinions to himself.

"No, dude. You shouldn't have. You better hurry if you're going to get back in time."

He shakes off his drooling and shoves his phone and keys in his pockets. "You want to come?"

I blink over at him. "To watch you change? No, man, I'm good."

He shrugs a *your loss* and starts toward the elevators.

I wait another few seconds before taking off on my own. My blood pressure has already jumped a notch or two since Eva's text. As if we don't have enough obstacles on our radar for tonight, she must have come across a new challenge. Will there be another unexpected guest we have to neutralize? Or, even worse, did Sandeke cancel? If that happened, this entire thing is a bust.

I find the room after a few false tries on locked doors. Hey, it's not like we drew a map the first time she dragged me here. My pulse rockets again at the memory of that blistering encounter. Wait, this isn't... no... is it? Just days ago it was *ethics this* and *what if we're caught* that. I still haven't decided where I stand on surprise office booty calls when I enter and close the door.

"Sorry. I came as soon—"

She cuts me off with a shove into the door and a finger in my face. "First of all, no misconceptions. This is not going to be a regular thing. This is reckless and stupid." Her other hand pushes down my back and latches onto my ass, locking us together. I hiss in a breath at the sweet friction, biting back a smile. Okay, so this *is* an emergency booty call. Update: I'm very much in favor. "Second of all, this is Pavlov's fault." Her lips crush mine, and she pulls back with a groan. "Just... we can't have any distractions tonight, and ever since you came into my office..."

See Marcos. Get naked. Yep, I get it. Also, is she pissed at how much she wants me right now? That's even more fun.

"Hang on, are you admitting I'm right about the relevancy of operant conditioning?" I say, my grin breaking at her clear distress.

"I hate you so much sometimes." She drags my mouth to hers. Her grip on my hair surges to painful levels, and I flip us around so she's the one pressed into the door.

"Do you now? How much do you hate me?" I growl, reaching under her blouse.

"So, so much," she breathes out, moaning when I find her nipple.

"We should have done this yesterday, you know," I say against the soft skin of her neck.

"We were busy... yesterday." She tilts her head, giving me full access. I take advantage, and within seconds she releases my hair to seize my belt instead.

"And we're not busy today? At work in the prime danger zone?" I'd laugh, but all nervous system functioning reroutes to my groin when she rips open the zipper and reaches in.

"I mis... calculated." Her voice is barely audible as she works my body into a frenzy of tension. My groan sieves out on its own. I've been trying to contain it, to keep the fire under control. Thing is, as incredible as this is, it can't go much further. I don't have protection—or a change of clothes—because, well, didn't think I'd need it for an impromptu secret meeting in a closet.

Okay, yeah, that's on me.

"What did you miscalculate?" Conversation. That will help, right? "Ah!"

Nope. I gasp against a fresh wave of desire. My hips seek hers now, pressing firm and hard through our thin layers of clothing.

"The power of operant conditioning. How quickly *want* can spiral into *need* and disrupt all brain functioning," she says.

Well, damn. "You... need me?" Despite the heat, the flare of insatiable tension, a smile cracks over my face. She sucks it away with another desperate kiss.

"You know what I mean," she snaps, lifting her hips and anchoring down hard again and again and again and... I lose the rest of my response as my vision clouds with distant stars. This is bad. So bad. Not bad. Good. So, so good.

She shoves me against the wall and drops to her knees, dragging my pants and underwear down my thighs. Her eyes go hot when they lift to mine, a devilish smile slipping over her lips just before they clamp around me in sweet agony.

"Oh shit," I gasp out, collapsing into the wall. This woman. Is amazing. I reach for her hair, desperate to sink my fingers into those luxurious waves, but her clip... and that bun thing she's got. Gah. I curl my fingers into a fist instead and bite through a groan as she works my body. Clenching my eyes shut, I imagine all the dirty ways I'm enjoying her that would absolutely mess up her hair and make her unpresentable for the rest of a workday. In my fantasy she doesn't kill me for it either.

"Eva, I'm about... to..."

Her fingers sink into my skin in acknowledgement, and I let myself go.

Breathing hard, I stare down at her as she wipes the corner of her mouth and straightens.

"Your turn," I say, drawing her to me. I love that I can taste myself on her, and deepen the kiss.

"Wait. What time is it?" She pulls back and fishes her phone from her pocket.

"Huh?"

She groans and shoves the phone away. "I'm so sorry, Marcos. I have to go."

"Are you serious?"

Her face pinches in apology, and I rest my hands on my thighs, shaking my head in disbelief.

I'm still catching my breath as she smooths out her clothes and hair. At least I didn't wreck that. What exactly was her plan for this rendezvous?

"We should have done this yesterday when we had more time—and less risk." My voice is strained, mirroring the look on her face. "This was..." Not enough. Too much? I shake my head again to clear it as I pull up my pants.

"I know. I told you. I miscalculated." She sighs, regret creeping into her features as she studies me. "Come here."

I hold up a hand, still trying to collect myself. "I can't just flip the switch as well as you, Eva. I'm not built like that. Literally." I wave over my open zipper, and the slightest of smiles flickers across her face, then mine.

"I know, okay? I promise, we'll finish this later. Long and slow. And no more closets at work. I just… will you come here? I only want to fix your collar."

I return a wary look, but allow her to approach this time. Just as she reaches for my shirt, I catch her wrist. Her eyes widen, then soften at my mock sternness.

"First of all, no misconceptions," I say. "Let it be clear for the record: I absolutely want to fuck you in a closet. Or anywhere you want." She laughs, and I trace her beautiful lips. God, I want to suck on them so badly right now.

She brushes her fingers along my cheek. "I know. Again, I'm sorry. I just… you make me uninhibited, Marcos. I don't know what happens to me when I'm around you. It's like these walls come down and this animal breaks out. All the rules change."

Wow. I love everything about that sentence—except how it's said in self-critique. "Well, I happen to love who you are when you're around me, so I vote for more of that."

"Really?" Her eyes search mine, tentative, vulnerable. I lean in and brush her lips with a soft kiss.

"I'm serious. You're a freaking goddess when you let go."

Her chest hitches, emotion welling in her eyes, and there's nothing in this world I wouldn't do for her in this moment. I pull her to me, loving the way her arms instinctively wrap around my neck. I wouldn't just follow her to a closet, I'd follow this woman anywhere. "Eva, I can't wait to con Denver Sandeke with you."

* * *

MAYBE IT's the weak chin or his cold, beady eyes, but Denver Sandeke in person is not what I expected from the photos. Then again, I also expected choirs, fireworks, and maybe a marching band to accompany the elusive billionaire mogul. I mean, *Denver Sandeke.* This guy is the Abram Fletcher of the business world. The inner MBA fanboy in me is baring a painted chest and fishing through pockets for a receipt or train ticket he can sign. The ethics-driven future CEO in me is punching him in the junk. Dude is a monster. Dude is also a king. A king monster? Somehow, that's worse. But there's no marching band blaring Sandeke's path through the restaurant, just a Barbie-like woman whose face doesn't seem physically capable of playing any instrument. *She's had work done*, would be a thing Mary Lou and her rummy ladies would explain in hushed tones while enjoying a "nibble."

I rise with the rest of the dinner guests as the couple approaches our table. I guess he's taller than I expected. Less man, more *presence*. And I mean "less man" in a non-poetic way. Something about how his icy blue eyes scan the group in instant appraisal has my skin crawling. Each of us was just categorized, sorted, and dismissed faster than his wife can blink. It's unsettling to see the moment you're reduced to expendable corporate fodder. Yep, Denver Sandeke actually makes me appreciate Reedweather and his sincere—albeit *failed*—attempts not to be an asshole. This guy? Unapologetic King Ass Monster. I force myself not to peek at the wire ball sculpture hiding our camera as I discreetly trigger it to record with my phone. I'd say my attitude toward taking this SOB down has escalated from moral duty to absolute pleasure.

And that's the joy fueling the smile he and his wife receive at this very moment.

"Marcos... *Oliveira,* is it?" he asks, shaking my hand.

Fine, so points for knowing *and* pronouncing my name correctly. One point. Half a point. Point-seven-five points.

"Yes, sir. It's great to meet you."

He nods, those steely eyes boring into me. "I've heard... things."

Damn.

Things?

If Reedweather is a business ninja, Sandeke is the Grand Master Sensei or whatever. With that one word he just owned me. Reduced me to an ant in his palm. Good things? Bad things? Relevant things? Irrelevant? All I know is I'm already on his radar, which somehow puts me in a weakened position compared to the status of someone unknown. There's power in "knowing" and right now only he has it. His expression is carefully stony, as if he understands this and intends to maintain that position. Sadistic. Yes, that's it. There's a gleam of sadism around the entire exchange that has my already-crawling skin burning hot with resentment—and maybe a twinge of fear. My guess is we're all little dots on his calculated how-can-I-use-them matrix.

Except there are things he doesn't know. In fact, there are things he doesn't know he doesn't know, which makes me a much more ferocious ant than he realizes. I'll stop short of saying "I could even bite" because *ew*.

Double *ew* at the bite-vibes I'm getting from his wife. Patrice, I think? And suddenly, I'm way more aware of the protective-slash-jealousy vibes I'm getting from Eva. What was she telling me about this woman? I try to remember the conversation in Eva's office this morning, but all I can recall are Pavlov's salivating dogs and Eva's incredible eyes. They're sending me an intense message now (her eyes, not the dogs), and I'm still trying to interpret it when Patrice takes my arm and pulls me to a seat beside her. Shit. How did that happen so fast?

I stare longingly at the spot beside Sandeke as Chad dives for it. Yes, Chad, the man who three hours ago was role-playing a swashbuckling hazelnut at his desk. *That* guy now takes the seat I've plotted, planned, and gave up sex with Eva yesterday to secure. Instead, I get Patrice on my left and Grant on my right with Eva across the table. Sandeke is at the head, flanked by Reedweather and Chad. What should have been an easy play has suddenly gotten much more complicated.

"So, Marcos, you look like a man who knows things. A man with *big* dreams," Patrice says, once we're settled. Her sly smile implies I should understand what those sentences mean. Do I know things? Yes. The things she thinks I know? I have no clue. Big dreams? Sure. *Big* dreams with an awkward emphasis on *big*? Probably not.

"I know the fundamental components of an action plan," I blurt out.

It's Eva's reaction I notice first. Surprise, alarm, then a hint of amusement. Crap, what was that? Patrice draws my attention next with a hearty chuckle and shoulder squeeze.

"Oh, you're a funny one. I bet you'd be able to keep a girl entertained all night," she purrs, leaning uncomfortably close. Wait... what?

I blink a response when my mouth opens to deflect and fails. "I'm actually not," I say finally. "I'm incredibly boring." My panicked gaze slips to Chad. "I'm obsessed with senators and nuts."

Oh. Well. That's one option for a deflection. Eva is snickering now, and I send her a helpless look that earns me nothing but a helpless return look.

"Ooh nuts. I *love* nuts," Patrice says, forcing my stare back to her. Of course she does. Probably senators too. Her fingers sink into my upper thigh, and I jerk away, crashing into Grant on my other side. I twist around and cringe at his annoyed look.

"Sorry. Spider," I explain.

"Spider?!" Patrice shrieks, jumping out of her seat. "What the actual fuck?!"

Um. Right.

Without thinking, I stomp my foot on an imaginary arachnid and use my napkin to swipe the non-existent spider guts off the floor before anyone can out me.

"I'll just…" I push my chair back from the table, holding up the napkin with the ghost-spider corpse. "Yeah."

And I run. Not *run*, but calmly flee the scene with my burial shroud and one hell of a mental shitstorm. Can't believe I'm going to say this, but Patrice is right. *What the actual fuck?*

Storming toward the restrooms, I make sure I'm out of sight before allowing any of the frustration to show. We worked so hard for this. *So* hard, and what do I get? A fake spider and very real molestation. I push through the door to the men's room, find a stall, and lock it behind me. Then I breathe. Close my eyes, pull in long, deep draughts of air, and surround myself with imaginary ceiling fans. Somewhere real spiders scamper through their real spider worlds, but here I'm an oasis of calm. I'm a paragon of peace. I'm a—

"Marcos?"

Shit. Eva? I suppress a groan and tap the back of my head against the door. Doesn't work because soon she's knocking on the other side.

"I see your feet. I can tell you're not actually using the toilet," she says.

"I have a unique style."

"You have a unique style of shitting?"

A smile sneaks onto my lips. "You said *shitting.* You never swear."

"Yes, I do. Just not often. And that's your takeaway?"

"You're the one who followed me into the bathroom. What did you think the take-away would be?"

"Marcos." I hear the smirk in her voice. "Open the door."

"I'm not coming out."

"Fine. Then I'll come in."

"Because that won't be weird."

"Weirder than you killing a fake spider and running away?"

My hand stalls on the lock. "How'd you know it was fake?"

"Because I saw what led to it. Let me in. Don't make me crawl under the door."

"You wouldn't."

"I would. Besides, this place is immaculate. The floor is probably cleaner than my countertop at home."

I sigh and click open the door. "I'm fine," I say. "Just recalibrating."

Her expression dims as she studies me. "She shouldn't have touched you."

I huff a dry laugh. "Whatever. You think that's the worst I've gotten? I was a stripper."

"Well, those others shouldn't have touched you either."

I shrug.

"Marcos, I'm serious—"

"I'm over it. Can we talk about something else? Like how we're going to salvage this disaster?"

Her gaze hardens on me, and I can tell she's not thrilled about letting the rest go. Still, we're cramped in a bathroom stall, already on borrowed time for a non-suspicious absence.

"Aren't you worried they'll think we're hooking up right now?" I ask, staring down at her.

"Not if it also means Patrice knows you're taken."

"I am?"

"If you want to be."

183

And then my hands are in her hair, my lips welded to hers. I press her against the door and groan into the kiss. How is this helping? I don't know, but I need it. She must too when she rolls her hips over mine, leveraging the unyielding strength of the stall to garner maximum friction. Sweet, sweet friction that has blood flowing hard and resistance going soft. Doors, man. I'm telling you. But just when my body catches fire and wholly commits, she pulls back, smug and determined.

"Hypocrite," she teases. "What was that?"

"A kiss."

"Exactly. A few hours ago, it was *no making out in closets. I'm not built like that.*"

"This isn't a closet. And that was completely different."

"Because the men's room is so much more appropriate?"

"Fine, but you gave into it," I point out. "And escalated it."

"Yeah, because you're amazing and make me break rules and I still want you as much as I did earlier."

"Thanks?"

She laughs and shoves my shoulder. "Okay, fine. Real talk? I want more than your body, Marcos. I want *you*. Always. Everywhere. Official, unofficial. You tell me, but I want this"—she taps my head—"and this." She rests a hand on my heart. "Those people in there have nothing on you. *Nothing.*"

Her smile, so sweet, so beautiful. Her eyes, so soft and hopeful. And I want her too. More than anything I've wanted in a long time. If she wants me to be taken, hell yeah, I'm taken. And suddenly I get it. The kiss. This moment. All of it. Tonight is a mission, but it's more than that. It's *our* mission. A testament to the incredible team we make. And despite the crappy start, she still believes in tonight—in *us*. She believes we'll pull out a win because I'm me and she's her and together we're unstoppable. Still…

"Are you really proposing to me in a men's bathroom stall?" I ask.

I totally accept that shoulder smack.

* * *

BACK AT THE TABLE, our fortunes have taken a dramatic shift. I return first to find an open seat beside Denver, with Chad and Patrice sulking in tandem where I'd been earlier.

"Mark-O, over here," Reedweather says, waving me toward Denver and him. "Mr. Sandeke is quite interested in my proposal."

He means *Eva's* proposal. Crap. I hesitate just a second until a hand presses into my back. "Just sit. Don't blow this," Eva hisses at my ear before taking her original seat. Her face is all polite smiles. I swallow and force one of my own.

"I took the liberty of ordering appetizers and drinks while you stepped away," Reedweather says.

I tuck myself into place between them. "Great. Sorry about that."

"The spider is... neutralized?" Sandeke asks, eyeing Patrice before resting his gaze on me. If he's concerned that his wife hit on a kid half her age in front of him, he doesn't show it. If anything, he's amused, which, strangely, makes it all worse. I can't help but wonder if she's a player in his game as well.

I swallow, not sure if I passed or failed the test. More unknown information he can lord over me.

"I believe so, yes," I mutter, arranging my new napkin on my lap. Let's hope this one gets to remain dedicated to food debris.

"I have to say, I'm intrigued by what Reed's told me so far. Targeting the millennials with their own zeitgeist. I like it."

He would. "I can jump into our deck now if you're interested," I say. Eva has the laptop, a strategic move we planned for this exact scenario when she was excluded from the conversation.

"Later, my boy. Plenty of time for business." I don't like the way he flashes another look at his wife before settling into a dialogue with me. Her advance must have been a test. I must have passed. I feel zero victory in that. "Tell me about yourself."

Somehow I sense my typical response to that request isn't the correct one right now. "I'm average at everything until I try it."

A startled look flickers over his face, followed by a more calculating appraisal. That's right, dude. You want to play me? You get one shot before I figure you out.

"Interesting. A quick learner, huh?" he says, a faint smile dusting his thin lips.

"Very quick. And adaptive."

"I sense that." His gaze plunges into me. "You're no trust fund kid."

"No."

"Not that advantaged kids can't be adaptive." Something darker settles over his features, and my brain goes *there*. Yes, this is why I research. Adaptiveness is preparation as much as instinct.

"Your son, Martin? He seems to be doing well for himself."

I guessed right when his face constricts before going blank. "He's an example of a kid who's squandered his advantages."

"How so?"

Shit. The server interrupts with a tray of drinks, and I feel Sandeke's hard assessment as we accept the deliveries. Scotch for me, apparently. Could have guessed that with Reedweather ordering. I also notice Eva is doing an admirable job of keeping the rest of the table engaged so Sandeke can focus on me. She's such a badass.

I must have successfully caught his attention when, drink in hand, he re-centers on me. "Perhaps that's enough pleasantries. Tell me about your proposal. I must say, I find Redburn an interesting choice for a partnership."

"They're one of the biggest names in the industry right now."

"And one of the most outspoken critics of *the establishment*. They're a rock band that doesn't even tour."

"Which makes them a perfect candidate for a livestream concert."

"Low elasticity."

"High demand."

"High risk."

"High ROI."

"What's your estimate?"

"Seven to one."

"Really." He crosses his arms.

I shrug. "You want to see the data?"

"I'd *love* to see the data. I think you're talking out of your ass."

"And I think if you want to reach a younger demographic already saturated with noisy consumer chatter, you need a louder voice. Preferably, one they're already listening to. Do you deny the trending power of influencers? Word of mouth marketing?"

Color filters into his cheeks, a burn of competition I recognize well. I resist the urge to rub my hands maniacally.

"Your entire premise is predicated on the assumption that Redburn would agree to partner with Sandeke Telecom. I happen to know they won't," he says, wonderfully glib.

Jackpot.

"Why's that? Everyone can be bought."

"Not everyone."

"Their lead singer starred in an underwear campaign. You think he has qualms about selling out?"

"It's more complicated than that."

"Yes, complicated by the fact that we're still thinking small. Sandeke Telecom is a giant and needs to partner with a giant."

"Agreed, just not *that* giant."

"Let me show you the numbers."

"I don't need to see the numbers."

"I'm telling you, sir. The numbers don't lie."

"They do when they're irrelevant!"

The entire table quiets at Sandeke's outburst, and he quickly waves away the attention with a flick of his wrist.

"Your numbers can't account for the intangibles," he hisses, leaning close.

"Like what? I've done my research. I know—"

"Oh you *know?* So you know my virtual daughter-in-law, who despises me and everything I stand for, writes for Redburn?"

Bam. There it is. I pull in a deep breath to keep the giddiness at bay. Pieces are in place. Crescendo is building. Camera is watching. And go.

"Kaitlyn Parker? She's your daughter-in-law?"

"Not technically. But she's Martin's longtime girlfriend. They have a child together."

"Really," I breathe out slowly, as if this is all news to me and not a carefully orchestrated opus. "Well, that certainly changes the game."

"It does. So as much as I appreciate your creativity, I can save us all a lot of trouble and assure you, a partnership with Redburn is not the future of Sandeke Telecom advertising."

"Hmm… well, maybe if you spoke to your son he could talk to Kaitlyn and—"

"My son hates me even more than she does. Why do you think *she* despises me?"

Because you're a King Ass Monster? "I'm sorry. I had no idea. I just assumed with your son following in your footsteps…"

"Following in my footsteps? What are you talking about?"

"He's in the telecom business too, isn't he?"

Sandeke's eyes narrow, and I remind myself this man is no Reed Reedweather. I'm not facing veiled racism and unveiled narcissism. This man is a clinical, scheming, highly effective snake.

"For now," he says finally. "But I assure you, his interest in the telecom industry is not one of filial bonding."

His brow furrows with just the right amount of genuine emotion to indicate his focus is on his son, not me. He suspects nothing from my line of questioning. I'm free to push.

"You know, that makes sense. I thought it strange he would start a satellite company when he could help you run your empire if he had an interest in telecom." I let out a harsh laugh. "Now that I think about it, you could almost argue he's in direct competition. Not that his little venture would stand a chance against a powerhouse like

Sandeke Telecom," I add, sounding irritated and then dismissive in appropriate succession.

Sandeke nods absently, his expression darkening further. "Yes, well, it's not as *little* of a venture as you might think. They have more assets than they should. They're also more stable and established than they should be at this point in a relatively new enterprise. He must have been working on this for a while. Long before they filed for incorporation."

"He's my age, right? They say college is where dreams are born and fostered. Could he have started strategic planning as a student?"

His brows knit again. "Probably, but the business plan was only dated four years ago."

"Oh, you've seen the business plan? I've written a few of those, actually. Although, my emphasis is on quality management systems."

That gets his attention. "Really," he says in a low, introspective tone.

"Yes. I know, weird passion for a twenty-four-year-old, but I love dissecting and reconstructing organizations in a tangible, referenceable format. Kind of makes you feel like God, building the lifeforce of a company. Its skeletal structure, respiratory, circulatory, and nervous systems all in one gorgeous document. I spent my last internship developing a QMS for Canterbury Sales."

"Canterbury Sales? The firm representing Brighthouse?"

"Yes. Oh, shit. They're your competitor too, huh? Don't worry, most of it was bogus for the purposes of modeling a structure their real personnel could replicate."

He smiles. "Yes, and we have a history of poaching employees from our competitors." He nods toward Grant.

"Wow. Grant worked for Brighthouse too?"

Sandeke's face scrunches into conspiracy-mode. I have a feeling his facial muscles spend a lot of time in this position. "Not Brighthouse. SAT Systems."

"Your son's company?"

He nods. "Yes, Martin doesn't know this is where he went, though. That's why we put him at Reedweather Media instead of Sandeke Telecom. For all intents and purposes, though, he's my number two even if his check comes from Reedweather Media. The beauty of subsidiaries, son."

"Wow," I breathe out, going thick with the awe. "That's brilliant. He probably knows lots of stuff about SAT Systems then."

Sandeke shrugs. Now *that's* smug. Eva and I have been doing it all wrong. "NDAs and all that. Of course he can't share any of that information with us." Yep, his eye crinkles in one step below winking.

"Of course," I laugh, almost-winking back. "Can you imagine, though?"

"Imagine what?"

"What it would be like to have complete access to your competition's entire QMS?"

* * *

IT'S LATE when the evening wraps, but Eva and I still can't resist a quick review of the audio. We end the night with three main takeaways:

1. *Smug*, as demonstrated by Denver Sandeke, is unachievable by lesser beings such as ourselves.
2. Patrice Sandeke was just as happy to *test* Chad in my absence. He was much more open to the exam and did *not* pass.
3. "It might be time to vet that Marcos kid."

"You like him, Mr. Sandeke?"

"He could be exactly what we need to use what we've got against SAT Systems."

"You want to send him in? Like a spy?"

"No. We already have the information. I think we just use him to decipher what we got."

"What if he finds out it's stolen data?"

"How could he? Kid's just an intern."

PART IV
TAKE ACTION

EVA

18—NASH ELLIS

EVA

They want to use Marcos. Of course my knight in shining armor is thrilled by that fact. This is what we wanted, right? Better than we hoped for. Not only do we have our evidence, they want to bring him in and hand it to him on a silver platter. Except, Marcos doesn't worry about trivial things like his own safety and well-being. He's already got his bags packed and funeral arranged. Me, slightly more concerned.

It's been two days since the dinner party. Two days of non-stop debating, debriefing, and discussing. (And sex, plenty of that.) What evidence do we have? What do we do with it? Where do we go from here? For the record, Sandeke passed on our pitch to partner with Redburn, but was intrigued enough to request an updated proposal with a different band. Guess we need to work on that too. Fake projects are a bitch when you're plotting to end corporate tyranny.

"I'm not comfortable with this," I say, clasping my bra on and adjusting the straps. Marcos latches his belt and checks the time again. Five minutes until Nash is supposed to arrive home. Guess it's time to relocate from the bedroom to the living room to wait for Marcos' elusive roommate. Also, I'm about forty-five percent sure he doesn't exist.

"You survived Nate. Nash is way easier to impress than Nate."

I roll my eyes as I follow Marcos from the bedroom. "I'm not talking about meeting your roommate. I'm talking about the yacht trip with Satan and Mrs. Satan this weekend."

Marcos huffs a laugh. "He just wants to use me," he tosses out in the most unconvincing argument of all time. "Come to think of it, I guess Mrs. Satan does too."

"Not funny," I mutter.

"A little?"

I glare at him, suddenly irritated that he looks like freaking Adonis right now. See, this is what I'm talking about. He's wearing a t-shirt and jeans, and it's everything I can do not to jump him and start the stripping war. On a yacht, sun-kissed, wet, and half-naked in a bathing suit with Mr. and Mrs. Lecherous Leech? I've seen this boy naked. And yes, I would pay dearly to see it again. His stripper financials make perfect sense to me. So, yeah, am I going to let that scenario happen to an employee on my watch?

Employee or boyfriend?

You know what, it doesn't matter. Neither one is acceptable. Case in point.

"What if I insist on taking you along?" he asks, tugging my hand until I drop to the couch beside him like putty. Legit. No bones. No joints. Just a mass of flesh and need that collapses against him.

I groan, more out of irritation that he can wreck me so easily and completely. One touch. One look. One toss of those sexy waves or glisten of those ridiculous blue-green eyes. So. Freaking. Irksome.

"They'd never go for that."

"You don't know that." He brushes his fingers through my hair as I lock my arms around his chest. I concentrate on the steady *thump* of his heart at my ear.

Thump.

Thump.

I brought him into this. This is my fault. Hell, I *wanted* this, didn't I? There I was, staring at those files and imagining a superstar like Marcos Oliveira swooping in and what? Getting cornered by Denver Sandeke in the middle of the ocean? No. I didn't think that part through. Maybe part of me didn't believe we'd ever get this far. I've been underestimating Marcos since day one. No more. He's too capable and efficient for this type of work.

"Let's just call it off."

"What?" he says with a laugh, pulling back. I glance up to study his gorgeous face. Murderous. Yes, that's it! I'm *murderous*. I could destroy anyone who'd hurt him. Sandeke, Grant, Patrice, my own father… Yep, line 'em up; I'll take 'em out. Do all future true crime stars have a moment where they see the documentary version of their impending bad decisions?

"We have enough evidence. Let's just hand it over to SAT Systems and let them take it from here."

"Are you serious?"

I give him the most serious expression I can muster from this position on his lap.

"I'm not walking away now. I'm *in*, Eva. Isn't this what we wanted? He invited me to join him on his fucking *yacht*!"

"Yes. In the middle of the Atlantic."

He laughs again. "What's he gonna do? Shove me overboard?"

"Patrice will be there. What will *she* do?"

Maybe I regret that strike when his expression dims. Just a tiny regret, though, because that expression is *exactly* why he shouldn't go.

"I can handle Patrice," he says dryly.

"That's my point. You shouldn't have to *handle Patrice*. The fact that we're talking about you not getting molested should be the end of this conversation."

His eye-roll isn't a good sign. "You're overreacting. You think I've never dealt with handsy women before? Hell, I've even dealt with *this* one."

Is he *trying* get me to scream right now?

"Would you still feel that way if we were talking about me and Denver? How would you feel about me alone in the middle of the ocean with Denver Sandeke?"

"That's completely different and you know it."

"Why?"

"Because I'm twice her size and won't have to live in fear. Should she touch me without my consent? No, of course not, but if I don't want her advances, I can stop them. I'm annoyed, not afraid."

I grunt. Why does everything have to be so freaking simple and complicated at the same time. *Kind Of* again. I'm getting so sick of *Kind Of.* "She could drug you. How would you like to wake up naked and tied to a bed?"

He shakes his head, the slightest of smiles drifting over his perfect lips. See, those are *my* lips. To touch. To taste. So help me if she so much as looks at them lustfully. "That was disturbingly specific."

"It happens."

"Does it, though?"

"You think *I've* never thought about tying you naked to a bed?"

His grin. Oh my god, I could smack him. "You wouldn't have to drug me to get me tied to a bed for you. Just ask."

"That's not the point." *Stay focused, girlie parts.*

"You're thinking about it now, aren't you?"

"Also not the point! Ugh. Marcos, I'm serious!"

He sighs and cups my face. "Look, I get your concern. It's sweet, really."

"It's not *sweet*. It's me being a professional. Your kind-of-*boss*. As your kind-of-boss, I don't want you in a dangerous situation, and the situation we're describing is what Hollywood movies are made of."

He grunts and drops his hands. "Well, I'm going. There's too much at stake, and I'm not a quitter."

His face hardens into the look I've seen before, the one anyone should dread in an argument with him. This is the expression of a boy who's faced incredible adversity. A young man who scoffs at tests of his resiliency. This is a warrior who's dug in and is determined to prove you wrong. Except I'm not wrong.

I straighten, and he seems just as surprised as I am that I'm digging in too. *But.* I'm desperate. So desperate that I'm willing to play my last card.

"You know, I'm starting to think this isn't about the espionage anymore. I'm starting to think you *like* being one of the 'good ole boys.'"

"Excuse me?"

I know. Low blow, but if it gets him off that boat…

"How can you even say that to me?"

I cross my arms, bracing against the power of his wounded expression. I need to protect him. I'm doing the right thing.

"You really think I'd sell out that easily? For one afternoon on some stupid yacht?" He swats the air in disgust.

I shrug. Meanwhile, my heart pinches in my chest. *No! Of course not!* it's screaming.

I force myself to picture Patrice's hand on his leg, Denver's cold stare tracing every detail of his face.

I thought there could be nothing more painful than getting my wisdom teeth out when I was seventeen, but that was before I had to injure Marcos Oliveira with words from the very same mouth.

"I don't know. I would have thought not, but here we are. I mean, I get it. This world is shiny and attractive and—"

"You know what? Just stop," he says, bolting to his feet. Those incredible eyes are narrowed in anger, blue-green irises dark and accusatory. "*You* brought me into this, Eva. *You* put me in this position. I agreed to it and I've been doing one hell of a job. I've endured one trial after another for this project, and now that we're at the finish line, you want to quit?"

"Not quit, just cash in. We got the info, Marcos. Don't you see? We're finished."

"Oh, we're finished?"

"Yes!" I push to my feet as well, breathing hard.

"Really. So what's Sandeke planning to do with the stolen info? Better yet, what has he done already?"

I clench my jaw, squeezing my fists in unison. It's a great question. I have no defense except, "That's not our problem."

Disappointment. Wasn't prepared for that. Anger, sure. I've been *trying* to get him riled enough to walk away, but disappointment? That's a whole other beast. I can tolerate him being mad at me, just not doubting me. My stomach drops like it did that first lunch at Kyle's club when Marcos wasn't sure if I was one of the good guys or bad guys. Unfortunately, I have no chance to fix this when the door lock clicks. Our gazes snap toward the interruption just as the door crashes open.

Nash.

We've been waiting days to make this introduction happen and now the timing couldn't be worse. It kills me that Marcos almost seems relieved. Has he already given up on this conversation? On me? Did my efforts to protect him backfire so horribly, he'll walk away from our relationship as well? I plaster a smile on my face, even though everything in me wants to slam my foot into their cheap-ass coffee table. Seriously, did they pull it from a dumpster?

Judge much, princess Eva?

Crap. Maybe I *am* one of the bad guys.

"Nash, this is Eva," Marcos mutters. Yes, mutters, and his roommate gives him a surprised once-over before focusing on me.

"Eva. Good to finally meet you," Nash says, extending his hand. I shake it, softening slightly as I take him in. Damn, to be a mouse in this apartment. Hell, I'd be a cockroach if it meant I could scamper around staring at these three all day. They're like a cast for a teen sitcom. Each with their role, each impossibly good-looking. Nash is clearly "the artist" of the group, complete with tattooed forearms visible beneath his rolled-up sleeves. He even has an eyebrow piercing and small gauges in his ears. I don't think he's actually wearing eyeliner, but with his thick, dark lashes contrasting a soulful blue gaze, it kind of looks like it. Dark hair curls out from under a beanie, which means it's at least as long as Marcos' medium-length waves. Nash's is much darker, however, almost black from what I can see. Did he participate in the stripper venture with Marcos and Nate? These boys would have cleaned up.

Oh, did I mention the guitar case he slings off his shoulder and props against the couch? It's true. Guitars make guys ten times hotter by default. For the benefit of everyone present, I try not to think about Marcos holding a guitar.

"How was the gig?" Marcos asks, dropping back to the couch.

Nash lowers himself to a mismatched chair.

Okay, I guess we're doing *this* now. Private argument officially tabled, I sit on Marcos' couch, careful to leave enough room for our relationship status to remain ambiguous. I don't actually know what he's told his roommates about me, and even if I did, that was before "the fight." At this point, I'm not even sure if we're co-conspirators anymore.

"Eh, fine. Boring crowd," Nash says. He pulls out his phone and starts scrolling like he's already forgotten about us. Shocked, I glance over at Marcos.

Nash, he mouths with a shrug and weak smile. The subtle apology is enough to make me want to throw my arms around him in relief. I'm grateful for anything that isn't hatred or disappointment from him right now. Wow, it's scary how important this person has become to me in such a short period of time.

"So, man, Kaitlyn Parker. She ever get back to you?" Marcos says, interrupting his roommate's texting.

"Huh? Oh. Yeah. Hang on."

Even Marcos looks slightly annoyed as we wait for our turn with *the* Nash Ellis. Funny thing is, he doesn't seem arrogant or full of himself. Certainly not to the level of the fancy suits in my world. No, just oblivious, maybe. Like there's only one second of time to consider in his existence and it's whatever this second happens to be. If Marcos is the quintessential strategist, Nash would be the opposite of that.

He finishes his text and scrolls to something else. "Here. 'Hey, Nash. We'll be in town next week. Want to meet up then?'" Nash looks up from reading the message and poses his hand on the phone as if prepared to type back our response.

Marcos flexes his fist and leans forward. "Cool, so she knows about us? That it's *Eva and me* who want to meet with her *and* Martin?"

Nash shrugs. "Yeah. I guess."

"Is that what you told her?"

"Yeah?"

"Okay, good. So when she says 'next week,' she means any day next week?"

His face scrunches. "Eh, probably not. They're pretty busy."

Marcos swallows and draws in a deep breath. "Okay, well, could you ask her which day, what time, and what location works for them?"

"Sure. But you probably won't get Abram."

"Fletcher? From Redburn?"

Nash nods.

"That's fine. We don't need him. The Redburn thing is off the table."

"Wasn't that the whole point of this?" Nash asks, focusing on his phone again. Crap, what's he typing? I have no confidence it's what Marcos asked him to type.

"No. That *was* something we were working on, but it's served its purpose so now it's irrelevant."

Nash leans back, clearly relieved. "Okay, good. Because you know I love you, dude, but that would have been one weird-ass favor to ask. Plus, the answer would have been hell no. Redburn and Sandeke Telecom? They hate each other."

"I know. It was never a serious idea."

Nash lifts a pierced brow. "Okay, so you *don't* want to meet with Kaitlyn and Martin now?"

Marcos shakes his head, then nods. "Wait, yes we do. The meeting with Kaitlyn has nothing to do with Redburn. It's about Martin's company."

"Hang on, that satellite thing?"

"You know about that?"

Nash shrugs. "I've heard Kaitlyn mention it. Just a heads-up, though, Martin's dad owns Sandeke Telecom and they *despise* each other. If you're gonna hang, probably shouldn't mention you work for him."

Marcos is obviously fighting back a smile when he mumbles, "Thanks."

Nash settles back into texting, and Marcos seems perfectly content to let him. Is this how they normally communicate or is he that desperate to avoid a follow-up conversation with me? Maybe I don't want to be a cockroach voyeur in this apartment. I'm not great with awkward silences.

"So, Nash. You're a musician?"

He looks up from his phone, a wry smile splitting his bored expression. "Yep. You're a… business person?" His blue eyes flash with an irony that makes it clear he's not stupid, just making a point.

"Yep," I reply. My attempt to bite back my own smile fails when I see Marcos' smirk. Point taken. Also, I'm back to cockroach envy because how fun is their roommate dynamic? Nash has zero tolerance for social norms and bullshit—basically, the very fabric of what composes Marcos' and Nate's eager corporate climbs. The fact that they openly acknowledge this with sardonic humor... have I mentioned teen sitcoms?

"Great," Nash says. "Oh, hey. Kaitlyn just texted back. You good for tomorrow at eleven at Bluesy Bean?"

"Tomorrow morning?" Marcos straightens in his seat. "I thought you said they weren't in town until next week."

"Yeah. And her text was from last week. So tomorrow's good?"

* * *

I'M THRILLED with tomorrow's meeting. Now Marcos doesn't have a choice. In less than fifteen hours, we'll be turning over our research to Martin Sandeke and making this entire mess his problem. No more scheming, no more handsy wives hitting on my man. Ugh, because he *is* my man, isn't he? Maybe not technically. Maybe it's too soon (and risky) for those kinds of labels, but the thought of any other woman touching Marcos the way I have makes my claws spring out with some alarming murder vibes.

He's at his desk in his room now, reviewing the stolen files for anything we might have missed as we prepare for our big meeting tomorrow. Nash took off again for *a thing in Chelsea.* Not to be confused with *the thing in SoHo* he just came from.

I lean over Marcos' shoulder, ostensibly to view the screen but really to read him. He doesn't seem upset anymore, just focused on his work. Also, as usual, he smells distractingly good. Pavlov is on notice.

"I'm sorry," I say softly.

He flinches at my voice, and I realize how creepy that must have been coming an inch from his ear. I move around his chair to lean against the edge of his desk and face him.

"I didn't mean that thing about you wanting to be one of them. I was just so worried about you and desperate to make you change your mind."

"I know."

"You do?"

He smiles and averts his attention back to the screen. "Yeah. I figured that out about five seconds after you said it. You were just trying to get me to back down. I know you wouldn't actually think that about me."

"Good. Because I wouldn't."

"It's fine. I'm over it."

"Okay. But I still don't want you going on that yacht trip."

A muscle moves in his jaw as he continues scanning his screen. "How about we see how the meeting goes tomorrow and then discuss? Martin might have an opinion on that as well. At the very least, he'll have advice."

"That's fair."

He really does seem over it when he returns his full attention to the files. "Hey, so I just noticed something weird. Check this out." He pulls up a window with a list of folder contents. Highlighting the first file name, he points the cursor at the date in the "about" info. "See that?"

"It was modified on February twelfth," I say.

"Yes. Now look at this." He highlights the next file. February 12. The next. February 12. He then opens a completely different folder and all of those files were modified on that date as well. "As far as I can tell, every file in this QMS was created or modified on February twelfth."

"Strange," I say, squinting at the display.

"Very strange. When do you think these were stolen again?"

"Hmm... probably mid-March? A few weeks before you started. That's when they showed up on the server."

"When did Grant start at Reedweather? Also around then?"

I nod. "Yes, pretty much exactly then. So these files were created a month before he started at Reedweather. What do you think this means?"

"I don't know yet, but I bet that date will mean something to Martin Sandeke and SAT Systems."

His eyes narrow back at the screen.

"Have I ever told you how sexy your brain is? And that smile," I add when it spreads over his lips.

He diverts his gaze back to me and scans me with a dark teal stare. I know that color. I *love* that color. It accompanies frantic storage room rendezvouses and *heated* behavioral psychology debates. It has no interest in stolen quality management systems.

"We're in pretty good shape for tomorrow, right?" The rasp in his voice chafes through my body, skimming the apex of my thighs. Yes, his *voice*. It's no wonder his touch can completely wreck me.

I slink toward him, straddling him in his desk chair. I want to feel him where I hear him. Abrasive and rough. Hot and hard. "The best shape," I whisper, wriggling into alignment.

He hisses in a breath when I find it. "Then I think we should move onto other activities and not make the same mistake as before." His hands spread up my back, firing heat in sharp vertical streaks. The cicadas surge back. Swarms and swarms of fluttering, buzzing cicadas.

"It would be the responsible thing to do. We can't afford distractions tomorrow." I gasp a violent inhale when his mouth finds my neck. Wrapping my fingers in his hair, I guide him over my skin, arching into the exquisite torture of him. Gah, I never want to stop touching this man. He's my reward and my punishment. My mistake and my victory.

He's also my future.

"Marcos?"

"Yeah?"

"I'm so glad this spy plot is almost over. I can't wait to fire you so we can be official."

He pulls back, his lips curved in the most delicious, wicked grin. "Are you sure? I was hoping I'd get to quit."

19—JERRY

EVA

One hour until our meeting with Martin Sandeke and counting.

As planned, I call Chad to my office for a super special project that will make his day *and* get him out of our hair. He bursts in less than a millisecond after I hang up, all determined gait and puffed-out chest. He takes the seat in front of my desk with an expression that's ready to receive the greatest of all universal truths. Does he really want this job that badly? I try to imagine being so sure and eager about anything as this dude is about nuts.

"Hey, Chad. I have a really important project for you if you're up for it."

"Absolutely, Ms. Reedweather. I just finished my presentation, so I'm wide open!"

"Great. I need you to head out of the office for a couple of hours and source some gourmet nuts for our final presentation to the board." He doesn't have to know there isn't a final presentation after the initial one. Or a board that oversees such things.

His eyes widen, and I swear he starts shaking. "Like, how gourmet?"

"As gourmet as you want. We'll put through an expense report for whatever you buy, so don't worry about that."

"Like, mass market brands or artisanal nuts?"

"Whichever you want."

"All kinds or just the normal peanuts and stuff?"

"I'll let you decide."

"Because acorns can be considered nuts."

"If you want to source artisanal acorns, go for it."

"I'm just concerned something like that could get pricey, but I'll do my best to be considerate of the company budget."

"I trust your judgment." *On this one thing.*

"Oh, you know what else would be interesting? Walnuts *in* the shell."

"Sure."

"Not even the half shell. I mean, the whole circle." He demonstrates a circle.

"Fine. Just—"

"I might have to go to a Christmas store for that. Seems like a Christmas thing, right? For decorative wreaths and sh... I mean, stuff?"

"Are unshelled walnuts a holiday-wreath thing?"

"I mean... they throw them in fires right? Yule logs and all that?"

"Um... are you thinking of roasting chestnuts?"

He freezes. All color drains from his face. "Oh my god. No." With a loud gasp, he bolts to his feet, eyes wild. "Oh my god. Omigod, omigod, omigod."

I stare at him in alarm. "What is it? What's wrong?"

"*Chestnuts,*" he draws out in a low tortured voice. "I totally forgot about chestnuts."

Oh.

"Gah! I'm so stupid!" He pounds his fist into his palm. Once. Twice. Three. Four. Five. "Chestnuts. Of course!"

I glance at my phone. Fifty minutes until game time.

"Well, tell you what," I say, interrupting whatever self-flagellation is still going on in front of my desk. "Why don't you take your laptop with you on your important errand. After you finish getting the nuts, you can find an inspiring place to work and finish the day there. We can push the presentation to Monday, which gives you plenty of time for edits. Sound good?"

"You'd do that?" he asks, his face flushing with relief. I almost feel bad that he's so terrible at marketing. It's not often you find talent for something so negatively correlated with enthusiasm. Oh well, Monday's problem now.

"Of course. Remember to bring the nuts."

"You want me to leave right now?"

"Yep. Now's great."

He nods and starts toward the door. "I won't let you down, Ms. Reedweather."

"Great. And Chad."

He stops mid-stride, twisting toward me.

"I don't want to see you back in this office until Monday, okay? You concentrate on your nuts."

"Will do," he says, adding a hearty salute.

Damn, I wish this campaign had the slightest bit to do with nuts.

* * *

MARCOS: **Chad's gone. Good job.**

Me: **Great. He won't be back today. We can take as much time as we need. We should leave in ten minutes.**

Marcos: **Shit. Incoming.**

I'm only confused for a second because soon my door is moving again. Except, this time the face poking through is one I've never seen in my office before.

"Jerry?"

The older man's gaze darts around the room like a nervous lemur. "Do you have a second, Ms. Reedweather?"

"Of course. Come in." I wave him in, but he still doesn't seem sure. "I have to get to another meeting, so if we can make this quick, that'd be great."

He nods, finally squeezing his large girth through a crack in the door rather than opening it all the way. He peeks back outside before shutting it behind him.

"Everything okay?" I ask, less concerned about his shifty behavior and more about whatever emergency would draw him away from Solitaire. I have to be perfectly honest. Jerry's been employed at Reedweather Media for as long as I've been alive, and I'm not exactly sure what he does. I asked Dad once and he responded, "Oh, Jer-bear? He's great, isn't he?" Beverly said his title is "Assistant File Manager of Operations." She couldn't tell me what that means except that his desk has to be near, but not necessarily adjacent to, the "Senior File Manager of Operations." He also requires a special ergonomic keyboard and one additional afternoon break for a reason that was declared confidential. By her expression, she just didn't know. Yep, for decades Jerry has sat at that desk playing Solitaire and being ignored. I'd bet a majority of our staff doesn't even know he exists. This is already the longest conversation I've ever had with him.

"I'm sorry to bother you, Ms. Reedweather. I just had a couple concerns I wanted to review with you."

I clench my fist and glance at my phone again. Seven minutes until we should be on the road in order to make it to Bluesy Bean in time. I want to ask if we can reschedule, but he's already in the seat Chad just vacated, smoothing out a crumbled piece of notebook paper. I sigh and settle back into my chair.

"Okay, shoot."

He flashes a weak smile before focusing on his handwritten list. A *list*. Fantastic.

"Right. Uh, first off, the hot water dispenser in the breakroom water cooler is running lukewarm instead of hot."

"Have you informed the office manager?"

"Yes, but she said to talk to maintenance."

"And did you talk to maintenance?"

"Yes, but they said I had to talk to the office manager. When I do that, she sends me back to maintenance, then back to the office manager, and so on, and so on. It's getting a tad frustrating."

"I see. And how long has this been going on?"

"Hmm… six years, maybe?"

I take a deep breath and jot down "water cooler" on a notepad in front of me. He seems legitimately grateful, so at least there's that. "I'll see what I can do. What else you got?"

"Okay, this one is bigger, sorry."

"Let me have it."

He smiles again, and I really don't hate Jerry. My sample size of known Solitaire experts is limited, but he seems like a decent guy.

"Okay, umbrellas."

"Umbrellas?"

"Yes. There's nowhere to put them."

"You can't put them in the coatroom?"

"I did that until Grant got upset because he said the moisture would ruin his leather jacket."

"Even though he wore the leather jacket on a rainy day that required an umbrella?"

"Exactly!"

I don't want to know how long *this* has been going on and just write "umbrellas" on the page. "Okay, well, I'll look into a permanent solution, but for now, you can leave it in the coatroom. If Grant gives you a hard time, just tell him I said it was fine and he can take it up with me."

He looks ready to hug me, and I release a tight smile.

"Thank you so much, Ms. Reedweather. You're a great manager."

"Thanks. You're a valued member of our team." Maybe? No one seems to know.

"Wow. That's so nice of you to say. And sorry to bother you with this. I know you have important manager stuff to do, like that nut play you all are putting together. It's just, the umbrella thing really got to me, you know? It doesn't even make sense, because last week it was pouring rain when he left for his Brighthouse job. Who was worried about his leather jacket then, *Grant*?"

My heart stops. "What?"

"Last week. That torrential downpour?" He grunts and shakes his head. "I was here late, finishing up a ga—work, and Grant was wandering around, blabbing on his phone as usual. Everyone else had left, and I don't think he knew I was still here, which happens a lot, actually. You know, it's funny, people always seem surprised to see me. Like, they pass my desk a thousand times, then one day—*blam!* They almost jump out of their skin when they realize there's a guy sitting there. There was this one time the janitor—"

"Jerry. Back to Grant, please. What about Brighthouse?"

"Oh, right! Anyways, nothing major, just thought it was weird he'd get all bent out of shape over my little wet umbrella when he had no issues walking into a monsoon for his meeting."

"He met with Brighthouse? Our competitor?"

Jerry shrugs. "Met? Nah, he definitely works for them. He had an employee ID number and security code and everything." His brows scrunch together. "Come to think of it, you might want to check that out too. Anyone who'd act that suspiciously over a leather jacket is probably up to shenanigans."

* * *

I GRAB MARCOS' arm on the way past his desk. "We're late. Let's jet," I say, pulling him toward the elevators. "Also, we need to talk."

209

20—KAITLYN PARKER

EVA

"Are you Kaitlyn Parker?" Marcos asks the woman seated alone in the Bluesy Bean.

"Yes. Where's Nash?"

"Where's Martin?"

"Martin?"

He sighs. "I'm Marcos. This is Eva. We're here to meet with Martin about a critical issue related to SAT Systems."

We stare at each other.

"Nash…" three voices mutter in unison as Kaitlyn picks up her phone to call Martin.

21—MARTIN SANDEKE

EVA

Kaitlyn is gorgeous, but not in an annoying, obvious way. In fact, there's an awkwardness to her that makes me think I might have found a kindred spirit, and she'd love Darcy and understand why having shirtless hot guys in your apartment is a perfectly acceptable reason to transform into a flustered half-IQ-point. After ten minutes of knowing her, I'm pretty sure I want to be her best friend, but manage to stop myself from blurting out confusing declarations. Why? Mainly, her significant other: Martin Sandeke. Serious, composed, almost standoffish, this dude is the opposite of Kaitlyn's authentic and accessible charm. He actually bears some striking physical similarities to Marcos with his athletic build, sun-kissed highlights, and startling aquamarine eyes, but the parallels end there. Where Marcos seems to go out of his way to ingratiate, Martin seems happy to inhabit his own manufactured island of aloofness.

In fact, it's not until we get past the initial pleasantries—largely carried by Kaitlyn and Marcos—and down to the gritty details of business that he shows any interest in the conversation. To be fair, I've met his father. If that was my control group for other humans, I'd be prickly around people as well.

"We weren't sure how to approach you with this information, but we thought you should have it," I begin, flipping my business switch to *confident* as I hand him an SSD drive. "This is everything we pulled off our servers before they were cleared. From what we can tell, it looks like your entire QMS."

A scowl spreads over Martin's face as he studies the drive in his hand before focusing on the laptop Marcos presents. "We also got video and audio of Denver Sandeke, Reed Reedweather, and Grant Worthington basically admitting to stealing all of this," Marcos says. "We included that on the drive as well so you have it."

Marcos plays one of the clips on the laptop, and Martin's expression deteriorates from stony to downright murderous. Bet that's how I looked when Patrice put her dirty hands on Marcos.

Interestingly, though, his face doesn't stay there. In fact, one could even argue there's a flicker of admiration in his expression when the clip finishes and he returns his attention to Marcos. He's definitely studying him with renewed interest.

"Denver isn't lying in that audio. He actually trusts you," Martin says finally. "In fact, they all seemed to like you. How'd you manage that?"

Marcos shrugs. "Just pretended to play their game, I guess. I've spent my entire life learning to work the system. Most people in authority default to assuming they belong there. As long as you reinforce that assumption, they have no reason to doubt you. It's actually easier to game a system you don't believe in."

Martin leans back in his chair, crossing his arms as he continues to evaluate Marcos. It's unlikely Martin Sandeke does besties, but if he did, I suspect my boy just got short-listed.

"You don't seem particularly shaken by any of this," I say, curious. Martin's gaze slides to me, and there's a definite return of skepticism.

"What'd you expect? That I'd collapse in horror? Throw a chair? Jump from a window? Sorry to disappoint you," he quips with a sardonic smile.

"Martin!" Kaitlyn snaps, smacking his arm. "Sorry," she says to me.

I actually like him more now and return his wry smile. "I mean, at least a string of colorful expletives. Maybe an obscene gesture or two. We've worked hard on this. Some payoff would be nice."

His eyes brighten a bit, his smile spreading. "My dad and Grant can go fuck themselves. Your dad too. In fact, they can rent a room and threesome-fuck each other all night. They should film it and use it as a promotional campaign." Kaitlyn rolls her eyes and smacks him again. He shoots a smirk at me. "Better?"

"Much," I say with a chuckle. A quick glance at Marcos, and I'm pretty sure he has a bro-crush on Martin as severe as mine on Kaitlyn. Guess I should have seen that coming. Martin and his innovative non-profit startup are pretty much the embodiment of what Marcos *does* believe in. Not too surprising he'd be up for the McPherson Genius Award. They're probably the same age, but Marcos Oliveira definitely wants to be Martin Sandeke when he grows up.

Martin sighs and leans forward again, ducking his head in a conspiratorial gesture. "Truth? I suspected Grant was up to something almost immediately after he came on board six months ago. Always leaving to take these weird calls. Shady shit on the servers late at night. I never totally trusted the guy, but didn't want to fire him without knowing his angle. I cut him out of all serious operations early on and basically just monitored him. When I found out he was talking to my father, I figured out pretty quick what they were up to."

"Wow," I say. "And you didn't turn him in?"

Martin snorts a laugh. "Turn him in? And launch an ugly, expensive legal battle, federal investigation, and very public corporate war with my competition at a time when I'm trying to fly under the radar? No way. I just let them do their thing and planted fake documents for them to steal."

I gasp. Marcos grins.

"February twelfth," Marcos says, slapping the table. "You cloned and altered your QMS on February twelfth."

Martin nods, again looking impressed. "Yeah. Took a whole team of trusted employees and an entire day of work, but yeah. I probably should have done more to hide the fact that all those files were fake, but if you're here, having this conversation with me, clearly they haven't figured that out yet."

"No, they haven't," Marcos says. "And since I have experience with quality management systems, it sounds like they want to bring me in to help them interpret yours."

"My fake one," Martin corrects with a sly smile. Marcos returns it. Yep, they're two bro-points away from a guys' weekend in Vegas.

"It would really screw them up to waste all their time and resources countering technology and an organization that doesn't exist." Marcos' voice holds a tinge of awe. "They think they have proprietary hardware drawings of your satellites and test scripts. Instead, they'll be studying, developing, and counteracting gibberish. The financials are all fake too?"

Martin returns a self-satisfied shrug.

Genius. Also, my stomach drops when I hear the unspoken conclusion hanging in the air around us. I see it too in the look Martin and Marcos exchange. It's settled. Marcos needs to continue riding this wave. Sandeke is already on the wrong track. Marcos can find out how far off and keep him there. He has to go on that yacht trip. I hate it, but there's no chance of talking him out of it now.

I'm also certain of another truth.

"There's something else," I say. Marcos must know what I'm about to disclose and offers an encouraging nod. I steady my gaze on Martin. "All that suspicious behavior you noticed in Grant? It probably wasn't just secret spying for Sandeke Telecom. We have reason to believe Grant actually works for Brighthouse. He's probably spying on Sandeke also."

Martin and Kaitlyn's look of shock quickly morphs into what I'm sure is the Martin Sandeke version of glee. "Grant is a plant from Brighthouse?"

"Sounds like a t-shirt slogan. Watch the rhyming, Lord Byron," Kaitlyn mutters, and Martin's expression shifts into amusement.

He cocks his head at her. "What would you prefer?"

"Hmm... spy, scout, mole..."

Martin focuses back on us. "Grant is a mole from Brighthouse?" he repeats dryly. Kaitlyn relaxes, now as satisfied with this twist as the rest of us. Martin shakes his head, studying the table in wonder. "This is amazing. Brighthouse is Sandeke Telecom's biggest competitor. The spy they sent after us is actually spying on them? Talk about Karma." His smile is genuinely friendly when it lands on me. "It took a lot of guts to go against your father. Your family business." Hey, maybe I'll be invited on that Vegas trip, too. I hope Kaitlyn goes.

I return his smile and shrug. "Our world may be draped in shades of gray, but sometimes right is just right. Marcos is the one who taught me the value of fighting a battle, even if you might not win the war."

Marcos meets my gaze, his eyes offering a clear window into the intricate maze that is his mind. Gosh, I'm glad I'm on his side of the war.

His fists clench on the table, his jaw set for a fight. "This proves the winners and losers in any equation are never a guarantee. Goliath only wins if David consistently backs down."

He's right. It's incredible how quickly this entire situation has turned on its head. I scan the group, enjoying the communal reaction as we bask in that beautiful image. It was a bumpy road getting here, but now that we've arrived? Pretty damn satisfying.

"Kind of funny that the monopolies who wanted to kill a startup could end up destroying each other instead. SAT Systems might be the only one to come out of this unscathed," I say, glancing over at Marcos. My intern. My partner. *Mine*.

Marcos grins back with all the radiance of a future CEO. A man who's determined to change the world.

That smile.

Note to the corporate monster: Better get ready for that smile. It's coming to take you down.

PART V
MEASURE

MARCOS

22—THE LOSER

MARCOS

Martin didn't have a ton of advice for me on how to attack this day trip with his father. It was obvious by the hostile cloud that settled over him that, while he endorsed our plan—and even appreciated the sacrifice on his behalf—he'd rather engage in a Nash-level artist-eye-gouging than endure such a trip himself. In fact, his guidance basically boiled down to: "Try your best not to murder anyone because prison sucks." Acknowledged.

My attempt to get Eva a ticket went better, and in fact, too well. As soon as we arrive at the marina, it becomes clear that our exclusive evil spy convention has morphed into a full-on couple's yacht party.

"This should be interesting," Eva says. "Also, is this a private yacht or a cruise ship?"

"I count at least three decks. Four, if you include a lower deck. It's going to be harder than we thought to keep track of everyone today."

"I'm guessing Patrice won't be a problem. She'll be keeping track of *you*," she mutters. "Why'd you have to wear that shirt?"

"What's wrong with my shirt?"

"Nothing, except you look even hotter than usual." She says this with such bitterness, I swallow the urge to apologize for being attractive.

"It's a teal button-down."

"Exactly. Do you not look in the mirror in the mornings and see what those colors do to your eyes? Plus, the sleeves. Don't even get me started on the sleeves."

I stare down at my sleeves—normal cotton fabric rolled up to the elbow like usual. "What's wrong with my sleeves?"

"Um… everything?" She waves her hands over my arms. "You have them rolled to maximum hotness length."

There are hotness lengths? That would have been helpful information at previous jobs.

"What should I have worn?" I ask with a smirk.

"I don't know. Pretty much *anything* else. Except a suit. You'd look ridiculously good in that. Or a bathing suit. Or any of the t-shirts or other button-downs I've seen you in… okay, fine. You could have borrowed a shirt from Chad."

"Actually, he would've loved that. He tried to get me to go home with him to watch him change the other day."

"What?!"

"I didn't. We had our impromptu storage closet meeting—oh crap. Is that J-Dawg?"

Eva follows my gaze to the giant bald man running security at the entrance to the boat. He's traded his black jeans and tightly fitted black tee for a black suit and aviator sunglasses, but it's definitely the man who has the power to ruin another important moment of my life. Our brilliant spy plan is quickly turning into a very bad idea.

"Yeah, he does lots of private gigs," Eva says, not sounding concerned. "Kyle hired him as a bouncer from the security firm Reedweather Media and Sandeke Telecom use."

She grabs my arm when I hesitate on the dock. "Wait, are you worried? We've already been through the stripper thing with him. He knows you work for me now. I'm sure everything will be fine."

"Yo, Reno! Ms. Eva! Small world!" J-Dawg shouts to us.

We lift our hands in a small wave as I cringe, and Eva scrunches her face in mock apology. "Or not," she whispers.

"He probably thinks I'm today's entertainment," I mumble.

Eva's smile grows, and I don't like the new glint in her eyes.

"No," I say, giving her a hard look.

"What? It's a good idea. We missed a golden opportunity, I think."

I roll my eyes. "Intern Spy isn't weird enough? Now we're moving on to Stripper Spy?"

"You could do a whole boardroom theme. Think of the potential for a water cooler prop!" Her arm tightens around mine with her grin, and I both hate and love how much brainpower she's devoting to that image. When her fingers dig into my bicep well beyond what's required for a polite stroll on a marina, apocalyptic prophesies for the coming afternoon begin flashing along the horizon.

"You've never done it for me, you know," she says as we walk.

"What, strip?"

She nods, her gaze darkening into hungry excitement entirely inappropriate for an office event. Damn. Wish I'd known about the sleeve thing a long time ago.

"Um, I've stripped for you several times now," I say. "In multiple locations."

"You know what I mean. You haven't *danced*. Or shown me the spreadsheet. I'm dying to see the spreadsheet."

Yeah, I never should have mentioned the spreadsheet—a problem for later. Right now, I'm more concerned about J-Dawg's grin at our approach.

"Oh, no way. You workin' Sandeke's party, Reno?"

I can't even look at Eva as I shake my head with what I feel is an entirely understandable scowl. "Yes, we're here for Sandeke's party. But no, I'm not *working* it. I'm Marcos, remember? An employee of Reedweather Media?"

Great, he looks genuinely confused again. Did nothing register from our previous encounter? But there's no time for a recap when Reedweather ambles toward us with a scotch in hand.

"I thought that was you, Mark-O! We've been waiting. Eva," he adds severely. Right. Still need to ask about that strange greeting she gets from her father. "Denver Sandeke only has the good stuff," he tells me in a serious tone, lifting his glass. "Can I interest you in a beverage?"

"I'd love a drink," I say, eager to escape before J-Dawg can point me to a dressing room or something equally incriminating. I offer a tight smile and step past J-Dawg just as he leans down.

"You're gonna clean *up* tonight, kid. Deep pockets." He pats his own with a knowing grin.

Reedweather's face contorts in confusion, and Eva grabs his arm.

"Rummy," she explains as she drags him away. "We'll be playing cards today, right? We're so ready to win some money." It's a good cover, and better than anything I had queued. My brain was stuttering between "uh" and "gah," about to settle on an unhelpful "ugh."

We've just rounded the final turn, the rest of the guests fully in view, when Reedweather yanks us to a stop.

"Wait." He's clearly no less confused than he was several seconds ago. "Has Mary Lou been playing high stakes rummy this whole time?"

* * *

Is HIGH STAKES RUMMY A THING? It is now, according to Eva, who wasn't a hundred percent sure she saw large amounts of cash being exchanged that one time last summer, but it sure looked like it. I don't feel bad about the lie since the thought of his wife as a rummy shark seems to only excite Reedweather. If this were a Tuesday, no sleeping area on this boat would be safe right now.

In other news, Sandeke brought Patrice, and Grant brought… someone. I suppose he could be carrying his own sequined clutch for today's aquatic adventure, but it seems more likely he's holding onto it for someone else. It suddenly occurs to me that the nature of this becoming a couple's party also puts Eva in the awkward position of being my date, not my boss, even though for the purposes of decorum and this spy mission she's my boss, not my date—while in reality, she's probably my date *and* my boss. I have no idea what to do with any of that. Eva seems unsure as well when she releases my arm and takes half a step away as we approach the other guests.

I'd like to pause to acknowledge that this yacht is the most glorious, ostentatious monument to wealth I've ever experienced. The main deck, where we're presently located (I think), is an indoor ballroom-sized lounge with an enormous TV screen, full bar, array of leather seating, and a short stairway that leads to an outdoor space. By the bikini straps showing from under Patrice's tiny sundress, I'm guessing the outside area boasts some sort of water feature. This is definitely a toy that screams, *I have too much money and ran out of islands to buy. How about a portable one?*

"Ah, Marcos. You made it," Sandeke says, his hand outstretched and primed for *The Handshake.* And...

Nailed it.

He lets go with the business greeting equivalent of orgasmic release, and my annoying brain wonders what a businessman stripper routine would look like. I cast a subtle glare at Eva for planting that thought, but she's busy at the bar, probably buying us time to sort out our relationship status for this event and giving me face time with Sandeke. That's definitely a boss move. Then again, I like her because she's smart and strategic, so it's also a date move. Her outfit, a modestly cut white pantsuit, could also go either way based on the fact that it suggests boardroom over yacht party, but still mercilessly draws my gaze to her butt—especially when she leans against the bar like that. Seriously, how long does it take to get a drink at a private party of eight? The bartender is enjoying her company way too much.

"Thank you for the invitation, Mr. Sandeke. This is a beautiful boat," I say, forcing my attention from Eva's magnificent rear to Sandeke's less-than-magnificent face. I don't know anything about Martin's mother, except that she must have had a pristine physical genetic code to pass on to her son. He was fortunate not to inherit his father's thin, crooked nose and suspect hairline, both of which make you positive there's some bully-style overcompensation going on in the ruthless tycoon. What do they say about inferior men owning superior yachts? Okay, fine. No one says that, but they should—based on this one instance right now.

"And so fortunate Eva could accompany us today." His tone doesn't support this statement, however. In fact, he sounds as if he views her presence as rather unfortunate. When his gaze flickers to Patrice, I shudder. Maybe Eva was right to be concerned about an attempted yacht-knapping.

"Yes. Eva is a tremendous asset to the team." Can't hurt to cement her position as well.

"Well, hopefully not so *tremendous* that we can't steal you away this afternoon. I have big plans for you."

Ah, so this is where Reedweather learned his creepy killer clown grin. Sandeke doesn't include a finger gun, though, which I find disappointing.

I swallow and force a return smile. "Looking forward to it."

"But don't you worry. There will be plenty of time for *play* as well."

Okay, well *now* I'm worried as Sandeke saunters away to greet Grant's date, who's finally returned from wherever she was. I ignore the fact that she looks exactly like Grant and join Eva at the bar.

"Grant's date just came back holding her phone," I whisper. "Don't look. They're facing us."

"But Grant had her purse."

"Exactly. Which means she definitely left to make a call, not to go to the bathroom or something."

"That woman over there? She was on her phone," the bartender interrupts. We stare at him in surprise and he shrugs. "I heard her a minute ago when I went down to get more glasses. It sounded intense."

The staff. Of course! They're going to be the key to our surveillance today. Guess that also means I'll have to pay J-Dawg another visit.

"Intense, how?" I ask. "Angry intense? Eager intense? Intrigued intense?"

"Hmm." He glances toward the stairs to the lower deck, presumably where glasses are stored and intense phone calls are made. "I guess... kinda like... *intense* intense? I heard a few words, though, if you're interested."

We nod, mirroring his conspiratorial slant over the bar. "What words?" I ask when he seems overly caught up in proper spy posturing.

"Oh. Um. She definitely said the word 'leverage'... although now that I think about it, maybe it was beverage? She did ask me for a chardonnay on her way by. Also, she said 'lighthouse.'"

That one's more promising.

"Are you sure it wasn't *Brighthouse*?" Eva whispers.

He thinks for a moment and shakes his head. "No. Maybe. No. Definitely, 'light-house,' which makes sense because we're on a boat. It actually sounded like *kite-house* but that's not a word. Right? I don't think so. But I guess maybe in Scandinavia?"

No. On multiple levels, no.

"Well, thanks," I say. "If you learn anything else that might be of interest…" I slide a few bills his way, which is pretty much the most baller spy move yet. Eva seems impressed as well—or surprised. Sometimes I can't tell those two looks apart on her. Damn, I wish I already had a scotch in hand. And a cigar. I'd chew on the end and nod super-shrewdly right now.

"Hey, can I get a scotch neat, please?" I ask the bartender.

He nods. "What kind, sir?"

Crap. What were the kinds again? *Trivia* or something. No. Those are random facts about stuff. *Trivet*? That might be the thing for protecting tablecloths from hot pans. Dammit. Got way too overconfident in my spy game.

"Trivello, if you have it," Eva interjects. "I'll have one too."

"Thanks," I mutter.

She winks back, and suddenly I'm not sure which of us is the James Bond of this scenario. The bartender slides us our drinks, and we touch glasses in a quick spy toast before moving away from the bar.

"So we've got leverage-or-beverage and *kitehouse*," she says once we're a safe distance from our new "source." "Maybe not the nail in the coffin we were hoping for."

I smirk and sip my scotch. It tastes good. I think. I don't remember how to tell the difference between the good ones and the bad ones. Something about oak barrels? Or was that bourbon? Man, this shit is hard. Where's the MBA course on top-shelf drinking?

"No, but it could be a nail in something. File it. In this spectacle, you never know. Speaking of nail, I should talk to J-Dawg."

Okay, *that* look is definitely surprise. "To warn him about the stripper thing?"

I wince. "That too, but also to put him on surveillance duty. He'll be a gold mine of information. I'm going to buddy up to Sandeke and Grant today. You want to take everyone else and manage the staff spies?"

"On it." She squeezes my arm before we break off, a gesture that could also go either way on the boss-date scale. Her warm look, though—definitely date. "We make a good team," she says softly.

"A great team." My return look would do better in a bedroom than a boardroom as well.

She sighs, probably realizing what I suddenly do. We'll be seeing very little of each other today. In another universe, a romantic yacht trip with the woman of your dreams would be a fantasy cruise. For us? Just another tour of dirty business.

"Be careful, Marcos. And good luck."

"Don't need it. I've got you." I could add "doll" and touch the brim of an imaginary hat, but her smirk indicates the cheese factor was already beyond detectable levels. Plus, after the scotch fail, I don't deserve a cool spy hat.

"Okay, Double-O-Seven." She holds a hand up to her mouth and whispers. "FYI. You already got the girl, so I'll skip the slutty outfit if it's okay with you."

"*Okay* with me," I say, eyes wide. "Why, I *only* collaborate with women in tasteful pantsuits."

She grins. "You find this *tasteful*?"

"It'll look better on my floor tonight, but works for now."

"What genius plot are you two whispering about over there?" Reedweather calls with his patented amused-grimace face.

Eva and I exchange a sobering look before she leaves to distract him. I take off to find J-Dawg and get our tactical foundation secured. With the bartender and security staff on our side, we'll be able to cover a lot more ground. Maybe this won't be a disaster after all. I should also check into the food situation. Certainly, there has to be a chef or catering crew we can recruit.

I've just exited the main party lounge when cold fingers latch onto my arm.

"Where you headed, sweetie?"

I freeze, cringing at the grating voice. Sure enough, I turn to find Nosy Barbie completely embedded in my personal space. Did Patrice follow me out? Because I swear I saw her planted at her husband's side when I left. A chill courses through me at the thought that Denver had been watching me and sent her. Would a man who'd poach an executive and steal from his own son's company use his wife to seduce another potential asset? Yes.

Also... *asset.*

"Meet Reed's latest acquisition."

I'd found Mary Lou's word choice strange and off-putting, but not suspicious until now. Who was their last "acquisition"? Grant? And if I'm the next Grant, who or what am I being acquired from? For what purpose? Who are the true masterminds behind my "acquisition" and how does this affect Eva and everything we thought we understood about her decision to hire me? *Did* she hire me? Is she the ally I thought or... no, not possible.

Hashtag *spy drama.*

"Sorry. Did I scare you? You look confused." Her fingers slide from my arm to my chest, and I pull away, firing a stiff look at her.

"You're so jumpy," she titters. Not sure I've seen tittering before, but that's definitely it. "Promise I don't bite. Hard." Her grin bares teeth that definitely, definitely intend to bite. I step back further.

"I'd prefer if you didn't touch me," I say. "I'm not interested in any contact with you. Especially, biting."

Her impish smile morphs into something higher on the derision scale. Personally, I'm proud of myself for holding back my initial instinct of throwing her overboard. She should be grateful.

"Interesting." Her tone is cold, her gaze sardonic as it runs over me. "Was that your stance last summer when you took your clothes off for money?"

Well, that's not good.

Somehow I manage to hold my hard expression. "Actually, it was. In fact, keeping your hands to yourself is a general rule most people learn in first grade. I'm sure there's an instructional video somewhere if you need remedial help."

She crosses her arms, glaring at me with the fire of a woman not used to being scorned—and maybe there's something else. I soften a bit the longer we face off, searching her nearly unreadable features for an emotion my instinct is telling me should be there. In the briefest of blinks I think I see it. If she knows about my past and intends to use it against me, I've got nothing to lose anyway.

"Who told you about that?" I ask.

She shrugs, her expression less certain at my calm response. "About what?"

"My summer job. I'm sure Denver vetted me before inviting me here. Did he find out and send you?"

Her fingers press into her upper arms until I fear they'll leave bruises. Her foot taps an uneven rhythm on the floor. Pieces are starting to fall, I just need to arrange them in place. When her lips press into a puckered cloud of resistance, I sigh and wave her over to a bench. Unnaturally arched brows rise even further.

"Just sit. Maybe we can help each other," I say, still impressed that I've made it this far without hurting anyone. Martin would be proud.

She directs her disturbing, plastic stare at me for several more seconds before finally slapping her arms down against her sides and marching toward me as if she's throwing a temper tantrum against herself.

"What?" she hisses, perching on the edge of the bench and snapping her arms back into pretzel status. Maybe that's their natural form and it's really all other shapes that should be viewed with suspicion.

"You want to hear my theory?" I ask, keeping a careful distance between us.

"What are you talking about?"

"I think Denver sent you to test me at the restaurant. I passed by rejecting your advances then, and now he's tasked you with seducing me for real. I also think you're scared because you know it's not going to happen and you don't want to go back to him empty-handed."

I can tell by the slight adjustment of a facial muscle that I'm touching something on the other side of that mask.

"What's your point?" she says.

"My point is, if you tell me his endgame and what you're supposed to bring back to him, maybe I can help you deliver."

By the sudden flare of heat in her eyes, she did *not* interpret that the way I intended.

"Not the sex part," I mutter. "The information part. This is ultimately about information, right?"

Okay, she's still confused. Could I have misread this entirely? Then again, maybe her face only does angry and confused.

"Come on, Patrice. I'm not an idiot. Even if you *were* legitimately interested in an affair with me, you wouldn't pursue it directly in front of Denver. He's obviously involved."

She throws her arms up, once again giving in to the toddler tantrum method of interaction. "Fine! He wants to know what you know."

"What I know about what?"

"Martin's company!"

"Who's Martin?"

"His son!"

"He has a son?"

"Yes!"

I wince. "Okay. You can stop yelling, though."

She folds her arms again. "Yes, his son started a rival company for the telephones or whatever and he's mad about it, and Grant thinks you might know something because you wrote a paper in college, but Reedweather says you're cool, and yes, Denver researched you, but he couldn't find anything useful—about *that*—so he wants me to find out what you know."

"About his son's company?"

"S'what I said."

Sure. Along with so many other words. And yes, I'm taking a risk with this strategy of complete ignorance. I've already spoken to Denver about Martin and his company, so he knows I have some background knowledge, but I'm banking on the fact that

Patrice is only interested in answering a broader question: am I a threat? For the benefit of her limited intellect, the less I know about *anything* the better. Ignorance will translate into approval.

"And he said you were a stripper, which means you're probably a man-whore and would be easy prey."

Oh. I squint at her, curious that anyone could say that sentence in such a bored, nonchalant tone. "I see. Well. I'm not."

"Yeah, I'm getting that," she grunts.

"Do you? Because I'm concerned you're not grasping the difference between a means of financial income and a personal character trait."

"Pfft. Whatever. Fancy words don't impress me."

I also question that because she looks kind of impressed right now. Well, as much as that one cheek muscle can shift in an *impressed* gesture. "Okay, so just to recap. Denver wants to know what information I have about his son's company. What's the company called again?"

"SAT Systems."

"Huh. Sounds like an academic testing firm."

She snorts a laugh. "Right? That's what *I* said!"

"And it's a telecom company?" I pull out my phone to pretend to look it up. The headline I find instead stops my heart, then kicks it back into gear at an accelerated pace. No way. Would Grant be so obvious? Now I'm even more impatient to conclude this distraction and get back to my main conspiracy that just fired ten times hotter.

"Yeah. They make weather balloons or something," Patrice says, twirling a lock of stiff bleached hair around her finger.

"Weather balloons?"

"I don't know. Something science-y."

Are weather balloons "science-y"? I guess.

"It says here they provide high-speed internet service to underserved areas via satel-lites." Also, I so don't care about that anymore. I *have* to get back to Sandeke and

Grant. Still can't believe Grant played right into our hands. I'd given him way too much credit as a double-triple agent.

"Oh. Yeah. Satellites. Sure. That sounds right."

"Cool. I'll bookmark this and check it out later." When I lower my phone, she's staring at me with the evaluative look I was hoping for. Perfect.

Three.

Two.

One.

"You didn't even know Denver had a son," she says in a distant tone. It's more of a statement, so I just shrug.

After another moment, she sighs and pretzels her arms again. "You know, I *told* Denver there was no way you knew anything about this stuff. You're too pretty to be smart."

* * *

WITH PATRICE'S amended seduction complete, I continue my search for J-Dawg. One last set-up piece, and I'm free to cannonball into the pit of corporate piranhas that first brought me here. After scouring every deck, I finally give up and return to the party, only to find J-Dawg stationed at the entrance of the room I'd left. He winks when I approach, and I pull in an irritated breath.

"Ready?" he asks. "You look great, Reno."

I clench my jaw. "I'm Marcos. A marketing intern," I remind him. Again.

He nods with another wink. "Totally. I like it."

"No! I mean... never mind."

Hearty laughter drifts toward us, and I glance over to find the men guffawing over something rich or business-y while the ladies smile politely at their sides. No one seems to have noticed me yet.

"Could you do me a favor?" I ask my "friend."

"Dude, for you? Anything. Whatchu got?"

"It's just, people aren't always honest to my face, you know?"

"Because you're a stripper? People are bastards. You know that, right?"

"Right. So if you happen to hear anyone mention me, could you let me know what they're saying?"

He peeks over the bridge of his sunglasses to study my face. "You sure you want to know that shit?"

I smile. "Oh, I'm sure."

"Because you hear some pretty strange stuff when people forget you're there. It could get ugly."

I hope it does. "All good. I want everything. And thanks." I tuck a few bills in his pocket. "For your troubles." Heck yeah. I've always wanted to say that while doing that.

His grin widens as he taps the now-thicker fabric of his jacket. "I got you, kid."

Man, I wish that exchange had been filmed. Epic spy shit right there.

Anyway… piranha time.

The main conversation dies when I approach, and I plaster a smile on my face. "Just explored the boat. You have quite a gem here, Mr. Sandeke."

His gaze flickers to his wife before resting on me with a rueful smile. "I do, don't I? I'm glad you had a chance to… *explore her*."

Interesting. Wonder what Patrice told him. But Eva's stare has me concerned. She has to know I didn't actually do anything with Sandeke's wife, right?

"Thank you, sir. I'm looking forward to learning from you." Particularly, what you think you stole from your son and what you plan to do with it. "In business school, you're quite the celebrity."

"Oh? I'm flattered. Your future is set if you stick by me," Sandeke says with an unpleasant undercurrent that involves a sinister swirl of his glass.

"That attitude will get you far in this business, Mark-O," Reedweather adds, less unpleasant and pointing his glass at me.

Note to future CEO self: Learn the art of glass gesturing.

Grant doesn't seem to have any interest in my education and glowers into his.

"Sorry to ruin the party with business," I say, "but I just read something and would love to hear your thoughts. Apparently, Brighthouse is launching a summer campaign that involves a promotional partnership with Larinda Scott."

Sandeke's expression darkens at the exact moment Grant and his date exchange an alarmed look. I knew it. She's not his girlfriend; she's his colleague. They're almost definitely Brighthouse spies working this party as much as Eva and me. Is anyone *not* here to draw blood? Maybe Mary Lou, who keeps fiddling with her blue yacht boa and exchanging glassy stares with the olive in her martini.

"Oh, the country singer? I love her!" Patrice chirps. Her brows return to their normal scowl when Denver glares at her. "I mean, if you like overly produced talentless pop-tarts." An interesting critique coming from her.

"Marcos, have you seen the sundeck?" Sandeke asks in a very clear message. *We need to talk.*

"Not yet, but I'd love a tour. This is my first time on such a fine boat." I ignore Grant's murderous glare—and the fact that I'm speaking in strange old-timey language again. It's Mary Lou, I'm telling you. She fluffs her boa and flexes her gem-coated fingers like she senses I've drawn on her power.

"Oh, it's a sight, Mark-O!" Reedweather says, clearly missing everything that just happened. No surprise there. Eva smiles stiffly at her father.

"Actually, Dad. Would you and Mary Lou like to play cards while they chat about boring business stuff? Patrice, care to join us?"

Mary Lou perks up for the first time since I've seen her today. Patrice reluctantly grunts her acceptance after a silent warning from Denver. "There's a nice table by the hot tub," she says. "It has inserts for your drink glasses."

"Oh, but is it protected from that awful sun?" Mary Lou asks as they start toward the stairs. "The sun ages you, you know. I've avoided it for seventy-eight years and look at me now."

"The sun is the worst. That's why I *only* tan in tanning booths. You'll love the fully adjustable awning..." Patrice seems more invested once she realizes she can show off her wealth and share her vast knowledge of tanning salons. Their voices fade as they disappear up the stairs, Reedweather and Eva right behind them.

"Audrey, wouldn't you like to join them?" Sandeke asks Grant's date.

Let me just say that *Audrey* isn't in the same spy league as Eva. She's completely spy-obvious when her expression clouds over and sweeps from Sandeke to Grant in unsuppressed ire. It's so far from suave, I'm concerned she's exposed them, but Sandeke seems too immersed in his angry haze to comprehend the silent Brighthouse spy tiff. Grant finally wins, and Audrey marches toward the stairs in a gait eerily similar to Patrice's tantrum-stride.

Two floors above the party lounge, the sundeck offers an impressive view of the water on one side, the city on another, and the dock below—which it doesn't appear we'll be leaving. I suppose that will come in handy if our cover is blown and we need to make a run for it.

"So those bastards stole our campaign of the year. How did they beat us on this?" Sandeke barks as soon as we settle into our chairs.

Campaign of the year? He wasn't even sold on the idea after our initial dinner pitch. We still haven't presented him with the revised proposal he requested. Funny what concept envy can do.

"And Larinda Scott. How the *hell* did they get Larinda Scott?" He points his drink toward Grant, sloshing it with each empathic gesture. "We've wasted enough time. We're moving forward on Marcos and Eva's proposal. Immediately. I want Eva running point and signing the biggest name she can get. Bigger than *Larinda Scott*. Bigger than fucking dead Elvis if she can get him."

"But, sir, our budget—"

"I don't care about the budget. This was *our* idea and I want it."

"But Brighthouse—"

"Fuck Brighthouse! We're going to make their little campaign look like a yearbook ad. If they book a concert hall, we book a stadium. If they plaster their image and slogan on an airplane, we put it on a spaceship. Got it?"

Damn. He's ready to bankrupt himself over his ego. Good to know. I study Grant, who's doing an admirable job of looking concerned. Is he secretly doing jumping jacks that Sandeke has clearly lost it over this? Or is he worried his stolen campaign has backfired into a full-on war. Hmm... maybe his expression isn't an act. Neither of them will benefit from a massive PR clash. In fact, there'd be only one winner:

SAT Systems. While these two behemoths battle it out on a (now intergalactic) scale, SAT will sit comfortably under the radar—right where they want to be. Martin can take an entirely different promotional approach and come out as the innovative, responsible darling of the industry.

"What do you think, Marcos?" Sandeke asks, drawing me back to the war room chaos.

What do I think? This is amazing. Perfection. Everything worked out better than I could have hoped on that first day I stumbled upon some suspicious documents that made me queasy.

"You don't have much of a choice, sir. You have to go after Brighthouse with everything you have."

Grant shifts uncomfortably in his chair, which only encourages me further.

"And I think you should absolutely put Eva in charge of this campaign. It was her idea to begin with, and no one will give this project more attention than she will."

Sandeke nods to himself, considering my words. "We're at war, son. We are at war." After a silent deliberation, he seems to settle on something in his head and leans down to pull a laptop from a briefcase under his chair. Is this it? The moment Eva and I had been hoping for since we recorded their conversation at the restaurant? He must have been intending to bring me in on the espionage if he had the laptop stored and ready.

He fires it up and studies the screen. "What I'm about to show you is strictly confidential. No one can know about this. Do you understand?"

My heart races, and I wipe my palms on my pants. "I understand."

The laptop crosses the divide between us in slow motion. It feels like a hundred pounds in my hands, and I pull it reverently into my lap. I almost lose my cool when I glimpse the first familiar document.

"We obtained these files from SAT Systems just over a month ago. We understand you have experience with quality management systems from your coursework and previous internships. We asked you here thinking you might be a valuable asset to interpret this one. What can you tell us about SAT Systems' operation?"

* * *

So, there it is. This is the industrial machine I've spent my entire life striving to join? And now I'm stuck at a crossroads, beckoned down two directly opposed paths. So which is it? Take a private jet to my CEO dream or trudge the harder route Eva believed I would choose. Coast or fight? I could tell Sandeke the truth right now and earn the support of a man who could deliver every "perk" turned entitlement I've grown to expect in my short glimpse into the good ole boys' club. One sentence and I'm *in*. Or...

I'm an orphan again. Standing in the hall of a rundown boys' home, staring left toward my lone, bullied friend Nash and right toward the impossible trials that await if I choose the hard way. So what do I do? What do I tell the bullies as they wait expectantly for the latest member of their twisted club to accept the status quo and take what's mine at the expense of everyone else? Who is Marcos Oliveira, the man driven by a spark forged by darkness?

And right then, with a yacht beneath my feet and the empire of Denver Sandeke at my fingertips, my choice becomes clear. Maybe this bizarre internship has taught me the most important lesson of all: *nothing* about business and *everything* about myself.

So I tell them. Every detail about SAT's operations—all of which is supported by the documentation they stole and is therefore one hundred percent inaccurate. I tell them lies based on the fake hardware design specs planted by Martin. Lies like, SAT's "propriety" technology is nothing to worry about and looks just like every other satellite out there. I tell them the financials are strong but show they don't pose much of a threat. Having not seen SAT's real financials, I'm going to guess they're strong and *do* pose a threat. I tell them their org chart seems top heavy and unsustainable with operations unnecessarily spread over multiple locations. I reinforce Reedweather's initial critique that their advertising budget seems unusually low. I *very* clearly point out that their strength seems to be in R&D, which could pose a long-term problem for them if none of their research pans out into profitable ventures. Therefore, that should be the main point of attack.

Over the next hour, I confidently tell them many truths based on what I know are lies and reinforce over and over how incredible it is that Sandeke has procured this information. I feed their egos while subverting them in every way I can. I end by suggesting he commission a task force to study the hardware drawings and test scripts. I estimate he'll need at least four engineers full-time for two months to start. Let's call this chunk of wasted Sandeke resources a moral fine in place of the legal one they should be getting from the federal government.

236

But the best part about the whole thing? Grant is rabidly absorbing every damaging fabrication from my mouth right along with Sandeke. I watch him take vigorous notes, knowing these red herrings will be sent off to Brighthouse and force those cheaters down the wrong path also. They, too, will be investing their money and energy to counter fake technology while ignoring the actual threats posed by SAT Systems. Meanwhile, Grant will continue to siphon real information from Sandeke Telecom to feed his own corporate beast. Sandeke still has no idea his number two has betrayed him in the same way he betrayed Martin, which leaves Brighthouse as only a partial loser in this battle.

The real loser coming out of Denver Sandeke's insidious attempt to ruin his son?

Denver Sandeke.

23—THE WINNER

MARCOS

The bartender had a lot more words for us before we left yesterday's very productive yacht party: caterpillar, vestibule, keratin, and my favorite, rye bean. Okay, so my bribe was wasted on that source, but J-Dawg's paid more dividends. He overheard Grant telling Audrey I was "going to be a problem for Brighthouse," which officially confirmed their spy status and his antagonism for me. It also led to J-Dawg's theory that Grant wanted to get into the stripping game. In J-Dawg's opinion, I shouldn't be concerned by the competition. Grant was not "man candy." Also, "Brighthouse is a stupid name for a strip club." All of this proved extra-confusing for J-Dawg, who then heard Sandeke tell Grant he had no intention of ever hiring "a goddamn stripper." J-Dawg, flustered and angry, assured me he'd set them straight if I wanted to change their minds about the gig. I assured him I was good.

So Sandeke is officially the slimy bastard we thought. No news there. As suspected, every word out of his mouth was a lie intended to seduce me until he got what he wanted. I'm even more glad I gave it to him.

Now I'm in Eva's room alone while she consoles her roommate over a recent breakup in the kitchen. Apparently, Axl Rhodes collects model girlfriends like his model girlfriends collect couture clothing. I admit, I'm mostly focused on the rumor that girl-bonding involves individual pints of ice cream because I'm starving. I pull out my phone to text Eva.

Is it true that distress in women leads to ice cream consumption?

Eva: **Do you want ice cream?**

Me: **Yes.**

Eva: **Despite your annoying stereotype, I will bring you ice cream if we have it. Sit tight. Five more minutes. *kissy face***

Kissy face… love it.

I toss my phone on the bed and pull up my laptop to work on my internship class assignment. I should have filed at least two progress reports by now, but really, how do I explain this experience? Every sentence I type sounds more and more like a ridiculous romantic comedy that would get me expelled.

"Reedweather Media is a circus. Sandeke Telecom is evil incarnate. There's a three-way spy scheme involving everyone. Also, I'm sleeping with my boss."

I huff a dry laugh, delete it all, and start again.

What have I learned in my time as an intern? That I don't fit.

For far too long, capitalist enterprise has been a zero-sum game of winners and losers. Corporations compete for consumer attention, employees compete for promotions and wages, and the result is an environment where greed is rewarded over innovation, and cheating is rewarded over merit. Discrimination runs rampant in a system that regurgitates itself. Incompetence will always thrive when self-promotion and sycophantic connections dominate the landscape. Who really wins in this scenario? Individuals who learn the game and are willing to manipulate the system. Who loses? Everyone else. Employees, consumers, taxpayers. Dreamers. Entrepreneurs who still believe an idea, hard work, and passion should be enough to succeed.

But I can't discuss any of this with "mentors" at my internship. No, my path to gaining career equity is by drinking scotch, smoking cigars, and telling powerful people what they want to hear. I guarantee a future by emulating the past and keeping those in power comfortable with the status quo. I suppress my ideas so as not to disrupt the tranquility of the yacht party, and I always, always, ignore the truth in favor of the preferred narrative of those who control my fate.

So what have I learned in my first couple of weeks as an intern?

I've learned this isn't a path I want to take. I've learned there are new directions I want to explore, new questions to ask and values to pursue. What if capitalist enterprise wasn't a zero-sum game? What if CEOs answered to employees and consumers instead of just shareholders? What if the boardroom cared about the breakroom and the living room as much as their own pockets? What if "the bottom line" wasn't the bottom line but a means to a greater, more equitable end?

There's much to love about our system. I love having the freedom to pursue my dreams and be rewarded for my creativity and passion. I love that enterprise can change the world and make it better. That's why the question that's come out of the last two weeks isn't how this internship can help me succeed, but when do we revise the definition of success? When do we ask what kind of opportunities we can create for each other and the next generation of entrepreneurs? When do we stop fearing competition and embrace the innovation and drive that fuels it? How do we build a system of win-win collaboration instead of win-lose war zones? I've spent my last two weeks in a corporate war zone, and you know what I've learned? There are no winners.

I don't know the answers to these questions. Maybe there aren't any, but I know I don't want to be a person who stops asking. I don't want to accept a flawed system and learn how to manipulate it to my advantage. I've learned I want my legacy to be the person known for asking, "How can I make this better?"

I also learned I hate scotch.

Gah, I really do.

* * *

"So we didn't have ice cream, but I brought you a yogurt," Eva says, handing me the cup and a spoon.

I smirk and set it on the desk beside me. "Thanks. Probably better for me anyway. How's Marisya?"

"Eh. She'll be okay. This is her seventh breakup since February."

I glance over from the desk chair, and she shrugs. She leans over my shoulder from behind, tucking her arms around my chest. I reach up and squeeze her wrist, rubbing my thumb over her skin as she scans my screen.

"A school assignment?"

"What have I learned from this internship so far. I'll probably need to edit some of this out so my advisor doesn't fail me, but damn it felt good to type."

She quiets, leaning further into my shoulder. "Wow. Is this really how you feel?"

"One hundred percent."

Her arms tighten around me. "You're going to do amazing things one day, Marcos Oliveira."

"Just not at Reedweather Media."

Her laugh echoes at my ear, and my grin widens. "Gosh, I hope not. Speaking of, I'm probably going to fire you tomorrow. We need to get you as far away from this as possible now that it's over. You cool with that?"

"I'll bring a cardboard box for my stuff."

"You mean that zipper portfolio and one pen you brought?"

I turn my head to meet the prettiest dark eyes that glitter when they tease me.

"It's a big portfolio."

"Is it now? How big?" Her voice lowers from teasing to mischievous, and heat spikes through my veins. Firm hands push down my chest and grip the hem of my shirt. "You owe me, you know," she whispers at my ear.

"For what?" I hiss in a breath at the sudden shock of pleasure when her fingers sink into my abs. They drift lower, and I instinctively tense into her touch.

"For six hours on a yacht without you."

"Hey, I was masterminding the final phase of our action plan."

"Yeah, while I was masterminding the most boring afternoon of cards and pointless conversation. Have you ever listened to an entire list of services offered by The Poised Peacock Salon and Spa?"

Touché.

"Well, in that case..." I capture her wrists and remove her hands from my body. Her disappointment flares into anticipation at my playful grin. "Get comfortable on the bed, Ms. Reedweather. I'd like to introduce you to my old friend Reno."

* * *

My only problem with getting fired today? Eva's doing it after lunch, which means I still have to sit through Chad's big presentation. You know, the one he did all by himself since his intern partner (me) completely slacked off and was no help at all. I don't argue any of those points. One, that's our cover for my impending release. Two, I want zero association with what's about to go down. I'm already concerned by the vast collection of pretentious nut packages littered over the table. Several employees have claimed one and munch obliviously while we wait.

Eva shoots me a glance from across the conference table that reinforces the urgency of my break with Reedweather Media. "Reno's performance" from last night still burns in her eyes, and I'll admit her performance afterward is probably seared into mine. I'm almost positive she had a third orgasm when I finally showed her the spreadsheet. In turn, I laughed for six minutes when she explained why her father always greets her with "Eva" in that weird, severe tone. Apparently, she made the mistake of explaining once that he needs to treat her like a colleague and not his child when other employees are present. This resulted in a string of awkward encounters that has gradually been whittled down to the single name uttered with the gravity of a malevolent dictator greeting his archnemesis.

"Journey with me to a wet land," Chad begins in a wistful tone to the packed conference room. He waves his hand in front of his face, then breaks character just long enough to click to the first slide. My mental picture of the Florida everglades is shattered by a deep ocean scene featuring an elaborate coral palace. Literal coral palace. Because is that…?

"Behold, a kingdom of mer-nut-people!" He pauses to allow for gasps of wonder and excitement. His expression droops slightly at the numb stares he gets instead. "We… have…" He clicks to the next slide. "King Chester Chestnut, ruler of the entire underwater kingdom of Macadamia." That is definitely a chestnut with a crown and a long tail fin.

Click.

"His devoted wife: the stunning Queen Ava Acorn." Wait, is that supposed to be Eva? His mer-acorn-queen does look suspiciously like our boss. I glance over to find her brow furrowed somewhere between horror and confusion, so "stunning" seems about right.

"The princess," Chad continues. This mer-royal doesn't get a clear identity. Click. "And our evil villain: Lord Brighthut." No photo, just the name in giant block letters.

Brighthut is italicized and underlined in case we didn't get the reference to Brighthouse.

He waits for a beat, ostensibly for a chorus of amusement at the cleverness. Nope. He keeps clicking. "Throughout our enchanted kingdom, we find plenty of nut references."

Click.

A slide entitled: "Nut References."

Click.

"The Enchanted Walnut Pools." Halved walnuts connect in a strange network that resembles a human brain more than any kind of swimming facility. Then again, what would a mer-person swimming facility that's not the ocean in which they live even look like?

Click.

"The gilded cashew throne." Yep, that's a mer-nut-king wedged onto a cashew.

Click.

"The vast almond quarry." Where mer-nut-people mine for the critical almond supply required to maintain the delicate balance of the coral reef ecosystem.

Click.

"And of course, the coco-*nut* carriage garage." Cue laughter. No? No one? But a coconut is neither a vehicle nor a nut! Also, if I *had* participated in this campaign, I would have used the walnuts for mer-carriages instead of unnecessary mer-swimming pools. So far, that would have been my only suggestion because this is the most amazing thing I've ever seen. God, I wish Nate were here. On second thought, keep the walnut pools. I hope they give summer swim classes. Would that be the equivalent of humans renting out patches of grass and charging for "walking lessons"?

"But despite the utopia this appears to be, all is not well in Macadamia. No. Behold, Evil Lord Brighthut is on the prowl!"

Click.

Yep. That's a Brazil nut. Wearing a monocle. And is he smoking a cigar underwater? I'm just glad I won't be the one who has to explain to Chad how water works. Two more hours and I'll be blissfully unemployed.

"Tis but morn in our bucolic Macadamia." Can an underwater location be "bucolic"? "The mer-nut-people have gathered from around the kingdom to view the highly anticipated seahorse race, sponsored by Lord Brighthut."

Click.

A crowd of mer-nut-persons has indeed gathered in front of a massive projection screen that shows a line of seahorses. I guess they don't watch live sporting events in Macadamia—a convenient fact for a telecom marketing firm. Corralled in individual gates, the seahorses appear ready to charge beneath the careful guidance of the pine nut jockeys strapped to their backs. On a towering platform beside the screen stands the half-blind Brazil nut villain (i.e., me) with a triumphant gleam on his face.

"The crowd roars with excitement. A countdown blares over the speakers in a bone-chilling *three-two-one*! You can *feel* the expectation. *Taste* the exhilaration. The alarm sounds and..."

Click.

The next slide is a canvas of indecipherable static.

"Oh horrors! Oh aghast exclamations of all types! Lord Brighthut and his inferior streaming service have failed the mer-nut-people!

"Furious, they revolt. Amidst a nightmare of chaos, they toss produce at the screen. Women and children flee in a cacophony of screams. King Chester Chestnut looks on in horror. Queen Ava Acorn faints." Eva rolls her eyes. Glowers. Didn't think she'd like that one. "And just when it looks like all hope is lost..."

The entire room flinches at the sudden trumpet blast from a speaker Chad produces from behind his laptop.

"Ta-da! It's the Warp Wizard, sliding in to save the day!" Sliding, because apparently that's what you do when you find a rainbow that inexplicably takes on concrete properties that allow it to be ridden from the top of the ocean to the sea floor. "Yes, the Sandeke Telecom Warp Wizard waves his wand to restore a high-quality picture using Sandeke Telecom's new Warp Speed service!"

Click.

Chad emulates the hoarse roar of his mer-nut-society as the Warp Wizard looks on victoriously from the platform vacated by the disgraced Lord Brighthut. I search the image for my evil clone and find him on the ground, glaring up in defeat. Also, he now has arms that are crossed.

"But this is just the beginning, folks."

Click.

"Action figures." Mer-nut-characters are lined up with giant dollar signs positioned strategically around them. A child in the lower right-corner grins rapturously while holding the bottom half of a mer-something. The top half of the toy conveniently disappears off-screen. There are no stock images of children playing with mer-nuts? Impossible.

Click. "Cross-promotion." Is that supposed to be a mer-nut-King-Chester roller coaster?

Click. "Expansion." Another storyboard with what looks like a mer-nut battle reminiscent of his initial concept. Yep, there's the white Bengal tiger and more physics-defying underwater snow.

Chad straightens abruptly, a wide toothy grin frozen on his face. No muscle moves except for his eyes that scan the stupefied audience with increasing alarm. The confusion in his eyes doesn't match the expectant smile clenched over the lower half of his face. He resembles a disoriented beauty pageant contestant who didn't understand the question.

And just when I start to feel bad for the dude... applause. Hearty and hollow and generating from one pair of hands.

"Bravo! Bra-*vo!*"

We all turn to find Reed Reedweather, III on his feet, palms slamming together with the approval of a thousand review boards. Are those tears in his eyes? He shakes his head and comes around his chair to start the long procession toward Chad. The rest of us look on in bewilderment as the two men embrace each other, their cheeks wet with... I don't even know at this point. Are they high?

"My goodness, son. That was—" Reedweather shakes his head again in mystification. He's not alone in that, I guess. The difference is, he seems to think a mystifying campaign pitch is a good thing. "Art," he breathes out finally. "Art in its truest form."

Chad swipes at his eyes as Reedweather grips his shoulders and turns him to face him. "Chad Smith, will you accept the full-time position at Reedweather Media?"

"You mean... I—I—win? I'm the winner?"

All eyes snap to me as my rival stutters through a response.

"You are, son. You've proven you have what it takes to be a Reedweather champion!"

The men hug in a fitting embrace for this public engagement and turn to face the rest of us. Reedweather lifts Chad's arm like he's the victor of a wrestling match.

"Ladies and gentlemen, our latest addition to the Reedweather family!"

Then Reedweather sees me.

His face pales.

His arm drops to his side.

His eyes bulge like his brain just caught up with the scene and can't believe what it's discovered. "I'm so sorry, Mark-O." His voice is strained, defeated. "It's just... the Warp... Wizard. He had that hat. You all saw the hat?" he asks, pleading with everyone else in the room. His attention rests back on me, begging me to understand his impossible choice, the irresistible power of the hat.

I steeple my fingers over my lips, staring back with a devastating blast of *Thoughtful Appraisal.*

"I see," I say finally, then go silent again for another expert display of the *Thoughtful Pause.* Reedweather backs up a step; Chad shrinks in his skin. Once I'm convinced they've suffered enough, I push myself to my feet and stride toward Chad, hand extended. "Well played, my friend," I say, tightening my palm firmly around his and squinting until he flinches. He flexes his fingers when I let go and shoves his hands in his pockets while staring at the ground. "Now, if you don't mind, I have some packing to do and exit paperwork to complete. Beverly? Shall we?"

I lift two fingers in her direction.

The startled HR Director stares at me in awe. Then rises from her chair.

24—THE REAL WINNER

MARCOS

Trust me, you dodged a bullet. Just promise you'll remember me when you get to the top.

I smirk at the text from Mark and open the one from Eva.

How's your first day of unemployment going? Any blowback from the university?

I'm about to respond with something snarky about meeting her in the make-out closet of her building for a different kind of blowing when my phone rings with Martin's number. Strange. We already gave him the update Saturday night after the yacht party.

Pushing up from my couch, I pace toward the window to answer it. "This is Marcos."

"Marcos, hey. It's Martin Sandeke."

"Martin, great to hear from you. What can I do for you?"

"I'm hoping a lot, actually."

My pulse picks up, and I shift the phone to my other ear. "Yeah? Look, I'd love to help, but I just got let go from Reedweather and—"

"No, not with the spy shit," he says. "Bigger. I've spent a lot of time looking into you since our meeting and I liked what I saw. A lot. How would you like to get in on the ground floor of an innovative non-profit about to blow up the telecom industry? I want to do things differently with SAT Systems and I need people who think differently by my side. People who aren't afraid of a fight and aren't afraid to ask questions."

I've learned there are new directions I want to explore, new questions to ask and values to pursue.

"You still there?"

I swallow the emotion in my throat, excitement building in my chest. "Yeah, sorry. Just... a lot to take in."

"Right, yeah. I get it. Well, hey, think about it. I'll be sending over a formal offer, but I wanted to chat first. I've been swamped with the business development side of things, particularly international markets that are demanding all of my attention. Plus, now I'll have my hands full with this McPherson thing and could use marketing help on that as well. But what I really need is a Director of Operations I can trust to run our core business and the main Manhattan office."

Did the oxygen just get siphoned out of this apartment? Is this a joke from Eva? Nash? Eva isn't that cruel. Nash isn't that motivated.

"Wow. Really? But..." What? This is too perfect. This is everything I want. My chance to make a difference. To ask those questions and work with a young, driven entrepreneur like me. Someone I actually *do* respect.

"Hey, I have to run. Just do me a favor and at least look at the offer. Let me know what you think."

I finally suck in enough air to speak. "Thank you, Martin. I'll definitely look it over and give it my full consideration. When would you want me to start?"

He grunts a dry laugh into the phone. "As far as I'm concerned, you already have."

* * *

"Wow. This is incredible," Eva says, scanning the offer letter from SAT Systems. Seated on my bed, she balances the laptop on her thighs while I lie beside her. I stare up at the ceiling, reviewing everything in my mind for the hundredth time since Martin's initial call. True to his words, the offer letter showed up in my inbox a minute later. Six-figure salary, attractive benefits—everything a new MBA grad could want, and more.

Except this time, it's the *more* that got my attention, the warmth and excitement that coursed through me as I ignored the offer letter and thoroughly researched the firm instead. So much potential. So much evidence in support of Martin's ingenuity and drive to buck the trend and think for himself. Is there a better fit for me at this stage in my career?

"What are you going to do?" Eva asks, closing the laptop and placing it on the nightstand. My girlfriend slides down to join me and takes my hand. I lift it to my lips and hold it there as I consider my answer.

"I already responded," I say finally, a smile creeping over my lips.

"You did?" her gaze snaps toward me, and I turn my head to meet it.

"Yes."

"But... did you accept or reject? What if you get better offers? Did you negotiate? You know those offers are always negotiable, right? And the benefits. Health care looked good, but the retirement package—"

I squeeze her hand, laughing. "All of those factors are irrelevant to me. What's the thing you always say you like about me?"

Her nose scrunches as she thinks. "Your eyes?"

I roll those and tug her hand. "Come on. I'm serious. You say it all the time."

She sighs, a smile tickling her lips. "Your instinct."

I nod. "Exactly. My instinct."

"So what did your instinct decide?"

"To me, instinct isn't just about knowing what decision to make. It's about understanding myself and deciding what to value and believe in beyond the decision. I want to make a difference, Eva. I want more than to benefit from the status quo."

"Good. I love that about you."

I stare at her, gripping her fingers. "*You* taught me that. You should be pursuing a better career path right now too. You deserve the world, and instead, you're staying on at Reedweather to run Sandeke's stupid campaign and keep an eye on those cheaters?"

"Only until we're sure this thing is resolved," she reminds me. "A year tops, and I'm out. I've been thinking. Maybe it's time I stop *talking* about starting my own firm and actually draft the business plan instead. Finally do things the way *I* want to do them. What do you think?"

"I think we should start tonight." I study her shining eyes and shake my head. "You're a badass, Eva. You know that? It's your courage to follow your conscience that showed me I want to be a person who takes a stand too."

She traces my cheek, smiling with the light I so admire in her. "I need to finish this, and I'll be able to do a lot of damage from the inside before I go. You know, you're going to be a great Director of Operations, Marcos. SAT Systems is lucky to have you."

Surprised, I shift to face her. "I only said I responded. How'd you know I accepted?"

She laughs and kisses me lightly. "Come on. You think you're the only one with good instincts?"

No, I'm definitely not. *She's* the one responsible for all of this. Evangeline Reedweather and her action plan rescripted my life, not to mention several international corporations. My brief stint as an intern may have been a circus, but with everything that came out of it, it's hard to argue it wasn't a wild success—especially when it comes to the woman sitting before me. She's not just everything I want in a girlfriend, she's someone I admire as a person and a professional. Maybe I found my mentor after all.

At some point while we've been talking, she shoved up my shirt and now traces the script on my ribs like she has so many times. I know she wonders about my past, all the things I hide in my quest for a better future. And there's no doubt about it—I want a future with this woman. I want everything with her. Can I have that if I don't *give* her everything in return?

Her finger slides over the word "darkness," sending chills through my body.

"I never felt like I belonged anywhere," I say quietly. She glances up in surprise, her gaze resting on mine. I swallow and drag in a deep breath. Am I really going to do this? For a brief moment of panic, instinct tries to shut my throat. She reaches for my hand and laces her fingers with mine, tugging lightly in encouragement. With that single sentence and one look, she knows what's coming. Somehow our deep connection means she always *knows* when it comes to me. Clearing my throat, I close my eyes and let the darkness return. "Since I was a kid, I thought knowing where I came from would help me feel whole. Like, if I could just meet my birth parents, I'd find the missing piece of myself that would allow me to fit somewhere else."

Her hand tightens around mine, and I blink back old emotion.

"When they declined to meet me, it felt… I don't know. Like all hope was lost. It was validation of all my insecurities growing up. That I was nothing. That I didn't belong, and now that they refused, I never would. That I wasn't *important*." I shake my head to silence her when she starts to protest. "I know. I mean, logically, I know that's not true. I told myself their decision was a reflection on them, not on me. That there could've been a million reasons they didn't want me in their lives. It's just… when you spend your entire life as a blip in a system, a checkmark on someone's task list, you start to believe that's all you are."

When I dare a look back, her eyes are clouded with silent tears. Tears for *me*. Tears laced with sadness, love, and affection, because maybe…

"God, Marcos. Do you have any idea how important you are to me?" she says, swatting at her eyes. She almost sounds angry in her desperation for me to understand. "I fought my feelings for you as hard as I could and still lost. I risked my entire career because I couldn't imagine letting you go and nothing seemed as important as having you in my life." She shifts to face me, forcing my gaze to hers. "And now, I can't imagine a life without you. The best thing that ever happened to me was finding those stupid stolen files because it brought us together. You belong. Here. In this moment. With me."

Tears burn behind my own eyes as I study her, absorbing the words I've waited my entire life to hear. "You belong." *I* belong. And suddenly, I want to tell her everything. Maybe I never felt like I fit because I never let myself. I held back, afraid of rejection, of confronting my past. But now, I want her to *know* me. Need her to understand the pain of being tossed from foster home to foster home. The fear and confusion of Bellevue and my feud with Billy Stanton. The agony of having my heart ripped out when my birth parents said no. And the beauty of the brotherhood formed with Nash and Nate when we locked into a bond of mutual survival. I want her to *know* me, because for the first time in my life, I believe someone could actually love me. I know I could love her. Maybe I already do.

I touch her cheek, searching her face in awe of everything she is and everything we'll be together. Maybe the missing piece was never meant for me to fill. Maybe it was an open space for someone else—I just have to let her in.

"My story isn't pretty, but it's yours if you want it," I say with a weak smile.

She cups my cheek, projecting everything I've come to love about her with one look. "I want it more than anything, Marcos."

I pull in a ragged breath and nod. "Long version or short version?"

Her eyes soften with such hope, promise, and yes—love. "I always want the long version with you. Always."

* * *

NATE and I just left the gym when my phone buzzes with a call. I glance down, surprised to find Sandeke Telecom on my screen. I turn the display to Nate, who gives me a disgusted look.

"What could they want? Didn't they just fire you on Monday?"

"That was Reedweather Media, their subsidiary."

"Same difference. You gonna answer it?"

I stare at the screen for another second and accept the call. "Marcos here."

"Mark? Is this Mark Oliver?"

I swallow a retort at Beverly's distinctive voice. Seriously?

"Sure is," I say, because why the hell not?

"Oh fantastic. I'm Beverly Harris, the new Vice President of Human Resources at Sandeke Telecom, and I have excellent news for you, Mr. Oliver! I found your résumé on your university's Career Development Center internet website."

"*You* did? Huh. Interesting." I *knew* she was the one responsible for getting my name wrong "in the system."

"Yes! And I'm pleased to inform you that you've been selected for Sandeke Telecom's world class internship program! Our program is famous for developing future business leaders who enjoy long, successful careers. We acquire the best of the best to breed the best of the best and are recognized as the pride of the industry! Congratulations, Mark! Big things are about to happen for you. Would you be able to come in for an interview tomorrow at ten?"

I bite my lip, pulling to a stop in the middle of a crowded Midtown sidewalk.

"Mr. Oliver? Can I put you down for tomorrow at ten? Mark?"

Note to future CEO self: Hire the real Mark Oliver. Dude could use a break.

"Mr. Oliver? Did you hear me? This is your lucky day. Are you ready to start the first day of the rest of your life?" Yes, I remember seeing that plaque on her desk. It coordinated well with the stack of brochures she probably never read. Brochures that no longer interest me and hopefully never will.

I smirk and lift an imaginary scotch glass to the heavens. "Thanks, Beverly. But I think I'm gonna pass."

The end.

ABOUT THE AUTHOR

From angsty and dark to snort-laugh funny, Aly writes romance from her soul to yours.

Thank you for taking this journey with me. I would love to hear from you! For updates, reveals, and more, subscribe to my newsletter and join my fun, laidback reader group on Facebook: Aly's Breakfast Club.

Aly Stiles
PO Box 577
Trexlertown, PA 18087-0577

Find Smartypants Romance online:
Website: www.smartypantsromance.com
Facebook: www.facebook.com/smartypantsromance/
Goodreads: www.goodreads.com/smartypantsromance
Twitter: @smartypantsrom
Instagram: @smartypantsromance
Newsletter: https://smartypantsromance.com/newsletter/

OTHER BOOKS BY ALY STILES

THE SAVE ME SERIES
available in Kindle Unlimited

RISING WEST

FALLING NORTH

BREAKING SOUTH

CRASHING EAST

THE WRECK ME SERIES
available in Kindle Unlimited

ASHTON MORGAN: Apartment 17B

THE HOLD ME SERIES
(Written as Alyson Santos)

available in Kindle Unlimited and audio

NIGHT SHIFTS BLACK (NSB #1)

TRACING HOLLAND (NSB #2)

VIPER (NSB #3)

LIMELIGHT (NSB #4)

AN NSB WEDDING (NSB #5)

STANDALONES
available in Kindle Unlimited

YOUNG LOVE

TRAITOR (TWISTED FATE #1)

HAUNTED MELODY

PARANORMAL BOOKS BY MOIRA HALE
Available in Kindle Unlimited

GIFTED (Gifted, Vol 1)
CURSED (Gifted, Vol 2)

ALSO BY SMARTYPANTS ROMANCE

Green Valley Chronicles

The Love at First Sight Series

Baking Me Crazy by Karla Sorensen (#1)

Batter of Wits by Karla Sorensen (#2)

Steal My Magnolia by Karla Sorensen(#3)

Fighting For Love Series

Stud Muffin by Jiffy Kate (#1)

Beef Cake by Jiffy Kate (#2)

Eye Candy by Jiffy Kate (#3)

The Donner Bakery Series

No Whisk, No Reward by Ellie Kay (#1)

The Green Valley Library Series

Love in Due Time by L.B. Dunbar (#1)

Crime and Periodicals by Nora Everly (#2)

Prose Before Bros by Cathy Yardley (#3)

Shelf Awareness by Katie Ashley (#4)

Carpentry and Cocktails by Nora Everly (#5)

Love in Deed by L.B. Dunbar (#6)

Scorned Women's Society Series

My Bare Lady by Piper Sheldon (#1)

The Treble with Men by Piper Sheldon (#2)

The One That I Want by Piper Sheldon (#3)